End of the
LUPINE
SEASON

End of the
LUPINE
SEASON

LAURIE OTIS

Little Big Bay LLC

LITTLE PLACE ~ BIG IDEAS ~ ON THE BAY

www.littlebigbay.com

END OF THE LUPINE SEASON

Author: Laurie Otis

Cover: Roslyn Nelson

Editor & Designer: Roslyn Nelson

Printed in the United States of America

ISBN: 978-0-9968071-1-1

Library of Congress Control Number: 2016908584

Publisher: Little Big Bay LLC
littlebigbay.com

END OF THE LUPINE SEASON

is dedicated to

to women everywhere

who secretly long

for the freedom

of a fresh start.

Table of Contents

Prologue

"One sorrow never comes but brings an heir."
(PERICLES) WILLIAM SHAKESPEARE

*T*he moon was full, but even so it was a black night as the wind gusted and sent clouds scudding across the sky to cause sudden and frequent eclipses. Strangely, the gale hadn't produced rhythmic waves, but rather the surf seemed a confused boil responding not so much to the wind as to unknown forces beneath its surface.

Two Island policemen walked the beach with flashlights and tapes cordoning off an area from the foot of the cliff descending stairs to the woods on either side of the beach and back to the shore, the lake itself providing the fourth side of a rectangle. A crowd, standing motionless, had gathered along the edge of the cliff some 100 feet above; the squad cars parked behind them captured their shapes in spinning lights and silhouetted an eerie, ghost-like audience.

The object of attention was a person sprawled in the sand about 10 feet from the last stair. It was hard to identify as a person: no human form was discernible. It looked more like a shirt and jeans carelessly cast aside by some impetuous swimmer in a hurry to take an impulsive midnight dip in Lake Superior. A woman and a man struggled down the stairs with a folded stretcher and rushed to kneel by the body.

"You can't do this one any good," the officer in charge said. "You'd best see if you can take care of Gudrun over there." He pointed to a middle-aged woman slumped in the sand. Her graying hair had blown wild in the wind, and she held her arms clasped tightly around her body, her hands on opposite shoulders in what was more like a lover's embrace than the usual tightly folded arms denoting withdrawal or protection. She stared straight ahead and rocked back and forth slightly. "I think she's in shock," Nelson said as he returned to measuring distances from stairs to body, from body to shore line, and from body to woods, all of which he was carefully recording in a small notebook.

"You okay, Gudrun? Are you hurt? What happened? Where does it hurt?" There were no responses, and the medics settled for laying a blanket across her shoulders and trying to convince her to stand.

Chapter 1

"To sigh to th' winds"
(THE TEMPEST) WILLIAM SHAKESPEARE

udrun Carlson stood on the town dock in Bayfield, Wisconsin. A thin, short girl, she clutched the lapels of her gray, cloth coat together, shielding her neck. The wind whipped the waves into whitecaps and sent the green water boiling up over the weathered planks of the pier causing eddies to simultaneously swirl around her shoes while perversely forming a dampening spray over the rest of her body. It was the May first and Lake Superior was in the throes of an early spring storm, hardly distinguishable from a winter storm except that instead of blowing across fields of ice, the gale had open water to beat and stir and slam with fury against any interfering solid object.

The wind tore at her coat as if to whip it from her body. What was this wild place and why was nature so furious with it? Other prospective ferry passengers were huddled inside a makeshift shelter of piled barrels, but Gudrun braved the elements, her eyes constantly darting across the horizon for the first glimpse of the boat which would take her to Madeline Island for her first real job. She was taking no chance on missing this boat and having to wait an hour for the next trip.

As she squinted toward the horizon, Gudrun was able to silence the wind in her mind and daydream of other May Days in St. Paul. It was a skill born of a shy little girl's boredom and loneliness and perfected over the years to escape the dullness of a solemn, restricted life. She thought of the May baskets they had made at school and the excitement of her classmates when they contemplated how many they would need in order to leave one on every friend's doorstep and the agonizing decisions as to what treats would be in them.

From an early age, Gudrun had an eye for color and was "very clever with her hands." This came from a mother who considered compliments to be the seed of conceit, a sin ranked high in a long list of character traits to avoid. But Gudrun secretly treasured what she considered her one attribute and basked in the attention her pastel baskets had brought. She smiled slightly as she thought of the misshapen, garishly-colored paper constructions smeared with fingerprints and bulging with paste lumps which sat beside her lavender and pink creations. She had carefully formed several shapes from tiny rectangular market baskets to perfect cones with handles, meant to be hung on a doorknob.

Nearly everyone talked about going to the dime store for candy corn or jelly beans to put in their baskets. Gudrun knew this would not set well with her mother, so that night she innocently suggested they make a large batch of sandbaklsse for the coming church dinner. She helped her mother press the buttery dough into the molds shaped like shells and flowers and carefully tipped them out when they had baked to a faint golden color. After they had cooled, she placed them carefully, to prevent breakage, in a clean, empty syrup pail with a tight lid. Mother always saved syrup pails for storage. The airtight covers kept her baking fresh and preserved the buttery taste of the cookies. As she worked, Gudrun surreptitiously held a few cookies back from the tin to put in her baskets.

Somewhere she had read that May baskets were meant to celebrate spring and should contain the first flowers of the season; but there were few flowers on the first of May in Minnesota and especially not in the heart of the city. She was pleased with how her cookies peeked out of her pretty baskets and thought they would taste much better than violets or candy corn and jelly beans for that matter. Mother viewed her handiwork with a tight-lipped expression but said nothing. Later, as she opened her Bible for the nightly reading, Mother remarked coolly, "Maybe tonight we'd better concentrate on verses about false pride." Gudrun felt her face color, but couldn't reply because of a familiar lump that had formed in her throat—a lump she often felt, but didn't know whether to label as shame or anger.

Amidst these thoughts also lurked the memory of a little girl's sadness when she couldn't think of anyone to be the recipient of those carefully-assembled expressions of friendship. She thought of a couple girls from school who were nice to her, but she didn't exactly know where they lived. A boy from her class lived down the block, but she also knew that the custom of leaving a May basket on a boy's door involved chasing and kissing, something that surely would not set well with mother and left her feeling sinful for having let the thought enter her mind.

When the baskets went undelivered, Mother suggested that they take them to the Mission; "they shouldn't go to waste." Gudrun complied and honestly tried to feel fulfilled with doing the Lord's work. "As much as ye have done it unto the lowliest, so have ye done it unto me." She felt a deep sense of shame for her feelings when she stood at The Lord's Table Mission and watched her beautiful baskets distributed to the day's unfortunate. One old man with the bulbous, pitted nose of an alcoholic turned the basket in his tremulous hands and then, glancing around furtively, crumpled it and put it in his pocket. A thin woman with dark circles under her eyes tried to eat the crisp cookies although she obviously had no teeth. Gudrun turned in revulsion as the woman dipped the cookie in her coffee until she could suck the mushy result without chewing. Suddenly, she didn't want to remember any more!

She could hardly see through the mixture of mist, spray, and rain, but at last a small boat appeared, diving down into the trough of one wave and appearing on the crest of another. It looked so small and assailable in the midst of the fury that Gudrun wondered at the wisdom of entrusting her body and soul to its doubtful safety. As it tumbled closer, she was able to read the lettering on the side: "The Nichevo." Even its name sounded foreign and unreliable. However, without allowing herself further thought, when it docked she scrambled aboard, even though it wouldn't leave for another half hour.

She quickly surveyed her surroundings. There were rain-streaked windows on two sides, leaving the front and back of the boat open for loading and unloading of vehicles. An upper level was contained by a railing and furnished with metal benches bolted to the floor—obviously a pleasant place to ride in good weather. There were no vehicles on the lower level, and the wind kept the metal deck constantly awash with water and debris churned from the lake bottom. Benches were attached down along either side under the windows.

Gudrun tried to select a sheltered spot in the middle of one side without sitting too near any of her few fellow travelers.

She sat hugging herself for warmth, trying not to make eye contact with anyone until her fare had been collected and the Nichevo had begun its heaving and pitching course out of the harbor. Taking her purse from inside her coat and undoing the clasp, she held a much-folded letter just inside the opening to prevent any stray backlash of wind from snatching it away. She read it again, this time to validate her reason for exposing herself to this terrifying experience.

Miss Gudrun Carlson
1420 Rice Street
St. Paul, Minnesota

Dear Miss Carlson,
After talking with you the other day and checking your references, we feel you would be the right person for the housekeeping position at our summer home on Madeline Island. Both Mr. Gendron and I were impressed with your grooming, your reticence, and the fact that you are Scandinavian. We have always found that Scandinavians make excellent domestic help.
We would like you to go to the Island on the first of May and spend the month cleaning and stocking the house for our occupation on the first of June. The handyman has been instructed to see to the lights and heating and advise you as to supplies and ordering procedures for groceries, etc. He will be there to greet and provide a key. A list of instructions is enclosed.
Also enclosed is a money order for your train fare from St. Paul to Bayfield and a small traveling allowance. As we discussed, your wages will be 20 dollars a week plus room and board, and you will have every Wednesday off. I am looking forward to a satisfactory relationship. See you in June.

Your Employers,
Mr. & Mrs. James Gendron
540 Summit Avenue
Minneapolis, Minnesota
P.S. Bring warm clothes. It's still cold up there in May!

CHAPTER ONE

Gudrun knew the letter by heart. She had always worked with her mother cleaning offices in downtown St. Paul, but this was the first job she had ever found on her own, and she was inwardly excited but very nervous. She had taken the streetcar to the public library to look up reticence in the dictionary and found it to mean, "silent in temperament." She guessed that must be good, then, although her eighth grade teacher told her when she graduated that she must be more outgoing and talkative to succeed.

She was suddenly cold and very conscious of the fact that she hadn't eaten since she had left St. Paul some eight hours ago. There had been sandwiches for sale on the train, but two suspicious looking men were sitting across from her, and she hadn't wanted to take her purse out to get any money. She was also rather desperate to use a bathroom, another thing she hadn't dared attempt under their scrutiny.

She had turned into a general store on her hurried walk from the train station to the dock, however, and took a bag of peppermint candy out of her coat pocket to quiet her rumbling stomach. As she munched the sickeningly-sweet, pink pellets, she thought about how glad she was to have almost reached her destination. This was the first time she had ever been out of St. Paul except for the church picnics when the whole congregation took a special train ride to Taylors Falls for a day in the park by the St. Croix River. It had been so much fun and exciting, but she hadn't been alone then. Her mother and all the other members had been with her.

She allowed herself to daydream about those days. She could almost feel the hot sun on her back as she waded in the water, and the cool river bottom silt as it squished between her toes. Once when she was still little, she played all morning with a boy named Jalmer Johnson. They waded close to the wooden dock and around submerged rocks to collect snails and small, flat river clams. Gudrun remembered how comfortable she felt with him. He was friendly and unguarded, and she liked the way he kept a constant stream of conversation going about the contents of the water, where the snails spent the winter, and what happened if you pried a clam shell open.

"You know you're walking in loon shit, don't you?" he suddenly asked innocently. She had been so shocked at his language, she couldn't answer, but ran to her mother where she sat doing fancy work with the other church ladies and whispered in her ear. Her mother told her to go get her shoes on and play with the girls.

After awhile, she noticed that Jalmer was sitting by himself on a bench in the Pavilion looking forlorn and sad. His freckled face was streaked with tears, and his eyes were red-rimmed. After that, he never talked to her again, but avoided her whenever he saw her. In time, he quit coming to church altogether. Mother said he was no good from the time he was little and the Johnsons couldn't do a thing with him. She said they should pray for him but not have anything to do with him. Gudrun often wondered how they would know if their prayers were doing any good if they never saw him, but always assumed that mother and the church knew best. Now she wondered what had ever become of Jalmer. Maybe he was in jail or on skid row on Washington Avenue. Perhaps if he had been more reticent, she mused, things would have turned out better for him. Even so, when she thought about it now, she wished she hadn't repeated what he'd said to Mother.

She was jerked from her reverie by a sudden reversal of the boat and was surprised to see them already backing up to another long dock on what she assumed must be Madeline Island. The wind had picked up and was rocking the boat so that she had to concentrate on walking without staggering and alighting without falling.

A light sleet had made the gale even fiercer, and she leaned into the wind as she walked up the dock carrying her cardboard suitcase (printed to look like alligator skin) and clutching her purse under her coat. She felt cold to the bone. Nothing could warm her, not even the knowledge that within that purse, snuggled against her chest, was a letter that named her as employed, by virtue of her reticence and lineage.

As she reached the road and began to wonder where to go, a small man jumped out of a rusty, once-green pickup and hurried toward her with the help of the wind. "You Miss Carlson?" he shouted over the howl of the gale. She nodded. "I'm Arne Peterson, the handyman. I'll take you up to the Gendron place." Gudrun thought briefly that anyone could say they were the handy-

8

man and make off with her to do unthinkable things, however, she was so cold, tired, and hungry, she threw all caution to the raging storm and climbed into the warm cab.

Once inside she ventured a look at Mr. Peterson as he slammed the truck into reverse, with a scraping sound, and started down the road away from the lake. He said nothing more after the greeting, so Gudrun knew, along with the familiar name, that he was of Scandinavian background. He was early middle-age and appeared to be of fair complexion, but you couldn't see the color of his hair since it was completely covered by an incredibly greasy baseball cap. His coveralls were very greasy too, and although he looked to be of spindly frame, his chest appeared oversized for the rest of his body. Gudrun suddenly realized he wasn't deformed when she saw jacket and sweater cuffs protruding from the coverall sleeves—highly advisable in this weather.

The road was unpaved and bumpy, but the wind seemed to grab the small truck and toss it around more than the numerous potholes that dotted the driving surface suggested. And though the heater hummed and gave off an unpleasant metallic smell with the warmth, this small refuge in the storm took on a rather cozy atmosphere and Gudrun found herself hoping it would be a long ride so she could thaw out a bit before tackling the next unfamiliar experience.

They appeared to be only a few blocks out of the village, which she later knew was La Pointe, however, when Mr. Peterson slowed down and turned into a long driveway leading back toward the lake and the storm. As she maneuvered her suitcase through the truck door, she looked with a sinking feeling in her stomach at the rambling, clapboard house that appeared to have some sort of decorative porch railing on the roof. *That's an odd place for a porch,* she thought, but had little time for speculation what with getting herself and belongings inside and running back out to help Mr. Peterson carry in boxes of groceries and cleaning supplies.

The kitchen alone was almost as big as the tiny apartment that Gudrun and her mother had shared on Rice Avenue in St. Paul. An enormous gas stove that included a griddle and hot water reservoir dominated one wall. There were built-in cupboards and a large hanging copper rack which suspended every conceivable type of cooking utensil and apparatus within easy reach of both the stove and long, centered butcher block table. A large, commercial refrigerator sat opposite the stove topped by its round generator, which was humming tonelessly in preparation for the perishable foods.

Arne set the last grocery box on the table and stood waiting for Gudrun to finish her inspection and turn to him. All signs showed that he had clearly decided to speak again. "That's it then, Miss Carlson. My wife says you'll be tired and in need of a hot meal, so you might as well come eat with us. Our place is the little one just in back of and to the left of this here house."

Gudrun didn't see how she could meet, let alone eat with any new people but she didn't know how to refuse. Without a conscious thought, she said, "I don't want to put you to any trouble." Her mother always prefaced any remarks she made with this phrase.

"I don't want to put you to any trouble, Mrs. Nelson, but your mending won't be done until tomorrow."

"I don't want to put you to any trouble, Miss, but could I buy this spool of thread?"

"I don't want to put you to any trouble, Pastor Lundquist, but here's my tithe for this month."

It was clear that Arne was uncomfortable too, but he shrugged and muttered, "We'd be eatin' whether you came or not."

"I'll clean up then, and come over," she managed. The idea of cleaning up at this point clearly startled Arne. He stared for a couple seconds, shrugged again and left. Alone at last, Gudrun ran to find the bathroom. On the second floor, the third door she opened revealed a large, narrow room, complete with a stool, a huge, clawed bathtub, and a sink with a wide lip, which held all manner of pretty bottles, puffs, and soaps. Gudrun was so overcome with the elegance that she almost forgot her urgency.

She allowed herself a few more minutes to explore before she went to bare the Petersons. The living room, dining room, and bedrooms were like pictures in a magazine of movie star's summer homes. There was an abundance of ruffles, cabbage roses, and brightly colored chintz. Gudrun was almost dizzy with the colors and prints and lack of food.

The living room extended across the front of the house as did a screened porch. She could see wicker and metal porch furniture piled against the inner wall and covered with canvases. But beyond that she could see the lake that she had so recently crossed. It was a deep, blue-green shade and still boiled and frothed with dirty foam. She felt rather sick to her stomach and homesick simultaneously, but hadn't she just crossed that angry water, and hadn't she been on a rolling, swaying train all day? At this point, one motion caused the same vertigo as another.

The Peterson house was a winterized guest cabin on the Gendron grounds. Gudron decided immediately that Mrs. Peterson was not Scandinavian. She met her at the door and ushered her into one small room that served as kitchen, living room, dining room, and bedroom. "You must be near starved!" she shrieked "although you sure don't look as if you eat much anyway." This was said as this five-by-five person whom she had never laid eyes on guided her arms out of her coat sleeves and gave her body a noticeable once-over with her eyes.

"I don't like to trouble you," Gudrun automatically murmured. The shriek this time was accompanied by an uninhibited laugh. "The only way you can trouble me is if you try to take my man, and I'll even loan him to you if you ask in advance!" She laughed long and hard while Arne remained stoic behind his newspaper. Gudron felt the color rise from her neck. *What a crude woman! And I'm supposed to live for the entire summer next door, let alone make it through this horrible meal?* Sensing her embarrassment, Willow Peterson tried to make amends. "Don't mind me, honey! My people don't have a lot of the hang-ups you Scandihoovians do, so I just speak my mind."

"Your people?" Gudrun offered.

"Indians! I'm Indian, can't you tell?"

In her own self-consciousness, Gudrun hadn't really looked at her. Now she noticed the long dark hair and the somewhat lined, brown face. Mistaking her silence for disapproval, Willow shrieked, with a tinge of hostility, "Don't you like Indians?"

"No, no!" Gudrun hurried, as she thought, *It's not that you're Indian. The Lord God made us all. It's just that good Christians don't talk like that.* And frantically she wondered what her mother and Pastor Lundquist would say to this small, dark harridan who made her so uncomfortable.

But Willow seemed to immediately forget any imagined insult and became cheerful again. "My name's Willow. Well, it's really Sweetwillow, but nobody calls me that any more. When I was little, they called me Sweet, but nobody would call me that now either!" The last statement was delivered with another whoop of laughter while she held her arms wide and surveyed her own ample frame.

"I'm Gudrun Carlson. I'm happy to meet you." She held her hand out. Gudrun was startled, but strangely flattered, when Willow ignored her hand and hugged her instead.

"We'll have to fatten you up," she said as she steered her to the table. "I've got a nice venison stew goin' here. Have you ever had venison? My people can take deer when they need it; they don't need to wait for huntin' season. You put a few wild onions and some potatoes with this, and you've got somethin' worth puttin' down your gullet. Sticks to your ribs too." There didn't seem the need to reply, so Gudrun sat and smiled, occasionally nodding her head, while Willow conversed with herself.

Besides the stew, there was a flat, crusty bread and a bowl of greens shaped like little violins. "They're fiddleheads," Willow explained, "They'll turn into ferns in June. Then they're no good for eatin', unless you're a deer." Again the laughter. In spite of the unorthodox descriptions and explanations, the food was delicious, and Gudrun ate ravenously and enjoyed herself. But when she had finished, the heavy food, long day, and nervous exhaustion left her almost paralyzed. She felt her chin drop to her chest several times as she fought to stay awake and keep abreast of Willow's constant chatter. "Hey, you're asleep on your feet, or should I say ass, since you're sitting down." Again the laughter! Gudrun was too tired to be shocked. "You go on to bed. We can have a long chat tomorrow, and you can tell me all your secrets." Gudrun felt slightly uneasy at the prospect of that, but obediently said her goodnights and left the warm cottage.

CHAPTER ONE

The cold air awakened her as she walked the short distance to the main house, and she became aware that the gale had become a mild breeze, and the sky was evidently clearing, since a sliver of a moon drifted in and out of clouds. *What am I doing here?* she thought. *Why didn't I stay in St. Paul where I was safe? What possessed me to leave everything I know?* She fumbled in her pocket for the key and let herself into the kitchen. She planned to go straight to the room designated as hers on the instruction sheet, but stopped as she noticed the moonlight coming through the living room windows. She slipped the latch on the door to the porch and stepped to the outer screen.

She looked over a sheer cliff, 100 feet above the water. The lake had calmed to a soft ripple and moonlight caught and defined huge boulders and tall pine trees along the shoreline. She swallowed with difficulty around a lump in her throat, but this time it wasn't the result of shame or anger but awe. This was the moment that marked the beginning of her lifelong love affair with the treacherous inland sea. She had read about the Atlantic and Pacific Oceans, but surely nothing she had ever read could compare with this. It frightened yet attracted her at the same time; it exhilarated and lulled her; it caused her heart to beat faster but her muscles relax. She wondered if she had lapsed into "make believe."

Gudrun fell asleep as soon as her head hit the pillow. Her physical and nervous exhaustion, along with the heavy meal, acted like a sedative; she slept soundly in strange surroundings, something she didn't think she could do and was not even visited by fitfulness or dreams.

Chapter 2

"And so, good morrow, servant."
(THE TWO GENTLEMEN OF VERONA) WILLIAM SHAKESPEARE

She awoke the next morning when the sun pierced through her closed eyelids. She looked around the room for several seconds before she remembered where she was; she had been too tired to take much notice of her surroundings the night before. The room was small but clean, with a single bed, dresser, rocking chair, and a small table which she realized must be meant as a desk. But the best feature, in her mind, was the source of the blazing sunlight: full length French doors that opened onto a small, railed balcony. She grabbed her coat, which she had carelessly thrown over the rocker, and pulled it on as she stepped outside.

The unpredictable, but ever changeable Lake Superior weather had held to its reputation. The sky was blue, the wind sharp but soft, and the only testimony to the raging storm of yesterday was a thin crust of snow which was already melting under the strong rays. Clumps of daffodils and another small blue flower, evidently encouraged to bloom on previous, milder days, were beginning to revive and were half-heartedly lifting their heads off the ground, willing to make one more attempt at spring. Gudrun heard the slap of waves, and, although her room didn't front the lake, she remembered her fascination of the previous night and raced back through the house and out onto the front porch.

Pastor Lundquist had always described what it was like to be filled with the Holy Spirit. It was joy and peace, coupled with excitement; it was laughing and crying both at once; it was an inner feeling of warmth and realization that, "God truly was in his heaven and all was right with the world." He and many members of the church professed to be, "filled with the Holy Spirit," and Gudrun wished for that feeling more than anything else. She longed for the release offered by that kind of religion, but seemed to be mired in the "war against sin" with its endless number of "thou shalt nots."

When she was younger, she had asked Mother when she was going to be, "filled with the Holy Spirit." Mother said it would happen when she was free of sin and had accepted Christ as her personal savior. She thought she had accepted Christ, but there were so many sins! When she was happy about her good school grades, Mother often accused her of being prideful; if she wanted something, she was warned to guard against covetousness; if she ate a lot, she was reminded that gluttony was a sin; if she wasn't hungry, she must consider her body a temple and keep it in good shape for the time when that elusive "Holy Spirit" might deign to enter. As the years passed, Gudrun quit asking, but she often noticed that many from the church, including Mother and Pastor Lundquist, were not always, "filled with the milk of human kindness" and seemed to have, temporarily anyway, lost the Holy Spirit.

But as she looked at the lake that morning, Pastor's words came back to her, and such a joy welled up inside her that she almost felt she should kneel and pray. The sun made paths across the waves like liquid silver which trickled and ran into new and ever-changing tributaries; The shoreline was a rosy-colored steep rock cliff with tall evergreens and mosses growing on top of it—some even growing out of the crevices in the solid rock walls. If you looked another way, you saw nothing but water with the occasional island seeming to float untethered on the surface. Unaware that she had spoken out loud, she whispered, "What hath God wrought?"

"Are you up yet?" Gudrun jumped at the sound of a loud voice, and before she had identified it in her mind, she was confronted by Willow Peterson, who was standing in the living room doorway holding a pan in her hands. "You didn't hear me knock, so I just used my key and came on in. I figured you'd be sleepin' in this morning, seein' as how you had such a rough day yesterday. But I made this corn bread, Arne is off to work already, and figured we could have some coffee and chew the fat a little. You know, it's so lonesome up here, and even though you're younger than I am, how old are you anyhow?, I need a friend, and I figure you do too, what with not knowin' anybody and everythin'."

This explanation was delivered in one breath, and Gudrun, who stood with her mouth agape, suddenly realized she was barefoot and in her nightgown and scurried for her bedroom. "You don't have to be shy with me; I've seen plenty of people, men and women, with fewer clothes than that on."

Gudrun peeked around the door jam. "I don't want to put you to any trouble, but I'll just take a minute to dress, then I'll come make coffee." But Willow wasn't having that. "Heck! I can talk while you're dressing." With that, she deposited her pan of corn bread on the nearest flat surface and followed Gudrun to the bedroom where she plopped onto her unmade bed. She continued a running commentary laced with questions, which she didn't expect to have answered. " What's it like to live in St. Paul?" Gudrun slipped into her small bathroom with her clothes. "We went there once to visit a cousin, but we had to take a streetcar and I puked my guts out right there, all over the floor. Nobody was very nice about it either, and this guy said somethin' about drunken Indians and I just lost it; turned and puked all over his shoes. He deserved it! I got sick because I couldn't stand all that swayin' and rockin'. But, you know, I just couldn't like that place after that, and I never went back. You ever feel that way about any place? Course, I suppose you being raised there and all, it's different. Where'd you work before? You like workin' for rich people? It's okay with us I guess. They get under your skin once in awhile with all their fancy-schmancy ways, but you learn to ignore it. You graduate from high school? I never did. Just didn't seem important to me. Then I met Arne and that was it, a married slob with nowhere to go. But he's okay. You wouldn't know it to look at him, but he's pretty good in bed, and he don't hit me or nothin'. Course, if he did, I'd prob'ly flatten him and he knows it! We ain't got no kids. I wish we did, but they just won't come. That's why most girls get married around here, cause they're knocked-up, but maybe there's somethin' wrong with me, or Arne. Who knows!"

Gudrun wanted to forestall any further conversation along those lines, so she hurried out of the bathroom and led Willow to the kitchen. She made coffee in a large enamel pot, using a raw egg to clarify it as Mother had taught her. The kitchen was arranged so efficiently that she had no trouble finding things and worked as if she had always been there.

The two new friends sat across from each other in the breakfast nook by a window facing what looked like a prospective vegetable garden. The cornbread was cut and buttered, and cups of coffee steamed between them. "This is the best coffee I ever had. Did I see you put a raw egg in it?"

"It's the Swedish way; it makes it clear and lets it be strong without being bitter."

"It'd be especially good for a hangover then, huh?" she whooped.

"You ever been married?"

Gudrun reddened. "No, I never have."

"You want to have kids?"

"I'd like that someday, if the Lord blesses me with a Christian husband."

"You're really into this religion stuff, ain't you? Actually, I'm pretty religious myself, only I believe in the Indian ways. You know, with spirits and such."

"You mean like the Holy Spirit?"

"Ya, I guess you'd say that. You know the lake has a spirit, and the land, and the animals. When Arne shoots a deer, I always thank it for givin' us food before I cut it up."

"But surely you can't think the deer hears and understands you!" Gudrun had blurted this out without thinking and quickly tried to soften her statement without offending a woman she—surprisingly—was enjoying. "Do you mean you thank God for the food?"

Willow shrugged. "It's all the same. It's talkin' to the spirit world any way you look at it."

Gudrun knew that Mother would never have accepted this casual approach to prayer, but she found it comforting and somehow more fitting for the "loving God" they always talked about before they started begging for forgiveness.

"You live alone in St. Paul?"

"I lived with my Mother, but she died two months ago."

"Hey, I'm sorry!" Willow touched the hand Gudrun had curled around her coffee cup, and she felt a sudden warmth that she couldn't entirely attribute to the hot liquid. And then a strange thing happened. All the feelings and grief that she hid from the Pastor and the ladies of the church suddenly spilled out of her mouth, and she found herself telling this strange, coarse woman things she had never told anyone and had hardly dared admit to herself.

"She got cancer, and no matter how much I prayed and cared for her, she just got worse and worse and wasted away to practically a skeleton. How can God let that happen to a good, Christian woman? Pastor said that God wanted her in heaven with him, but why did he make her suffer so before he took her?" The hard knot in her chest burst like a boil, and she felt the pent-up poisons drain from her body as the tears she had not shed ran down her cheeks and fell into her coffee.

Willow moved beside her and cradled her with one arm, rocking slightly. "You think too much about this stuff, kid, and you want too many answers. We're never goin' to know the answers. We just take life as it comes and find enjoyment where we can, and when the bad stuff comes, you just swallow it and go on." Gudrun cried silently, but more profusely than she had ever cried before, as Willow, the woman who would never be a mother rocked, made soft, hushing noises and patted her hair.

Gudrun didn't "take a day to get to know the place" as Willow had suggested, but dutifully faced her first day on Madeline Island by beginning at the top of Mrs. Gendron's list of chores that must be accomplished before the house would be ready for the family's arrival.

She judged the fresh, sunny weather perfect for airing the heavy, lined drapes from the living and dining rooms. She watched the patterns of flowers ripple on the clothesline as the lake wind caught them; they danced as if waving on long stems in a field.

Her morning's confession to Willow had left her with a feeling of release from a burden she had harbored for months—a burden of repressed grief and a burden of fear that she blasphemed God when she questioned her Mother's torture. She felt light and happy as she perched on the stepladder and washed down the painted walls and many-paned windows in preparation to rehang the drapes at the end of the day.

At noon she cut a slab of the remaining cornbread which she ate as she explored the yard. Steep steps crudely etched out of rocks and traced by a swaying rope railing deposited her at the base of the cliff on a sand beach 20 to 30 feet wide. The winter storms had left sand pockets filled with debris and an almost unbroken, wavering border of driftwood along the edge of the waves. Gudrun poked the debris with a stick and was fascinated with the small snail shells, shards of colored glass polished dull and smooth by the sand and water, and small bits of driftwood which once had been branches or roots, but now became birds or snakes when held to the light. Over the summer, many of these discoveries made their way to Gudrun's bedroom, propped on a windowsill or kept in a jar of water where the sun could catch and reflect the colors and textures of rocks and glass. While beach combing, she often unaccountably thought of the impulsive Jalmer Johnson of her childhood and mused that he would have loved this treasure trove.

And so May drifted by, each day allowing another check mark on Mrs. Gendron's list and another discovery on the beach or in the small village of La Pointe down the road. Gudrun found an ample supply of yarn in the general store and selected several skeins for a cardigan. No matter how pleasant the days, she found that the nights were cool; and while not requiring the winter coat she had brought from St. Paul, the blue sweater she knit was worn nightly.

"That blue is the same as your eyes," Willow declared when she first saw Gudrun's handiwork, "you should always wear that color. I wish I could knit like that."

"I could teach you," Gudrun offered, "I'm sure you could learn." And so began the knitting lessons with Willow's brown eyes riveted to the needles she held as she laboriously transferred knots of yarn from one to the other.

"I'll never get the hang of this," she often declared in frustration, but Gudrun always remarked that she could see progress as she took the needles to loosen stitches that Willow had pulled too tightly.

"You just have to relax your fingers more and move in a regular rhythm." Gudrun could hear her Mother's voice in her ears.

"Relax and move with the rhythm? Sounds like dancin' to me."

"I've never danced, but I suppose it's something like that," Gudrun conceded, and here again she could almost imagine what her Mother would have said to that comparison. But she was flattered that anyone would think a skill she possessed was worth emulating, and she often looked in the mirror when she put on her blue sweater and blushed as she silently agreed with Willow that the color was becoming.

Gudrun had her first best friend, and, as the days went by, it mattered less and less to her when Willow swore or made crude comments. In fact, after a week or two she ceased to notice them and increasingly admired her lack of inhibitions. The shared confidences, the sudden happy recognition of common feelings and interests; even the guilt-free disclosures of character or behavior flaws were new experiences for Gudrun, and she embraced the relationship and her Island life, sometimes wondering if this was the much touted "born-again" feeling she had heard so much about during all those endless Sunday sermons of her childhood.

Gudrun would always remember the long spring evenings with Willow and Arne, eating wild game dinners prepared with fresh herbs she had never tasted before. Sometimes she would cook for them at "the big house," and her neck and cheeks flushed pink when Willow rhapsodized over the creamy sauce she had made for the fresh lake trout or exclaimed over the flaky pastries she had perfected over the years of her mother's tutelage. Willow's conversation was as imbued with Indian legend and spirituality as Gudrun's was with Scandinavian folk tales and Christianity. And often, as they shared and compared their thoughts, they would burst into laughter when the realization of the many similarities would surprisingly dawn on them.

One day, Gudrun selected a soft shade of yellow yarn at the La Pointe store and began to knit after she had said goodnight to Willow and Arne. It was a feeling she couldn't name. To find a way to thank Willow for being her friend? To thank her for liberating her from the constant obsession with sin? Or was it just to be able to do something that pleased someone? Gudrun took up the yarn at every spare moment and knit as if she'd been given a deadline. Gradually the skeins became a soft garment the color of butter, and she sewed matching buttons down the front.

She wrapped the sweater in a piece of tissue and tucked it inside the knitting bag she was seldom without. She was to give Willow another knitting lesson while Arne was off at his Wednesday night card game with his cronies. She felt nervous for some odd reason, and when she finally gave Willow her gift, she reverted to the self-deprecating, "I don't want to trouble you" beginning.

"Are you back to that?" Willow shouted, "I thought we were friends? If you're troublin' me, I'll damn well tell you and you don't need to ask!" She acted angry. Flustered, Gudrun pressed the tissued parcel into her hands and mumbled,

"I thought yellow would look nice with your brown eyes. You should wear yellow."

Willow slowly drew the sweater out of the tissue and let it fall to its full length. It was a long cardigan with raglan sleeves and a circle of rosebuds worked around each buttonhole.

Gudrun watched tentatively as her friend felt the softness with her rough, plump hands and traced with one finger the perfectly wrought cables that decorated the front panels.

When she finally turned to Gudrun, her brown eyes swam with tears and her voice was one that Gudrun wouldn't have expected to hear from her: soft and full of sadness and immediately Gudrun was embarrassed and ashamed too. At that moment, she wished she could take back her gift; for in some way, Willow seemed diminished and vulnerable. "Nobody ever gave me anythin' this beautiful before in my life," she said as she hugged Gudrun with such exuberance that she could feel the buttons on her own sweater dig into her chest.

Then Gudrun sighed with relief as Willow became herself again and stood at the darkened window to get a full-length view of herself as she pirouetted, hands on hips, loudly humming "Ain't She Sweet." Their friendship was to last until Willow's death, and Gudrun rarely saw her without the sweater. Over the years, the color dimmed and it bulged in places to conform to Willow's ever-changing shape; and even though Gudrun knit other sweaters for her, the butter yellow thank you from a young girl's heart remained her favorite.

Chapter 3

"So well I know my duty to my elders."
(THE TAMING OF THE SHREW) WILLIAM SHAKESPEARE

As the days grew warmer and the to-do list shorter, Gudrun began to dread the coming of the family and her relegation to the servant role again. "They're not so bad," Willow would assure her, "They're pretty fair about giving you time off, and they're not fussy and complaining."

And so, one warm afternoon they arrived. Gudrun had met both Mr. and Mrs. Gendron at the interview. Mrs. Gendron was pleasant and happy; Mr. Gendron, who was a St. Paul lawyer, shook her hand formally and said, "How do you do, Gudrun?" He seemed not to remember he had met her before. There was a fourteen-year-old girl, Francis—pretty but belligerent about something—and a four-year-old boy, Jimmy, who was being yanked around the yard by a huge, black dog that looked more like a bear than a canine. Gudrun realized the family was aware of the similarity when she heard the dog's name.

"Heel, Ursa!" the boy screamed as the animal charged to sniff one tree, rock, or patch of ground after another, never stopping long enough to let the boy regain stable footing.

"He's been cooped up in that car for hours," Mrs. Gendron apologized. "He's usually much better behaved. At any rate, let me assure you that he will not be part of your responsibilities. He belongs to the children, and they must take care of him." The last was delivered in a shout and directed, with a tilt of her head, at each offspring in turn.

"I never wanted that smelly, old thing," Francis whined. "I don't see why I have to take care of him or why I had to come with you at all. You've ruined my summer!" Gudrun stood in amazement as the girl burst into tears and ran out of the kitchen.

"I'll do her share if he can be my dog alone," came a quiet voice at Gudrun's elbow. She turned to see an exertion-reddened face almost lost behind tortoise-shell glasses, now perched slightly askew on the bridge of the boy's nose. The magnification of his eyes gave him a startled expression, which Gudrun was to learn was his natural look and not the result of his recent foray around the yard. Ursa howled from his tether in the back yard as the boy extended his hand formally, as his father had. "How do you do. I'm James Gendron, Jr., but my parents call me Jimmy to prevent confusion."

"And what shall I call you?" Gudrun asked as she knelt to his height, suddenly blushing when she realized her question might be construed as being forward. He seemed stunned at being asked for his opinion and even glanced in his Mother's direction before answering.

"Jimmy will be fine," he said as he smiled broadly. Gudrun would always remember Jimmy for his brilliant smile, which was the most sincere she had ever seen.

The first impressions were made and remained surprisingly intact over that summer and many summers to come. Mrs. Gendron was talkative and agreeable, clearly in charge even though she seemed constantly flustered, as if life was too much to handle. Mr. Gendron made many trips back and forth to St. Paul; but when in residence, was aloof and preoccupied, usually preferring to be closeted in his study rather than on the beach or the porch. He always looked somewhat alarmed when he encountered Gudrun cleaning or cooking, and his eyes momentarily glazed as he mentally scanned his brain before he remembered her identity and function.

Gudrun was a servant to Francis. All requests were delivered as orders and no pleasantries ever exchanged. The beauty and seclusion of the Island were as nails in the coffin of her social life, which as she readily told any listener, only thrived among her friends at the swimming pools and summer parties back on Summit Avenue. Francis' emergence from puberty would eventually improve their relationship; but they would always remain, if on a friendlier level, servant and mistress.

Jimmy, on the other hand, would become Gudrun's constant companion, following her like a puppy (with Ursa smiling and drooling at his heels) and chattering constantly about learning to read, going to school, what he would be when he grew up, and asking questions, few of which Gudrun could answer although this didn't seem to bother him.

Gradually the family settled into their summer vacation life and Gudrun's days were full with cleaning and cooking. Willow handled the laundry and helped with some of the heavier chores and on nights when Mrs. Gendron entertained Island or visiting St. Paul friends.

Gudrun, within boundaries, began to think of the house as hers and initiated cleaning and baking before being told, confirming Mrs. Gendron's wisdom in her choice of a "reticent Scandinavian." The Saturday night buffets at the Gendrons became the most sought after invitation on the Island or in Bayfield. The huge roasted turkey, stuffed with oysters and resplendent on its bed of parsley, dominated the table on these occasions.

Its only competition was the tall ring of orange rolls, which Gudrun had perfected from her mother's sweet dough recipe. She rolled uniform sized balls of the dough in a powdered sugar icing, heavily laced with orange juice and fresh zest, and then in chopped pecans. She then packed them in an angel food tin to rise and eventually bake. The result provided the centerpiece for the buffet table. Turned out of the pan and drizzled with the remaining orange icing, the crown of rolls made Gudrun famous in that rarified, summer circle where indulgences of all sorts were frantically pursued in the belief that they were as limited and fleeting as the balmy, fair weather.

On several occasions, guests of both genders would surreptitiously slip into the kitchen after dinner and offer Gudrun more money, or other enticements much sought after by local domestics, to work for them. Gudrun was flattered, but being satisfied and fiercely loyal to the person who had given her the chance to experience this new life, she humbly refused.

On her days off, or during any spare time snatched from her busy schedule, Gudrun continued her exploration of the Island and the lake Superior mystique that surrounded it as an aura, sometimes almost visible and many-colored as a prism. In the middle of June she witnessed for her first time yet another miracle of nature when the roadsides and meadows bloomed with the tall lupine flowers.

The many shades of lavender and pink were rivaled only by the varied combinations of colors that turned any untended area, no matter how bleak or neglected, into banks of purple spires. Gudrun could hardly believe that such a display was random, but the plants sprouted indiscriminately in fertile or poor soil alike, even pushing their way through fissures in the rock cliffs to stand, during their season, undaunted in the face of the lake wind and spray.

At first she was like a young lover, insatiable with her desire to possess, and, much to the amusement of Willow and the Gendrons, gathered armfuls of lupine that she distributed in every room of the house. But they didn't do well in vases. When in captivity, the tall stalks bent themselves at weird angles, seeming almost to be straining to escape their containers; and the all too sensitive Gudrun endowed them with emotions and refused to pick them after her first frenzied and thoughtless violation.

Jimmy, with the ubiquitous Ursa a step behind, found Gudrun emptying the withered flowers onto Arne's compost heap in the back yard. "Are we going to pick more lupine this morning?" he asked, hopefully, for his outings with Gudrun and Willow were quickly becoming the high point of his summer.

"Not this morning." She saw his face sag slightly, anticipating a rejection. She could feel his uncertainty sharp as a sudden pain. Was she going to be busy with her work, or did she really not want a kid hanging around? Gudrun identified with this awkward boy whose eagerness was often confused with pestering. His loneliness was almost palpable.

"I've decided that the lupine look prettiest when they're growing straight in the fields," she said as she gathered the empty vases. "But we can walk the beach and look for bobbers if you'd like." Relief and gratitude flooded his great, magnified eyes, reminding Gudrun of Ursa's adoring gaze when she stopped to pet him.

The lupine season came and went, and although Gudrun was sad to see the splendid flowers fade and die, other firsts in what she came to think of as her born-again life took their place. In their evil-smelling little fishing boat, Willow and Arne took her, with Jimmy and Ursa, to several other islands in the Apostle group where eagles and falcons nested and ferns almost as tall as a person made the small dots of land in the vast lake look like prehistoric forests. They explored the many and varied lighthouses still operating on the outer islands and fished for lake trout in sheltered coves, wading into the beaches to eat picnic lunches

The work was hard and tiring; but these domestic chores were Gudrun's special skills, and she reveled in them, gradually becoming bold enough to make menu or housekeeping suggestions that were met with grateful acceptance. She looked forward to Monday morning when Mrs. Gendron would sit in the breakfast nook with her, and, over a cup of coffee, plan the coming week's meals, entertaining, and housework. Her employer often concluded these sessions by saying, "You're making my summer an absolute joy. What did I ever do without you?" The same thought remained unspoken in her own mind, as she shyly dropped her eyes and smiled.

Toward the end of June, her trust in Gudrun prompted Mrs. Gendron to make a request that did not fall within the realm of her usual household duties. "I hate to take your evening," she apologized, "but Francis wants to go into Bayfield to roller-skate at the Pavilion on Wednesday night. I think she's meeting a young boy there. She's been so miserable here this summer that I hate to say no to the first thing she's shown any interest in. What I was wondering was, well, I hate to send her off unattended. Could you maybe go to the mainland that night and sort of keep an eye on her? Not so she notices, of course. I'd just feel better. You could take Willow with you, as if you two girls were on an outing?" Her pleading manner precluded any thought of refusal, and although Gudrun had no protective feelings for the arrogant girl (as she did for Jimmy) she agreed to assume the role of the unseen chaperone.

Chapter 4

"That love should of a sudden take such hold."
(THE TAMING OF THE SHREW) WILLIAM SHAKESPEARE

illow was delighted with the whole idea of the subterfuge, and chattered constantly as they rode the ferry to the mainland. She spoke in a loud, stage whisper about inconsequential places and events, lapsing into furtive remarks shielded by her hand and accompanied by glances toward Francis, who sat some distance from her two bodyguards, staring towards the horizon.

"Do you think we have to follow her everywhere? What if she goes off to neck with this guy? Should we watch?" (An idea obviously relished by Willow and made perfectly legitimate by virtue of their mission.) Gudrun hoped with all her heart that this decision wouldn't present itself.

"Shh! She'll know we're talking about her if you look at her like that."

"I don't care! It might do little Miss High-and-Mighty some good if she took a roll in the hay. She might not be so snooty and crabby."

"Don't say things like that! She's just a girl and she's our responsibility. Mrs. Gendron would never forgive me if I let that happen."

Willow snorted under her breath. "You might not have any say in the matter if it comes to that, unless you plan on wadin' in and throwin' a bucket a cold water on 'em!" Willow couldn't help herself at this clever remark and whooped with laughter before clamping her hand over her mouth. Francis, along with the other passengers on board, looked quickly at Willow, and Gudrun colored.

They kept well behind Francis as they left the ferry. The Pavilion was built at the end of the dock and extended out over the water. Before they left the boat, they could hear the lilting music and see the rays from the revolving globe suspended from the ceiling. As long as she lived, this memory of summer nights would lie softly on Gudrun's mind as she heard the strains of "Let Me Call You Sweetheart" intermingle with flickering half shadows as the light played on the waves.

A young boy of 15 or 16 stood at the foot of the dock and stepped forward as Francis approached. They greeted each other shyly and walked stiffly to the Pavilion. In the instant she turned to enter the door, Gudrun caught the expression on Francis's face and felt a rush of sympathy when she recognized the unmistakable look of self-consciousness and uncertainty.

"He's just a pimply kid!" Willow sputtered, seeming disappointed that Francis's date hadn't turned out to be a leering, cigarette-smoking predator. "You won't need to be worryin' about your responsibility tonight, Gudrun. That one won't be up for much more than a feel, if that."

From the top of the wall halfway to the floor, the sides of the Pavilion were comprised of shutters which, propped up and out, provided air for the skaters and a roof over the spectators who leaned on their elbows against the half wall and watched the circling figures inside. The faceted ball threw elongated diamond shapes across the floor, and a pale yellow crescent, shaped to resemble the moon and lit from inside, slowly traversed the ceiling on a thin track, as if orbiting a microcosm of music and light and movement.

Gudrun had never seen anything like it and almost forgot about Francis in her effort to accommodate the sensory bombardment caused by her first glimpse of what could pass for glamour. She lapsed briefly into her fantasy world and imagined she was gliding across the floor. "There they are," hissed Willow, "on the other side." Gudrun followed her pointing finger and saw the couple gingerly take the floor and join the other skaters. They were slow and hesitating at first; but the boy seemed to be giving her some instructions, demonstrating long strides, and soon they too were gliding and laughing with the others.

They watched for awhile—Gudrun in fascination, Willow getting increasingly bored. "I'm gonna go uptown for a beer," she finally decided. "You wanna come along and have an orange or somethin'? They ain't gonna be done for a long time." In the short time they had been friends, Gudrun had come a long way out of her church-imposed shell to either ignore or accept willow's excessive ways. But it was one thing to accept them, and quite another to join them. This Gudrun could not do!

"I'll stay here and watch," she offered. "Don't forget, we take the ten o'clock. ferry back." Now alone, Gudrun was free to step back into dreamland and skate once more, this time with an imaginary partner holding her tightly. She was so absorbed that she didn't notice when a young man left the circle and skated towards her until his skates bumped the wall and jarred her awake.

"Hello! Why don't you come in and skate?"

"Oh, thank you, but I don't know how."

"I'll teach you. There's nothing to it!" Without further argument, he motioned and coaxed her along the wall until they met face to face at the door. "Come on, I'll rent you some skates." Gudrun, never good at opposition, couldn't refuse but feared she would embarrass him and herself with her clumsiness. He kept a steady stream of conversation going as he sat her down, measured her foot, and tightly laced the ungainly rolling shoes to her feet.

She tried to stand but rolled backwards, then overcompensated and ended falling forward. He caught her in both arms, laughing uproariously. "It's like bein' on the Big Lake for the first time. You gotta get your sea legs! For awhile they struggled, looking at times as if they were engaged in some sort of slow and gentle wrestling match. Gradually, with his left arm tightly around her waist and their right hands locked and protruding in front like a rudder, they managed to complete a circle without mishap

"See! I declare you're a natural. I've never seen man nor woman get their sea legs that fast." He showed her the long, gliding stride that Francis's friend had demonstrated, and soon Gudrun was floating and smiling, but concentrating very hard.

Finally she felt confident enough to lift her eyes from her feet and sneak a look at her partner. He was taller than she, but not by much and very muscular. He was dark: brown eyes and black curly hair, with a smile that showed his even, white teeth.

He's very handsome, she thought. *I wonder why he's bothering with me.*

At this point he steered her to the refreshment stand and ordered two bottles of orange pop. They sat on a bench with their drinks. "Want some?" He had taken a small, flat silver container out of his pants pocket and was pouring some of the contents into his pop bottle.

"What is it?"

"Just a little booze to sparken it up a bit."

"No thanks. I don't drink."

"Me neither, just for medicinal purposes, and I feel a cold comin' on." He laughed at his tired, old joke and poked her playfully in the ribs. "My name's Cy Gaudette, What's yours?"

"Gudrun Carlson, I work over on the Island for the Gendrons, as a cook and maid." Gudrun couldn't believe she was freely offering this much information and immediately wondered if she was being too forward.

"Yeah? A cook, huh? Are you a good one, Gudrun?" He laughed again at his play on words and bumped her shoulder with his. "That's an odd name, Gudrun. What nationality would that be?"

"Swedish. I'm named for my grandmother in the old country."

"That a fact? I'm French. We been here since the voyageurs, but now I'm a fisherman and so was my dad. My boat's moored over there, The Sea Siren. You ever read that story about those sea sirens that lured that poor guy off course? That's her—that's who she's named after." He took another giant swig from his bottle and looked pensive. Gudrun thought he wasn't going to talk any more when he suddenly asked, "You ever cook fish?"

"At least once a week for the family; and if I go fishing with my friends, Willow and Arne Peterson, we build a fire and cook what we catch right on the beach. It tastes so good that way."

"You friends with Willow?" He laughed again. "Somehow you two don't seem as if you'd be friends."

"She's my best friend."

He drained his bottle and dropped it into the crate of empties. He took hers and set it under the bench as he pulled her unsteadily to her feet. "Come

32

on, let's skate!" Once again she was encircled by his arms and performed admirably. If she wavered in the least, his grip tightened and she couldn't have fallen if she'd tried. Sometimes he lifted her right off the floor until she was able to regain her rhythm. She was exhilarated beyond her wildest dreams and found herself wishing the night would never end.

But all too soon she heard the strain of "Good Night Sweetheart," and they skated slowly as the crescent moon had reached its destination and hung suspended and still in the ceiling. "Good night, Gudrun," he said as the music ended. "Will you be back to skate next Wednesday? You've got to practice, you know, or you'll lose your sea legs." His smile was a flash of white teeth in the darkness as they stood outside the Pavilion.

"I'll probably be here. It's my night off." It was a decision unusually quick for Gudrun.

"Then I'll see ya." He leaned close and she detected the sharp smell of liquor on his breath as he kissed her forehead. "Your eyes are the same color as that sweater of yours," he said as he walked away.

Gudrun stood rooted in a stupor. Was this real or had she truly gone over the dividing line and was confusing her dreams with reality? She started when she heard Willow's voice.

"Cy, you old dog, what you doin' in town? Ain't you out fishin'?"

"Gotta come in sometime or go nuts. Been skatin' with your little, blue-eyed friend."

"Hope you didn't scare her," she called over her shoulder, as they grew further apart.

"You okay, honey? He didn't say nothin' nasty to you, did he? He can get pretty raunchy when he's been drinkin'."

"He taught me to skate. It was a lot of fun." Gudrun suddenly remembered Francis and the reason they had come to the mainland. "Oh my gosh! Where'd Francis go? I can't believe I forgot all about her. Mrs. Gendron'll fire me if anything happens to her."

Willow didn't say anything but nudged her and pointed into a dark corner of the Pavilion near the water. They were in a tight embrace, kissing. The boy's hand had dropped casually below her waist, as if resting from the strain of holding her, and cupped one buttock through the skirt fabric. Gudrun instinctively moved towards the couple, but Willow took her arm and said loudly, "Come on Gudrun. We'd better hurry or we'll miss the ferry."

The embrace broke immediately and Francis ran up the dock. When they boarded the ferry, she sat in her original place, once again staring at the horizon, although in the dark, it couldn't have been much of a view. Gudrun could see her flushed face and puffy lips from where she sat and wondered how long they had been engaging in their activity.

Why hadn't she paid more attention to her? She should have noticed if she left the Pavilion.

When they reached La Pointe, Mrs. Gendron was waiting in the station wagon.

"I didn't want you to walk home alone in the dark," she called to Francis and then, "Gudrun and Willow! I didn't know you girls were in town. Would you like a ride?"

The following morning Francis came into the kitchen, supposedly to get a cereal that wasn't on the sideboard in the dining room.

"Don't forget to put out the puffed wheat," she commanded, "It's my favorite."

"I'm sorry, I thought you favored corn flakes."

"I like a little variety now and then, don't you?" The last was delivered with a conspiratorial tone, as she paused in the doorway holding the cereal box.

"I don't eat much cold cereal, so I don't know."

"What about men? That guy you were with last night didn't exactly seem like your type. I'll bet you didn't meet him in church." She laughed and left before Gudrun could reply. When Willow came to help change the beds, Gudrun told her about the encounter.

"What if she tells her mother?"

"So what? It was your night off, and all you were doin' was skatin', weren't you?"

"Well yes, but I was supposed to be watching her, not enjoying myself."

"We were supposed to act like we weren't watching her and were there on a night in town, which we did. Quit worryin', the Queen Bee was just mad she had the pimple face and you had a handsome guy."

"He is handsome, isn't he? Gudrun mused as she shook the pillows from their cases. Willow eyed her narrowly from her side of the bed.

"You fallin' for Cy? Cause if you are, you should know that he jollies-up lots a girls and is a pretty heavy drinker, to boot."

"Of course not! I just enjoyed the skating, and he was very nice and considerate. I'll probably never see him again, anyway. As you say, I'm sure he has lots of girls."

Willow was silent but looked worried. Gudrun's cheeks were flushed rosy and the beginnings of a smile barely upturned the corners of her mouth. *Please let him be there next Wednesday*, she prayed to the God who had heard only one other request from her: "Please make my Mother well."

But Gudrun wasn't quite as innocent as Willow suspected. Her lonely existence allowed plenty of time for fantasizing, or "make believe" as she preferred to think of it and as she automatically helped Willow with the morning chores, she grew quiet and allowed herself to slip into her alter universe where she skated with Cy under a real moon and twinkling stars. Willow's face tightened with concern as she observed for the first time her friend's emotional withdrawal from the real world, busying herself while she unconsciously hummed, under her breath, snatches of a melody: "Let me call you sweetheart, I'm in love with you."

Chapter 5

"Quickly dream away the time"
(A MIDSUMMER NIGHT'S DREAM) WILLIAM SHAKESPEARE

*G*udrun had been a lonely child, under constant scrutiny from a stern and over-protective mother and inwardly hounded during every waking hour, and in her dreams, by the threat of sin and its dire consequences.

School provided an intellectual outlet and Gudrun was an eager student, not overly bright, but so persistent that sheer effort afforded her a place academically at the head of the class. This honor garnered praise from her teachers but didn't help her make friends with her classmates; aside from her painful shyness, she now had to endure the agony of being singled out either for recognition or teasing, both equally abhorrent to her.

"Here comes 'punkin head'," her class's male ringleaders would taunt as she approached the school in the morning. "Is that why your head is so big, 'cause of your big brain?" Some of the girls stood in a tight knot giggling and spurring on the hecklers' clever gibes. They couldn't oppose the boys, and were also were jealous of Gudrun's success—a success she gladly would have relinquished to be one of them or even just one of the ignored who lurked on the perimeter of that magic circle of popularity, as did a majority of the school ground population, observing with studied indifference, relieved and passive in their anonymity.

Once, out of the corner of her eye, she noticed Jalmer Johnson leaning against the step railing surveying the scene. He looked straight at her, and for a fleeting moment, she imagined him coming to her defense. She actually saw him throw down the piece of grass he was chewing and leap at the largest tormentor, rolling in the dust with him until at last he would hold his bleeding face inches from the schoolyard dust and force him to "apologize or eat dirt!" But in an instant, the image vanished and Gudrun saw Jalmer continue to lounge languidly, and when he knew she was looking, slowly shift his eyes to a distant point on the horizon, as if the local drama was not worth noticing.

All her life she remembered walking through that gauntlet of sneering faces, her cheeks flaming and her eyes fixed straight ahead. Later she would ask permission to be excused from the classroom and hurry to the bathroom, there to gaze into the mirror and try to determine if her head was abnormally large. It was impossible to tell without another head for comparison, which left her staring forlornly at her mousy-colored hair, so tightly braided that it pulled the skin of her temples back and made her eyes look small and squinty; the mouth with a slightly full lower lip, resulting in a perpetually pouty expression; and a nose more straight and pronounced than she'd like.

That night she lay in the darkness listening to the drone of her mother's evening prayer. Earlier she had knelt by her mother's side and recited a long litany of sins she had committed that day. Sometimes she made up transgressions to please her: I envied Karen Ableman's sweater (she had really thought it ugly and poorly knit) or I felt pride that I had 100% on my spelling test (this was true, but she was not sorry for it). Gudrun knew that if her list were short, mother would say, "Well, Miss, you must be an angel that you haven't sinned today!" It was easier and took far less time to confess, ask forgiveness, and be excused for bed. Then she was free to think and mull over in her mind all the thoughts and questions that buzzed in her head like flies at a window, seeming like trapped insects butting against the inside of her skull looking for a way out.

Tonight she wanted to think hard about how she had seen Jalmer defend her at school. She knew he hadn't, but she also remembered completely removing herself from the whole encounter while she had imagined swift retribution justly administered. The feeling had been exhilarating. Gudrun reasoned it would be easy to repeat that exercise in any difficult situation, saving herself the taint of embarrassment while remaining calm and unruffled.

She snuggled further into the blankets and allowed her imagination to expand her earlier fantasy. Jalmer would hold the bully roughly by the nape of his neck and force him to stand in front of her. Through tears he would blubber, "I'm sorry, Gudrun, (no, Miss Carlson) and I won't ever tease you again."

After that, Jalmer would take her arm, solicitously, and inquire, "Are you okay, Gudrun?" to which she would smile warmly and reply, "Yes, thank you. You're so kind!" A delicious warmth spread through her body as she lay unmoving, for fear of breaking the spell, and she felt herself smiling. *It's so easy,* she thought. *I can make anything happen. I can even change the way I look, what I wear. I can make myself talk without stuttering and imagine myself making all sorts of clever and bold remarks to the "giggling girls" as they look at me enviously.*

On this day, Gudrun had discovered the land of fantasy where she would dwell, off and on, for the rest of her life. Her smile broadened as she continued to test her powers.

She perfected her power to withdraw into her own fantasy land. Mostly she imagined herself as wildly popular. All the girls wanted to eat lunch with her and complimented her on her clothes, which were always a light shade of blue. (Once a kind church lady had said her eyes were cornflower blue, and Gudrun had seized the compliment like a lifeline.) Parties in blue taffeta dresses occupied most of her elementary school daydreams and, of course, scenes of swift punishment for those who crossed her in any way.

At first she waited until she was in bed to lose herself in her thoughts, but the practice grew addictive; sometimes she would gaze into space in the middle of class and leave the school room behind as she soared, floating and twisting, in her fantasies. More than once Gudrun found the teacher by her desk talking to her and she had no idea how she had gotten there or what she had said.

In the apartment with Mother, she retired to an empty room and quietly spun the intricate plots with herself as the heroine. The stories grew involved and occupied more and more of her time. Sometimes, without her realizing it, the characters stepped into the world of reality, speaking and moving, causing Gudrun to mumble in response, rock back and forth, or smile and gesture to herself.

One day, as she was completely lost in communication with her fantasies, she heard her name called sharply and awoke to see her mother's shocked stare from the doorway, the pastor's wife, wide-eyed, standing slightly behind her. She felt the heat spread from her neck to her cheeks as she frantically searched her brain for a plausible explanation for her behavior, all the while wondering what she had been doing and how much they had seen.

"I was practicing a play we're having at school," she managed.

"Go peel the potatoes for supper," Mother directed, clearly not in acceptance but not wishing to press the issue in front of outsiders. Gudrun was glad to escape. She knew Mother wasn't done with her, but at least the interval gave her time to make her original story more convincing.

"Your teacher tells me you spend a lot of time daydreaming in school," she began later that evening.

"My grades are good."

"Pride goeth before a fall."

"Sometimes I'm done with my work before the others and go over it in my mind to make sure I haven't made any mistakes." Mother looked at her hard and long, and Gudrun knew she had to return that look, unflinchingly, to be believed. After endless seconds, Mother averted her eyes.

"When you act like you did today, people will get the idea there's something wrong with you. Do you want that?" Gudrun immediately thought of David Dahlberg, a boy from church, who drooled and spouted loud, unintelligible comments. People always whispered that there was, "something wrong" with him and usually accompanied their obscure diagnosis with a finger tap to the temple or the even more explicit gesture—the circling forefinger at the side of the head.

As a result of her near discovery, Gudrun was forced to lead an ever-expanding secret life. So it wasn't surprising that her awakening to womanhood would be conducted in a clandestine fantasy world that her mother or Pastor Lundquist would never imagine. The quiet, obedient daughter and pious church member suppressed and masked all the normal, sensual feelings of adolescence and lived through them in a dream world that only she entered.

There were babies born to couples in their church, so she knew from a fairly early age that the mothers carried them in their bodies. She knew this long before Mother quit explaining that the new mothers had "found" their babies behind a lumber pile at the nearby saw mill. Even then she hadn't challenged her mother but wondered that she thought her so dumb and unobservant that she would swallow such an improbable tale. Later, of course, she was told that God planted a seed in the chosen mothers, and this seemed entirely plausible. Lacking the "facts of life," but admonished early on about avoiding certain activities with boys, she got the idea that any function that occurred below the waist was shrouded in secrecy and somehow dirty or sinful.

When she was 11, she had her first menses. It came at school and she hadn't an inkling what was wrong. She knew she wasn't feeling well and when she went into the bathroom, she discovered the rust-brown stains that she knew must portend a horrible disease. Her ashen face convinced the teacher that she should be sent home where she lay in her bed, hardly daring to move, until her mother came from work.

"I have something terribly wrong," she managed to gulp through her tears. "I'm bleeding and I don't know why because I didn't fall or anything."

"Where are you bleeding?"

"Down there," came the shameful whisper and without a gesture her mother knew where "down there" was.

"Don't cry about that," her mother said, "It's the curse of all women to bleed down there every month. It means that your body is ready to have a baby when the Lord deems that it is right."

"Will I have a baby?"

"Not for many years and not before you have a proper, Christian husband."

This rudimentary explanation satisfied Gudrun, and any questions she had were curtly answered, always skirting sex. Her isolation from other girls her age prevented her from gleaning any information through the grapevine route, and it wasn't until she went to church camp the summer after seventh grade that the awful truth was revealed to her.

One talkative, older girl in Gudrun's cabin always initiated what she called "pillow talks" after lights out was sounded. The girls would gather on one bunk and giggle about boys and the presence or absence of breasts. Gudrun couldn't bring herself to participate mainly because it was breaking the lights out rule, but she lay quietly in her bunk and strained to hear every word.

"It's really not fair," one girl said loudly. "Women have to carry a baby for nine whole months and have it, and men only have to do that one thing." Gudrun could hardly keep from asking, but fortunately another less shy innocent was a "pillow talk" participant.

"What one thing?" she blurted. At first there was general laughter, then the girls warmed to their story and one by one the sordid details were recited. "That can't be true," the shocked innocent declared, "My mother and dad wouldn't do a dirty thing like that!"

"Ask them," came the reply.

"I can't, they'd get mad at me for even thinking a thing like that."

"At least you're an only child. That means they only did it once. I have four brothers and sisters," came another thin voice.

Gudrun knew instinctively that it was all true. It completed the puzzle with answers for many of her unasked or obscurely answered questions. She knew she wouldn't tell the counselor or her mother, for that matter, what she had heard. For one thing, she was too embarrassed to even think of the act much less repeat it; for another, she had always regretted telling on Jalmer Johnson at that long-ago picnic and didn't care to repeat the indiscretion.

And so, she harbored her secret and, from time to time, was able to learn a little more to add to her fund of knowledge. Eventually, without a word spoken between them, her mother assumed that Gudrun knew the facts of life and although Gudrun wondered how her mother thought she had learned them, it was their tacit agreement to speak of it no more. Her eighth-grade teacher talked in health class about the normal, healthy act of procreation, but the Bible verses stressed the wife's duty to her husband and the whole act of childbirth as Adam and Eve's punishment for their original disobedience, or, as it was referred to, "the original sin."

But then she began to have odd attractions to boys and craved their attentions, regretting that none were forthcoming. She thought of this as God's test of her obedience and vowed to handle it in her usual fashion by withdrawing into her own world and imagining long, intricate scenarios involving an acceptable, Christian husband.

She could shut out the world around her and dream of this handsome man who was just as disgusted by sex as she, but might agree to it in order to have beautiful, curly-haired babies. He was inordinately fond of her, however, and held her hand, kissed her, and hugged her tenderly at every opportunity. She never imagined them actually having sex, but sometimes dreamed of his hands caressing her body and his kisses on her neck and shoulders. Then she would awaken with her face hot and an indescribable pain to her pelvic region that wasn't so much a pain as a yearning.

"I can't control my dreams," she would rationalize to herself, but sometimes she couldn't distinguish between her day and night dreams and found herself in church or at school feeling the touch and experiencing the yearning. Her teachers were concerned about her withdrawal and preoccupation and spoke to her mother.

"I guess I'm just not interested in school any more," Gudrun defended.

"Then there's no sense in your going on to high school," her Mother said. "You might as well come help me at my cleaning jobs. At least you'll have an honest trade." And so Gudrun's profession was decided for her. She would have no further education beyond the required eighth grade and not much contact with her own age group; but no one, not Mother, the church, or even God, was able to take away the handsome, fantasy mate who remained faithfully at her beck and call.

Chapter 6

"A man worth any woman"
(CYMBELINE) WILLIAM SHAKESPEARE

or a while, Gudrun was determined that she would cure herself of what she began to view as her affliction. Maybe Mother was right. Maybe there was "something wrong" with her. If she could keep her mind occupied with tasks that required constant attention, maybe she wouldn't be tempted to escape into the dreamland, which sometimes seemed sullied with a film of sickness and shame.

She threw herself into perfecting her needlework. Under Mother's watchful eye, she set about learning every intricate loop and knot of silken thread which resulted in the beautifully embroidered flowers adorning growing stacks of pillowcases, table runners, and dish towels. She had to admit she enjoyed the pastime and began to design her own patterns and combine colors that elicited "oohs" and "ahs" from the church ladies. Best of all, Gudrun could tell Mother was pleased with her new interest and proud of her skill, although she didn't voice it for fear of appearing prideful. Gradually, she expanded her work to include knitting, crocheting, and sewing. As she grew older and more skillful, some of Mother's "ladies" (the women whose houses she cleaned) would hire Gudrun to decorate items or make garments for their families.

And so she forged the bars that imprisoned her behind the dull, gray walls of the relentless day-to-day and eroded her spirit by denying her access to the power she possessed to soften and alter reality.

But she felt a great emptiness in her chest—almost a grief for something that had died in her. She had experienced the rush of wind under the fledgling wings of her imagination, and the sensation was much too heady to still. Consequently, she furtively began again practicing her other, secret skill behind closed doors or in the privacy of her bed at night. She paid attention to every detail which might give her away: not to spend too much time in the bathroom so as to arouse suspicion; never to "escape" during church; and always to maintain the calm, expressionless demeanor of one without a thought or care in her head. As she grew older, she imagined herself talkative and interesting, with adults and peers alike in rapt attention to her every utterance. She fabricated whole conversations in her mind and knew them to be intelligent expressions of her thoughts on interesting subjects, all the while remaining silent.

And then came adolescence, when hormones coursed through Gudrun's body with as much fervor as those that caused the girls at school to primp and simper, betray their friends, and generally live a miserable existence worrying about dates, or the lack of same. The boys sparred in outlandish ways for attention, bragged of mostly phantom sexual accomplishments, and usually relieved their frustrations in the age-old manner, only casually wondering if they would go blind or lose that member that had suddenly become their most important, if troubling, appendage. It was at this point that Gudrun invented her lover who remained faithful for life, even cradling her in his arms at the moment of her death, allowing her the dignity of a fearless passage and shielding her one last time from the reality whose cruelties he had always enabled her to evade.

Gudrun experimented with making her phantom lover from boys she knew at school. But she soon realized that when she no longer fancied their attentions or even grew to dislike them, she then had to conjure up replacement boyfriends. She found the same to be true of celebrities; their fleeting popularity caused her to feel fickle. No, it was much more satisfying to mold him entirely from imagination, so he could remain steadfast and true. He was tall, six-foot-one (or two), blond curly hair, blue-eyed, very tan, and very muscular. His physical appearance mimicked the ideal man concept, but his face remained a blur to Gudrun no matter how hard she tried to settle on features for him.

His foremost characteristic was his overwhelming love for Gudrun, being willing and eager to sacrifice his own comfort and well being to ensure hers. She called him Glen after a boy who had visited school once but had left before anyone knew anything about him.

Over the years, the demands made on Glen changed. At first he was her knight who slew all her personal dragons and extracted vengeance. During her early teens, he patiently taught her all the things she couldn't do (many times because they weren't allowed by the church). They danced while other couples ringed the floor watching; they swam, their tanned bodies (now Gudrun could turn her pale skin and freckles to gold) plying the water in tandem; they rode bikes, picnicked, and played softball, always surrounded by beautiful, laughing couples who were their friends.

The immature longing of a young girl for a rose-covered cottage and apple-cheeked, dimpled babies put her hero through a time of storybook weddings and the appearance, as if by magic, of one adorable baby after another. However, when Gudrun, shocked and disbelieving, was finally advised of the facts of life, she mentally erased the weddings and babies, relegating him to his former role of knight in shining armor, ready to do battle for her, but only for the purest of motives.

Her suppressed sexuality finally did blossom, however, and at first shamefully, she began to imagine him naked, his body that of a slightly modified Adonis whose picture she'd seen in a magazine. Finally, she could no longer admire from afar; and, while safely tucked into her bed at night, she sent shy and tentative fingers to touch him with feather-like caresses that teased her own body into one tingling sensation. It was a sin of great proportions. Mother had told her never to touch herself "down there" except to wash; and she had obeyed, until now.

Her physical need for him grew as she became bolder in her explorations of the curves and crevices of his body. At night they would lay entwined, pressing so close that Gudrun could almost feel her skin merging with his and her soul entering his body. Her hands rubbed and fondled the quilted tufts of the mattress, as she kissed her pillow and he whispered, "I love you" to her parted lips.

Inevitably, the night came when he entered her after she was nearly mad from his probing and petting. Although Gudrun was orchestrating the whole drama, it came as a shock to her. She considered stopping short, but his hands gently chaffed the nipples of her breasts and she surged into the denouement of her dream, suddenly afraid when she realized that her lover had sapped her power and her fantasies now controlled her.

He still defended, admired, and loved her to distraction; but at night he demanded his payment. Gudrun rationalized that no sin was being committed since it all took place in her mind. She didn't even admit to unclean thoughts, since they involved no other human being. She was careful to arrange the twisted sheets of her bed before Mother saw them in the morning and soon came to accept her lover as an integral part of her life, her aid and comfort.

To all outward appearances, Gudrun was still the introverted, religious, smart (but blindingly dull) young woman who ate alone and spent the rest of the lunch hour reading a book. But as the school year wore on, they noticed a difference in her. She smiled more readily, and there was a softness about her that gave her a dreamy, almost ethereal quality. She was never irritable or short with anyone, and often extended shy compliments to the other girls, sincere in her admiration, but devoid of any bitter envy.

She became self-effacing but satisfied with her lot in life. She was pleasant company, as well as helpful and ambitious. In short, she became everything that Mother and the church had wanted her to be. She was even accepted by the girls at school (she was not a threat) and, miraculously, the teasing stopped. Sometimes her mother watched and envied her, secretly wondering why, with all the prayers she sent to heaven, she had never been granted the inner peace that shone in her daughter's face.

Chapter 7

"Now quick desire hath caught the yielding prey."
(VENUS AND ADONIS) WILLIAM SHAKESPEARE

And so the summer melted away, as Gudrun moved like a sleepwalker through her duties on the Island, seeming to live for Wednesday nights when she met Cy at the Pavilion. As he had predicted, with weekly practice, she became a fairly good skater. In fact, she felt confident enough to let him twirl her under his arm and even to skate with their bodies facing, as if they were dancing. Dancing was a sin in the eyes of her church, but Gudrun rationalized that this was much like the circle games they had played at Bible school so couldn't be sinful.

Her emotions almost overwhelmed her when she skate-danced with Cy. It was becoming harder and harder to distinguish him in her mind from her fantasy lover, Glen. He took on many of the mannerisms that she had imagined, and when she dreamed of Glen (which wasn't that often lately), he increasingly took the face of Cy, flashing his white teeth in a wide smile and nuzzling her cheek impulsively.

Gudrun softened. She sometimes thought of herself as a piece of the colored glass she found on the beach: once translucent and sharp-edged, she felt the knife like corners of her resolve become rounded and smooth with Cy's compliments; and her once clear thoughts became opaque and dulled by the intoxication of Cy's physical presence. The vivid colors of her aura turned muted and pastel.

Their relationship turned more physical each week. Gudrun worried about the liquor that Cy seemed to need; but, in her frenzy to explain away any doubts, she looked on it as a bad habit acquired from his association with the other young fishermen who occasionally showed up at the rink, attempting to lure him away to party. But, although he frequently spiked his orange from the silver flask, he never left her side. In her ardor and inexperience, she thought she would eventually change this habit.

After all, the liquor didn't cause him to stagger or talk wild or slurred, as Gudrun had seen in some of his friends, so she never thought of him as drunk. In fact, as the night wore on, the only change was his increased interest in her, a development she found pleasant and desirable.

The initial kiss on the forehead quickly became a fluttering but lingering kiss on the lips, tentative and shy, which belied Willow's warnings that, "he had much experience with the ladies." In fact, he seemed as nervous as she in the beginning. But, gradually, they both allowed their racing desires to overcome reluctance, and each week the physical relationship advanced so fast that sometimes, when she was away from him and the longing that was almost a pain was soothed by the salve of day-to-day duties, Gudrun thought, sanely, that they should slow down. After all, what was the urgency?

But then, they would meet again, and nothing in the world was as important as his kisses, which had now advanced from sweet to passionate, their mouths open and devouring in a hunger that was never satisfied.

Sometimes, when Cy stopped to pour liquor into his orange drink, he would lay his head in Gudrun's lap and talk about his life and his hopes for the future. "But why think about such things?" he'd conclude, as he reached for her again, "It ain't never gonna happen, and it just makes ya crazy thinkin' about it!"

But with the absorption of a lover, Gudrun didn't tire of hearing him talk about himself and what he had wanted to do. "You'll laugh, but I'd like to go to college. Of course, I didn't even graduate from high school. My Pa let me go through the eighth grade cause it was the law, then he took me on the boat to help him. There wasn't nothin' I could do. A'course, I never did too good in school anyway. But I missed so much, what with helping during herring season and all the other times he needed me. Seemed like the days just kept piling up, and pretty soon I was too old to go to school and too old to learn another way to make a living, such as it is!" He laughed and stopped to take a long pull at his bottle. "That's why I named my boat The Sea Siren after Pa died. She sure has lured me far off the course I'd planned for my life." He stared hard at the sand as they sat together on the beach.

"It's not too late," Gudrun said, wanting desperately to lift his mood. "You could study in your spare time. I'd help you! I've heard if you pass entry exams, lots of colleges will take you without a high school diploma."

"You go to high school?"

"No, I was like you. My mother thought it was more important for me to learn a job, so she took me out cleaning with her. It's okay, though, I like what I'm doing, so maybe she was right. I was good in school, though, I could help you."

"Aren't we a pair," he whispered as he rolled onto his stomach in the sand and reached up to pull her next to him. "but right now I got some other ideas of how you can help me!"

Willow was worried about, and not a little jealous of, the developing romance between Cy and Gudrun.

"She's gonna get in trouble! He's way more experienced than her!" she complained to Arne.

"Guess that's how ya git experience, ain't it?"

"Ya, but she's gonna get hurt. He ain't one for settlin' down with no one, and he'll just leave her in the lurch. It'll kill her!"

"Maybe she ain't that serious."

"Are you kiddin' me? She's swallowed that bait: hook, line, and sinker. She don't want to do much with us any more, and when she does, she's only half there." Arne permitted a slight smile.

"Maybe that's what's buggin' you!"

"I shoulda known better than to try and talk to you. You're nothin' but a cold Scandihoovian, and a man to boot. What do you know about feelins?" Willow slammed the door of their cottage and headed for the big house. It was an unusually hot and humid night, and the sky at sunset was a sulfurous yellow with the lake as flat and unmoving as if the seasons had momentarily advanced and frozen it into a sheet of clear ice.

She found Gudrun rushing through her evening chores in the kitchen. She scurried from work table to refrigerator storing covered bowls of food left from the evening meal, and scrubbing, with jabbing motions, at the surface of the butcher block with her dish cloth.

"What's the all-fired hurry? It ain't yer night off or nothin'."

"No, but Cy is picking me up in the Siren for a moonlight picnic." Gudrun couldn't keep from smiling when she answered, although she had recently been aware that her friendship with Cy was becoming a sore spot between her and Willow.

"I got news for ya! There ain't gonna be no moon tonight. In fact, it's gonna storm. You'd better stay off that lake when it decides to storm, it could kill ya!"

"Cy's a sailor. He probably knows the lake better than you or Arne." The minute the words left her lips, Gudrun knew she had hurt her friend's feelings. If Willow professed to know anything it was about the workings of nature and particularly about the proclivities of the big lake. "Cy will take care of me," she added, hoping to end the conversation.

"Don't you know everythin' all of a sudden! He'll probably take care a ya alright, if he ain't already done it!" Willow retaliated.

The two friends glared across the butcher block, Gudrun's face and neck flushed an angry red. At a loss for words, she reverted to the religious clichés of her childhood and hissed, "May God forgive you for your spitefulness!"

Both turned at a slight sound from the breakfast nook and saw Jimmy sitting there with a book open on the table. His glasses magnified shock and fright that turned to embarrassment as Willow slammed out the back door.

His voice wavered and his glasses further magnified tears starting at the corners of his eyes. "Don't be mad at Willow," he said, "She just misses you, and so do I." Gudrun put her arms around him but couldn't think of anything comforting to say. To her surprise, he brought his face close to hers and almost in a whisper said, "Please don't go out tonight. I'm afraid something terrible is going to happen!"

An overwhelming feeling of love and protectiveness welled like a great bubble in Gudrun's chest, but her feelings for Cy were different and stronger, and he needed her love and protection far more than Jimmy did. "Willow's just trying to scare me about the weather. It'll be okay. Everything will be alright with us too. We'll all go on a picnic tomorrow, okay?" He looked skeptical but was used to bowing to the wills of adults, so he nodded in agreement even though he knew that his friends, the weather, and his whole world, for that matter, were at cross-purposes, and he had no idea how to align them. Gudrun looked into his huge eyes again. "I have to go," she concluded. It was an urgency so strong and primal that no amount of common sense or prior bonding could influence her resolve.

She waited on the beach by the town landing, and had to agree with Willow that a storm was brewing. Heat lightning burst intermittently on the horizon and there was barely audible thunder. Otherwise the twilight sky was still clear, even though it remained the strange color.

Cy was late, as usual, and Gudrun waited on the beach by the town dock for half an hour before she saw the outline of the *Siren* materializing out of the dusk. It was now almost completely dark, and the lightning flashes were continuous and the thunder ominous. When Cy jumped off the bow to secure the boat to a piling, Gudrun could tell he had already been drinking. He balanced the all too familiar bottle of orange pop in one hand as he handled the rope with the other; she could see the outline of the flask in his back pocket.

"I thought you weren't coming."

He smiled and pulled her close with his free arm, attempting to kiss her right there in front of the ferry crew and passengers who were just alighting from a 'run.'

"Cy, not here in front of everyone."

"Why not? You ashamed to be with me or somethin'? Just cause you're a fancy cook for rich people? You're just a hired hand, and I've got my own business. I guess that puts me one step up the ladder from you, Goody!" This time Gudrun could tell he was drunk. His speech was uneven and loud, and his stance was unsteady.

"You know I didn't mean that," Gudrun whispered, "You know I think you're better than anyone." She was hurt that he had taken such a derisive tone with her. He had sounded like the boys outside the school as they called her "punkin head." But the thought that he might be so angry that he'd leave her overpowered any red flags that his behavior might have raised. "I was just anxious for you to be here."

"I was havin' a pretty good time with the guys at Junior's, so don't make me sorry I made the effort to come over here," he scolded. Gudrun had never been to Junior's Bar, but heard about it from Cy and Willow. All the fishermen hung out there.

He reared back and threw the pop bottle far down the beach, then turned to pull the rope from the piling. "You comin'?" he said as he jumped aboard the *Siren* that was already drifting away from the beach. Gudrun had to wade in the water with her shoes on in order to jump on board and couldn't believe that the ever polite and solicitous Cy she knew hadn't even bothered to extend a helping hand to her.

He busied himself maneuvering around the town dock and headed into the channel between La Pointe and Bayfield. Gudrun stood close to him, so longing for his touch that instant forgiveness erased her hurt. By now the still lake had become choppy and swells caused the *Siren* to rise and fall. Cy steadied himself by holding the wheel with both hands. "I'm afraid we're going to have a bad storm," she ventured. "Maybe we'd better not go too far."

He turned his head to look at her, and Gudrun could tell his mood hadn't changed. "You tryin' to tell me my business now, 'Goody?' I don't tell you how to cook, do I?"

"I'm sorry. Of course you know what you're doing. I'm just afraid of storms. I always have been ... ever since I was a little girl." Placing herself in a subordinate and vulnerable position had assured him that he was in control and instantly softened his heart. He gathered her against his chest with one arm and kissed her wetly on the mouth.

"Don't worry, little girl, I'll take care of you." The taste of liquor, slightly tinged with orange, lingered on her tongue, and no amount of swallowing quelled it. His words echoed in her head. She remembered that Willow had said almost the same thing an hour before.

"He'll take care of ya all right. If he hasn't already done it!" she felt sorry for arguing with Willow and for leaving Jimmy when he'd begged her to stay. "But I had to go!" she repeated in her mind, and she couldn't feel sorry she was here with Cy, not even in his present condition and state of mind.

They followed the shoreline from Bayfield toward Red Cliff. "I know a nice little beach on the Red Cliff shore. This is just a squall. It'll be over in no time and we can have our picnic." He steered the Siren into a small, sheltered harbor by a cliff. The water was deep enough to accommodate the boat, and he moored her securely to a tree that jutted from the side of the cliff. He cut the engine and busied himself turning knobs and flicking switches.

They huddled together on the bench in the tiny cabin portion and prepared to wait out the storm. The stench of fish was strong, but the wind seemed to freshen the air just when it would begin to stifle. Cy kept both arms tightly around Gudrun, seeming to take seriously his promise to, "take care of her."

Although they had kissed passionately and lain in each other's arms before, Cy had not touched any private parts of her body. She had taken this as a mark of his respect for her. But tonight his hands seemed to be everywhere. They cupped her breasts and ran up her thighs, invading "down there." She squirmed and changed position, pretending to seek a more comfortable spot on the bench. She was afraid any sign of protest would make him mad again, and she didn't want to risk that. When he released her, she gulped in air, unaware that she had been holding her breath.

"I think we need a little fortification," he said. He stumbled and giggled as the rocking boat tossed him against one wall. He returned to the bench with a bottle of red wine and fumbled with the cork and the tip of his jackknife. Just as he'd succeeded in extracting the cork, Siren heaved, and the dark liquid splashed onto the front of Gudrun's sweater. Cy didn't seem to notice as he righted the bottle and tipped it to his lips. He drank long, making gulping sounds and giggling, as the rocking boat caused the bottle to slip from his lips and spill wine down his chin.

"Your turn."

"You know I don't drink, Cy," Gudrun said quietly.

"Are you sayin' you're too good to drink with me?"

Gudrun was afraid his belligerent mood was returning, but he immediately turned sweet and coaxing. "Come on, honey! I just want to keep you from being cold; this'll warm you right up, and it tastes just like grape juice. You like that don't you?" He pressed the bottle to her lips and tipped it. She tried to keep her lips closed, but wine was running across her face and the pressure of the bottle finally forced her mouth open. She spluttered and coughed as she swallowed. He was right about one thing, it would warm her. She could feel the heat spreading down her throat and into her stomach.

"You know, even Jesus drank wine once in awhile, actually quite a lot. You remember that wedding where he changed water to wine? That was a neat trick!" He looked pensive.. "Bet you didn't think a dumb fisherman would know a thing like that did ya? Well, I'm a helluva lot smarter than people think. But if he could drink wine, so can you!" He tipped the bottle to her lips again, and, this time, she drank before it could spill. "Atta girl, now you've got the idea. You know, Goody, maybe I'll be a teacher. I taught you how to skate, now to drink wine. Maybe I'll teach you some other things tonight too. Don't you think I'd make a good teacher?"

"You're good at whatever you do," she said softly. She wished desperately that they were skating at the Pavilion, lying in each other's arms on the beach below the Bayfield town dock, or talking about their lives as they sat on a park bench waiting for the ferry to come. She wished desperately that he hadn't gotten so drunk, and that she knew how to handle this situation.

"You're damn right I'm good at whatever I do!" He took another pull at the bottle and pressed it to her lips again. If he had let her hold it herself, she could have controlled the flow, but as it was, she was only able to let the liquid flow down her throat, hardly tasting it at all and not able to determine the amount she was swallowing.

By the time Cy tossed the empty bottle into the lake, Gudrun's vision was blurred and her head was swimming. She felt set aside, as if wrapped in a fuzzy cocoon, and all movement seemed slowed. But even through the cocoon, she felt the thrill in the pit of her stomach when Cy clamped his lips over hers and rubbed his tongue across the roof of her mouth. She associated the flashes of lightning and the claps of thunder from the storm that raged around them with the colored stars that burst and faded when he massaged her breasts and the moans that she heard as he pressed his body down on her.

At some point she realized that he was touching her bare skin, but she couldn't remember removing her clothes. His hand cupped her pelvis as one finger explored. Her thoughts were wild and scrambled. Maybe this was really her dream lover, Glen, and she was in her own bed. But an eddy of wind brought a blown spray of rain across her face, the stench of fish to her nostrils, and a moment of clarity to her brain. Mother's voice rose above the wind, "To lay with a man before marriage is a sin!"

She tried to rise, but Cy's body covered her and his strong arms held her fast. He whispered in her ear. "Just go with it, Goody, it'll feel great, I promise you. I love you, and I won't let nothin' bad happen to you. You love me don't you?"

She managed to nod. "Then that's all that matters. Just relax and enjoy it. You've never felt anythin' like it, I promise you." The stab of pain when he entered her was numbed by the intense pleasure that radiated to every part of her body, even her fingertips. She threw her arms around him and clung to him as their bodies rocked in unison with the storm-tossed lake.

Chapter 8

"What light through yonder window breaks?"
(ROMEO AND JULIET) WILLIAM SHAKESPEARE

illow pulled her sweater close as she turned to answer the knock at her door. Arne had just left, and she couldn't imagine who would be visiting at eight in the morning. Jimmy stood outside, teeth chattering, nose reddened, and, of course, a startled expression. The storm of the night before had broken the unusual hot spell and left the Island scrubbed and fresh. The sky was a hard blue, and a breeze that was almost icy stirred the evergreens and the tall bracken which typically covered every untended spot of ground in summer.

"Mom says can you come over and do Gudrun's work this morning 'cause she's really sick?"

"What'sa matter with her?"

"I haven't seen her, but Mom says she looks like death warmed over."

Willow reached to turn off the burner under the coffee pot and pushed Jimmy ahead of her as she closed the door. "I knew somethin' like this was gonna happen! Nobody ever listens ta me!"

"Do you think it's something bad wrong with her, Willow? I know you're mad at her, but I don't want anything bad to happen to Gudrun."

"I ain't mad at her no more! She's just in love, and you can't talk sense ta nobody that's in love. Someday you'll figure that out yourself, but she ain't got no bad disease or nothin', if that's what you're afraid of."

"And you think she'll be our friend again?"

They were at the kitchen door, and Willow used the activity of entering and removing her sweater to ignore the question, although that thought was uppermost in her mind too. Mrs. Gendron was clearing away the family's breakfast dishes. "Willow, good! I'm glad you can fill in this morning. We can tend to our own lunch and dinner, if you'll put the house in order before you start your usual duties. We must all pull together in time of crisis, and hopefully, Gudrun will be on her feet again tomorrow." She sounded invigorated and decisive as a general preparing her troops for battle.

"What's wrong with her?"

"Some sort of stomach upset. She knocked on my door early this morning, as pale as a ghost, and said she'd been up all night. She looks terrible!"

Willow cleaned the kitchen and straightened and dusted the downstairs rooms. She checked the refrigerator to ensure that there were lunch materials and found leftover chicken and potato salad.

It was her day to change the beds and do the white laundry, but before she started, she made a cup of peppermint tea and a piece of unbuttered toast to take to Gudrun. She knocked on the door, then entered the darkened room. The empty bed was like a nest of twisted sheets, and a blanket trailed halfway onto the floor. Willow deposited the tray and busied herself straightening the bed, wincing inwardly as she heard the sounds of Gudrun's retching from the bathroom.

When she finally opened the bathroom door and saw Willow, she started to cry and walked into her arms with obvious relief, as if her friend possessed the cure for her miseries. "I was hoping you'd come, but I was so mean to you!"

"I wasn't exactly Mrs. Nice Guy myself! It's okay. Get inta bed and try this tea. Sometimes when ya been pukin' a lot, it breaks the pattern if ya put somethin' in your stomach ... at least ya'll have somethin' to puke up."

Willow held the cup with one hand, and Gudrun's trembling hand guided it to her lips. Her thoughts returned to the *Siren* and the storm, where her tortured brain had led her all night. How gently Willow held the cup on the edge of her lower lip, allowing Gudrun to tip and swallow, in contrast to Cy's administering of the wine bottle. The remembrance caused her stomach to convulse, and she turned her head from the cup.

"It's okay, ya took a couple swallows, and I'll leave it here in case ya want some more. I suppose ya don't feel like talkin', but what the hell happened anyhow? Never mind, we'll talk when ya feel better. I gotta get at the laundry before I get yelled at. I'll come in later to see how ya are."

Willow started out the door as Gudrun curled into a ball on the newly made bed, then remembered that she should take the clothes from the hamper. She tiptoed back into the bathroom and began to gather towels. She opened the hamper, and on top she saw Gudrun's blue sweater, a purple splash across the front. Unconsciously she picked it up to determine if she could get the stain out for her friend and unearthed a pair of panties, stained with pale traces of watery looking blood, the elastic stretched out of shape and twisted. She sat down hard on the floor and put one hand over her eyes. "Oh, honey! I was afraid of this. Why didn't you listen to me," she whispered to herself as she finished gathering the laundry and quietly left the room.

Willow peeked into Gudrun's room when she'd finished her work, but the form under the covers didn't stir and appeared to be in the same position as when she'd left hours before. "That's good," she thought, "she's getting some sleep."

Although bursting with concern and curiosity, Willow decided to leave Gudrun alone until she was well and able to seek her out. Gudrun would know that Willow had learned, or at least suspected, what had happened on the night of the storm. She had to force herself to stay in her cabin that night and not run over to check on her.

"You're nervous as a cat! What's up with you tonight?

"Nothin', I'm just worried about Gudrun. She looked awful today."

"So, go on over and check on her."

"No, I better not."

"You two still fightin'? It's not like you to carry nothin' in your craw. Usually once you've shot yer mouth off, it's over."

"Is that 'sposed ta be some kinda dumb-ass compliment?" She knew it was Arne's way of saying he appreciated that she didn't hold a grudge. "Oh, Arne, I'm afraid Cy screwed her last night." She plopped onto a chair, her face as despondent as Arne had ever seen it.

He was moved to lay down his paper, which was almost an appendage whenever he was in the cottage. "That wouldn't a made her sick, would it? Not yet anyways."

"It would her. You know how religious she is, always talking about sin and that proper Christian husband she was savin' herself for. She told me that her Mother said anyone who did it and wasn't married would be spoiled, and no proper Christian man would ever want her."

"So? Maybe her and Cy'll get married. He seems pretty interested."

"Ya really think Cy wants ta git married? And besides, what kinda life would she have if they did? He's a real drinker, and he's got a mean streak in him too. I seen him in a bar once when he slapped a girl he was with. I don't know what she said ta him."

Arne raised his paper, evidently feeling he had done all he could to assuage his wife's fears.

"That's the life a many an Island girl. You're just luckier than most." His slight smile flickered behind his paper, then gave way to shock as Willow threw the paper aside and clasped him in a vise-like grip

"Ya think I don't know that, ya big, dumb Scandihoovian? He returned the embrace which lasted for several seconds before they were interrupted by a knock on the door. When Gudrun entered, he folded the wrinkled paper neatly and said he had to go check his tip lines to see if he had any fish.

"Well, at least now ya look like you're among the livin'. Didja eat anythin'?" Willow filled the tea kettle as Gudrun sat at the table. She moved gingerly, as if her body were sore, and she was still almost totally without color except for her blue eyes, which tonight had a feverish quality to them.

"I had some canned soup and crackers. It stayed down. I just thought I'd tell you I can take care of everything tomorrow and thanks for today." She played with a loose string from the oilcloth which covered the table, her eyes riveted as if it were a most important task demanding all her attention. The silence lengthened, and when she finally had to raise her eyes, they swam with tears.

Willow stood beside her and pulled her face against her body, smoothing her hair. "Now ya wanna tell me what happened last night," she finally said.

"We got caught in the storm and put in over by Red Cliff. One thing led to another and … we had relations. Willow, he hasn't ever talked about getting married, but he said he loved me, and if he won't marry me I'm spoiled for anyone else."

"Is that what ya think made ya sick, cause if ya think you're knocked-up already, it don't happen that fast and even if it did, ya don't get sick that fast."

"No, no, the wine made me sick. We had a lot of it, and I'd never had any before, and, as God is my witness, I'll never have it again." She shuddered visibly while delivering the last statement.

"So, he got ya drunk so's ya wouldn't know what ya was doin'!"

"It wasn't like that. I wanted it to happen too." Gudrun knew this wasn't exactly true, but she felt the need to defend Cy to Willow, whose face had gathered like a thundercloud and was clearly ready to accuse Cy of rape.

"Okay, okay, Shh … shh … Gudrun, this happens to more women than not, an if ya get married to him fine, an if ya don't, that's okay too. Long as ya ain't knocked-up, cause then ya don't have any choice. I don't 'spose lover boy used anythin'?"

"What do you mean?"

Willow hugged Gudrun's head close again, and made clicking noises with her tongue.

"Lordy, lordy, I shoulda knowed ta talk ta ya!"

Gudrun, always shy and silent, talked even less and smiled little during the following weeks. Mrs. Gendron thought she was getting over her traumatic stomach flu and made every effort to lighten her work load, doing some things herself and calling Willow in often to help with the meals.

"Maybe you'd better make an appointment with the doctor in Washburn, dear. You should be bouncing back faster than this. I'll pay for it, if that's what you're worried about. I don't want you sick, and not just for the work, I want you feeling your old self again." Gudrun knew Mrs. Gendron was sincere and her concern touched a reservoir of sadness. Her eyes filled with tears. "Oh, my dear girl, you are worried. Now I'm going to make an appointment today and see that you get there. And I won't take no for an answer.

"I'll be fine. It just takes time. Give it time," she begged.

Chapter 9

"Of one that loved not wisely, but too well"
(OTHELLO) WILLIAM SHAKESPEARE

t first, she was too ashamed to face Cy and didn't go to Bayfield on Wednesday nights, staying in her room so the Gendrons wouldn't note any change in her habits and question her. To her initial relief, Cy hadn't attempted to contact her either. Then she began to wonder at his absence. Then she began to panic.

"I've decided we have to get married," she confided to Willow.

"Why? You think you're pregnant?"

"I don't know, but it doesn't matter! I've sinned and have to make it right."

"Are you back to that? Besides, once you've sinned you can't take it back, can you? Look, let's get you to the doc and see if you're pregnant. Once you find that out you'll feel 100% better. If you're not, you're home free, and if you are, then it's time to see what he's gonna do about it."

But strangely, Gudrun wasn't fearing pregnancy as much as she was grieving over her lost virginity and the fact that she was now deemed unfit for a good, Christian husband. Nothing a doctor could do would ever change that, and it invaded her thoughts like a fever that rose as the days passed. Overriding all considerations, of course, was the fact that she loved Cy, the first man who had paid her any attention and, conversely, the one who, in her eyes, had literally spoiled her for marriage to anyone else.

She decided she had to contact Cy. Maybe he was as ashamed and sorry as she, and thought she didn't love him. Maybe he would tell her he loved her, this time when he was sober, and beg her to marry him. Then everything would be alright. He wasn't exactly the Christian husband Mother would have approved, but she'd work hard to change him, and she did love him so.

Fortified with this fantasy, Gudrun and Willow rode the ferry on the following Wednesday night, Gudrun silent, knotting and unknotting a handkerchief, as the noisy islanders talked and laughed in anticipation of an evening on the mainland. Gudrun glanced at them thinking, "I was one of them just a few weeks ago."

As they'd agreed, Willow left her outside the Pavilion. "You sure you don't want me to stay with you?" She looked worried and touched Gudrun's hand as she shook her head and they parted. The shutters were raised and the music was playing. There were a few couples on the floor already, and the crescent moon had begun its spasmodic journey across the ceiling.

The summer sun allowed long twilights, and it was hard for Gudrun to distinguish between the dimly lit interior and the outdoors. She recognized his jaunty swagger, though, even with skates on, before she could distinguish any features. Cy had approached the bench and stopped to fill his orange pop bottle from his flask. Gudrun expected him to skate on, but he stooped to help a seated girl lace her skates. Then he pulled her to her feet, held the flask to her lips, and they skated away, both laughing and hugging each other.

She looked hardly older than Francis and was very pretty, with her short, pleated skirt flaring as they circled, a smiling face always directed toward Cy. Gudrun stood in a trance as she watched them perform one of the maneuvers she had mastered: he twirled her wide, then brought her close enough for a brief kiss. Gudrun could feel that kiss on her own lips as soft as the night breeze, and full of tenderness, not like those crushing kisses on the *Siren* that were more like a dull blow than a sweet promise. She couldn't move but suddenly wished she had when she saw them rounding the curve to skate down the side where she stood rooted.

The girl couldn't pull her gaze from Cy, but his eyes met Gudrun's and lit with recognition. They stopped abruptly in front of her. "Hi! Haven't seen you in awhile! What'cha been up to? Oh, this here's Dixie." Dixie changed her smiling face to an indifferent stare as she nodded, wordlessly at Gudrun. As they skated away Gudrun heard her say, "Who's that?"

"Just a cook for some rich people on the Island. I deliver fish there sometimes."

"She's kinda creepy." Then shared laughter.

Gudrun found a bench on the town dock and waited for hours until Willow came to catch the ferry. "Did you find him?"

"Yes! He's with a girl! He told her I was just a cook he delivered fish to, and they laughed." She felt as if she'd been punched in the stomach as she whispered, "The girl said I was creepy."

"That son-of-a-bitch!" It came out too loudly, and people nearby turned to look, but Gudrun was beyond being embarrassed by anything Willow could say. She was too shattered by Cy's betrayal to even notice anyone else.

They rode to the Island without talking and walked silently home from the ferry, but when they reached the path to Willow's cottage, Gudrun seemed to straighten, as if she'd come to a decision, and turned to Willow. "Will you come with me to a doctor?"

"Of course! You want me to make an appointment?"

"Have you been to a doctor around here?"

"Sure, lots a times. I know a good one in Washburn. He's old but he still knows what he's doin.' I hate these young guys. You know you always wonder what they're thinkin' when they look at you and …"

"He'll be fine," Gudrun interrupted abruptly with a voice so steady and cold it sent a chill up Willow's spine. This was little, mousy Gudrun who always meekly deferred to her every suggestion with profuse thanks and apologies.

"Are you okay, honey? You don't seem like yourself."

"I guess I'm not who I used to be. Oh Willow, I've really sinned! This isn't like overeating, or having bad thoughts, or any of the things I used to confess every night. Now I truly know the wages of sin, and I have to make it right before I'm lost."

"God, I thought you was getting' better about all that sin stuff. So you ain't a virgin any more! Big deal! It's human nature to screw, honey. Even your ma did it, and from what you say, she was practically a saint. You haven't committed murder or nothin'!"

"She was a married woman. Not only am I unmarried, now I find Cy doesn't even love me. And what if I'm pregnant?" Gudrun's resolve melted, and she covered her face with her hands, her shoulders shaking. This was more like the Gudrun Willow knew, and, with somewhat guilty relief, she held her in her arms, rocking slightly as she'd done on their first morning together in May.

And so, a week later they again found themselves on the ferry to Bayfield, this time wedged together in the cab of Arne's truck, as they'd need transportation to Washburn. Arne, who wasn't much of a conversationalist in the best of times, was too embarrassed to speak, and even Willow sat silently beside him, occasionally patting Gudrun's knee.

Although it was July and warm, Gudrun remembered the time in May when she'd first ridden in this truck. She could almost smell the heater, and feel again the coziness of the cab as they had bounced over frozen roads to her new life. She had loved her new life, but now it had gone wrong. She remembered another favorite saying of her mother's: "Be careful what you wish for, you may get it."

Dr. Olson was old but kind without being too personal. Gudrun had never had a pelvic examination before. Actually, she hadn't been to a doctor at all since she was little and had an ear infection. The pain, due to her inability to relax, was as nothing compared to her embarrassment. The wages of sin, she thought over and over again. Why did God make love and happiness so degrading?

When she'd dressed and sat facing him, he was all business. "It's a bit early, but I see no signs of pregnancy . In the earliest stages there's a slight discoloration of the womb that isn't evident, so I'm 99% sure you're not. Now, if you're experiencing symptoms we should probably explore some other avenues and find out what's going on."

Gudrun only heard him say she wasn't pregnant. After that she stopped listening to him. If she wasn't pregnant, she had no hope of getting Cy to marry her and absolve the sin. He clearly didn't love her. In all fairness, he hadn't spoken of marriage to her. When they talked about the future, he'd wondered about the possibility of getting some sort of training, so he could do something other than fish, which he seemed to hate. Now that she thought about it, he also hadn't spoken about love, except for that night on the *Siren*. The realization dawned that, like countless inexperienced, young girls, she had mistaken a man's attentions for love, when he had merely been enjoying the adoration of a good listener with the possible added bonus of sex, if he played his cards right. "I won't be needing any further tests," she almost whispered. "Thank you for your time."

Chapter 10

"One sin, I know, another doth provoke."
(PERICLES) WILLIAM SHAKESPEARE

*I*t was nearing Labor Day and with all the thoughts that churned in her mind, constantly adrift, never alighting on a conclusion, Gudrun hadn't faced the fact that her domestic situation would change within a matter of weeks when the Gendrons closed their summer home on the Island and went back to St. Paul for the winter. So it was like a sobering dash of cold water when one night after dinner Mrs. Gendron brought her cup of coffee into the kitchen and stood watching Gudrun perform the nightly cleanup.

"You've become like one of our family, Gudrun," she started. "Of course you'll come back to work for us in the city. I know that'll be nice for you since it's your hometown where you'll have friends and family. You'll have your own room, of course, and days off, and we can talk about a raise too. You've more than proven yourself this summer, and I know you'll have more personal expenses in the city." She stopped and looked inquiringly at Gudrun, waiting for what she clearly hoped, but also expected, would be her immediate consent.

Gudrun was flustered and blindsided by this new turn of events. "I … I'm not sure of my plans. I have to think. Things have come up …" Her eyes filled with unwanted tears and she turned her back to hide them. She had come to like and respect Mrs. Gendron and half of her wanted to unburden herself and ask for advice and help. But the other half argued, "Advice about what? Was she ready to tell her she was no longer a virgin? Would it be important to Mrs. Gendron that Cy had dropped her and already taken up with a new girl? Would she approve of lying to trap a husband?" Gudrun knew what all her answers would be, many of which Willow had already given her.

She scrubbed diligently at the butcher block and the silence lengthened between them until Mrs. Gendron said, in a voice that had lost some of its warmth with Gudrun's abrupt rejection, "It's your decision, of course, I just thought that since the summer had gone so well, we could make it a permanent arrangement. At any rate, we'd like you to stay an extra two weeks after we leave to shut the house up for the winter, if that's okay with you. Let me know."

There was no longer time for plotting and planning and agonizing over past sins and future transgressions. As soon as she could she ran to Willow's cottage. She knew Arne was playing cards at the tavern. Willow smiled when she opened the door. "How you doin'? I made an apple pie. I know it's not as good as yours, but ..."

"The Gendrons are going back to St. Paul, Gudrun blurted.

"Well, ya, the kids have to go to school. They leave every year this time. You knew that. Did she say somethin' to you?"

"She wants me to go back with them and live at their house."

"Hey, that's great, you've got a steady job, kiddo, and a nice place to live back where you were brought up." Willow's voice had taken on a jovial "all problems solved" tone.

"Just listen! I'm going to tell Cy I'm pregnant and that he has to marry me. He won't know it's not true, and I'll get pregnant right away and tell him the baby came early."

"You're crazy! What if you don't get pregnant right away? I ain't got pregnant after tryin' for years. Cy's no dummy, you know. Lotsa girls have tried to catch him."

"He won't ever suspect I'm lying. I know he won't. And once we're married, I'll be so good to him ... such a good wife ... I'll help him get a job doing something he likes, and he'll be happy. If I don't get pregnant, I'll tell him I was mistaken; and by then he won't even care."

"You're dreamin' girl! Cy ain't gonna fall for that!"

Gudrun was dry-eyed but distraught. She paced back and forth in the small Peterson cottage, her eyes darting wildly, focusing on nothing. She seemed to be plucking her words out of thin air, improvising the romantic scenario as she paced faster. She was in her fantasy land.

"Cy drinks because he's so disappointed in himself, if …

"Stop it!" Willow almost screamed and was clearly alarmed at what she perceived as the behavior of a mad woman. She pulled Gudrun onto a chair and sat down beside her, taking one of her hands in both of hers.

"Look, You go back with the Gendrons away from here and Cy, and every day will get better and before long, you'll wonder what you ever saw in that loser. I can come visit you in the Cities. You can show me the sights." She bumped shoulders with Gudrun and rolled her eyes in an attempt to defuse the volatile scene with the promise of high times. "Then next summer you can come back again and it'll be like it was before you met that bum." The latter inducement was promised not without a little anticipation on Willow's part.

Gudrun kept her hand in Willow's but turned to look deeply into her eyes.

"What is there for me as a housekeeper in the city? I keep their house clean and cook their meals? Maybe I help raise Jimmy like he was my own, with Francis always in the background reminding me that I'm hired help? Should I go back to my old church and kneel every night by my spinster's bed as I beg forgiveness for a list of imagined sins, because I don't have enough of a life to even be tempted to stray. I want my own home and children, and now that I'm spoiled for any other man, Cy is my only hope for that."

"What about lying? Isn't it on that 'thou shalt not' list of yours? You know, honey, when you start to lie all sorts of angles you never thought of come up, so you make up more lies to keep the story going. Then you start forgetting how you lied about certain things and your whole story falls apart like a plant with no roots. What if Cy buys your pregnancy but catches on after you're married? How happy do you think he's gonna be then? Animals don't think kindly of the ones that trapped them."

"Some sins are worse than others. I have to make things right, then promise God never to lie again. Please say you'll help me! You're the only friend I've ever had, and I can't do it without you." Willow looked hard at her but finally shook her head in resignation.

"What do you want me to do?"

"Arne has to help too." Willow started to protest, but Gudrun silenced her with a raised hand. "You and Arne have to go to Morty's early on Wednesday and be there when Cy comes in to drink. If you talk to him when he's sober, he'll be more apt to listen. And he'll be more apt to listen if Arne talks to him. He likes Arne. He's told me that lots of times." Gudrun began to embrace the plan.

"What are we supposed to tell him?"

"Just tell him I want to talk to him. I'll be waiting down on the beach where we used to meet. This way we'll catch him before he's drinking or with another girl. If I can just talk to him!"

"I can't tell Arne you're pregnant. He won't go along with helpin' to trap somebody who's kinda a friend of his. Besides, he already knows you ain't. He was along to the doctor."

"You'll have to tell him the doctor was wrong and that I am."

"You want me to lie to my husband? I ain't done that before."

"Please, Willow, I have to try. If he says no, I'll go back to St. Paul with the Gendrons and nobody will know the difference."

There was a touch of fall in the air when, once again, the trio of friends rode the ferry to Bayfield. It wasn't as crowded, since many summer people had left already in order to give themselves a few days before school started to prepare their offspring with clothes and supplies. The stoic Arne was not only speechless but notably agitated, jiggling one leg in an irregular motion.

"Either we'll send Cy down or we'll come back ourselves, if he don't come in Morty's." Willow spoke as if repeating the steps of a much-rehearsed plan, and Gudrun nodded without comment.

Her stomach churned as she sat on the familiar log beneath the town dock. She was so absorbed in repeating her own lines in this soon-to-be portrayed drama that she started at a sound close to her shoulder when Cy jumped to the beach from the dock.

"Hi! What gives? I ain't got much time. I'm supposed to meet somebody at the Pavilion before the skating starts." As Gudrun had planned, he appeared to be sober, but was as cold and uninvolved as a stranger. She decided to indulge in some innocent small talk, rather than leap to the serious right away. Maybe she could remind him of previous conversations, of sweet affection unmarred by baser instincts.

"It's good to see you. I've missed you. What have you been doing?" Gudrun cringed inwardly as she listened to herself. She might as well have said, "How's fishing? How's the weather? How's your new girlfriend?"

"Oh, not much. The goddamn fishing is lousy. I ain't gotten over your way much, the fish are moving more toward Outer Island. He plucked a long strand of beach grass, held it in the side of his mouth, and looked inquiringly at Gudrun; as if to say, "So, get on with it." Involuntarily, Gudrun blurted,

"Are you meeting Dixie?" He looked confused, then suddenly remembered that he had introduced her to Gudrun. He laughed and tossed his head in a dismissive gesture. His wide smile reminded her of the time he had first asked her to skate, and her heart filled with love and hope when he said,

"No, I'm thinkin' ol' Dixie is back in the Cities with her suited-up boyfriends getting ready for college." There was a tinge of regret or envy in his voice, then he threw the blade of grass to the sand and said, "So, what's up?" Gudrun knew she had to get down to business, because he wasn't in the mood to stick around and dredge up old times.

"Well, it seems … I mean… that last night we saw each other? On the boat? In the storm? Well, we had relations that night and now, it seems, that I'm pregnant." The first thread had been caste from which the tangled web would emerge.

He stared at her, giving himself time to absorb her words and to look deeply into her eyes for unspoken confirmation of her news. After what seemed like minutes to Gudrun but in reality was only seconds, cliché excuses rolled from his lips, one after the other. "I hardly remember! I was so drunk! It can't happen after one time! We didn't really do anything but some heavy petting. You only thought …" He concluded his initial reaction with the most offensive question of all, "How do I know it's mine, anyway?" Gudrun was suddenly ashamed of his inability to accept responsibility and the alacrity with which he tried to shift blame. Forgetting that she herself had initiated a deception, she warmed to the plot and felt righteous indignation as she hardened her resolve and her voice.

"You know I have never been with anyone but you, and that I was a virgin. Now I'm telling you what has happened, so that you can do the right thing," a cliché of her own.

"What do you want? What do you mean, right thing? Do you want money? Can we find a doctor and get rid of it? Let's ask Willow. She knows what the Island girls do when this happens."

"I have sinned once with you, and now I'm not about to commit murder on top of it. Either you marry me or for the rest of your days know that you've ruined my life and your child's life, and that the wrath of God will somehow seek retribution." She hadn't planned on enlisting religious epithets, but the wrath of God had become so ingrained in her subconscious that it slipped easily to her lips in her efforts to present a strong case. Her voice shook with conviction but remained strong as she delivered the sentence. She had risen to face him, and now Cy took her by the arm, lowering them both to the log and adopting a more friendly stance and tone.

"I'm sorry, Gudrun. I know you don't lie, and I know you were a virgin. But you don't want to marry me! I'm a heathen, a drunk! I barely make enough to keep myself alive. Sometimes I sleep on my stinkin' fish boat, 'cause I don't have money for a room. Sometimes I camp out on whatever island I'm near. You can't live like that, and a baby can't live like that. Just write me off to experience or damn me to hell or whatever you have to do; but for God's sake don't tie yourself to me or your life will be ruined worse than you can ever imagine."

"But you don't have to be like that! I can work, and you can get some training and then a good job. I'd help you, because I love you. We'd be a family and it would be your salvation. You have it in you to be a fine man, and when you're not so disappointed or have such a poor opinion of yourself you won't need to drink. You'll see …"

"I can't handle this right now," he gasped and turned to leave. Before he jumped to the dock, he turned and said, "I gotta think. I'll get in touch with you." It seemed as if he were mulling over an expensive purchase or trip and not a serious life change. Gudrun had to say something to cement the obvious threat she presented him.

CHAPTER TEN

"Don't think too long," she said quietly. "I'll be going back to the Cities with the Gendrons before long. They like me, and with Mr. Gendron being a lawyer and all, he'll know how to handle the situation if you don't." It was the final play that Gudrun had hoped she wouldn't have to make. Unknowingly, Mr. Gendron had become the father figure and provided the legal weapon for the proverbial shotgun wedding, a term Gudrun had heard Willow use when she talked about some Island nuptials.

A week went by with no word from Cy. Mrs. Gendron was busy packing, and although Gudrun had agreed to stay on and close the house, they hadn't spoken again of the proffered permanent position. She was amazingly calm and ready to follow the family to St. Paul, as she'd promised Willow if Cy didn't come through but she had to wait until the very last minute, hoping against hope. Already she'd extended the mental deadline she'd assigned several times, all the while knowing that her chance of employment would disappear with the Gendrons, since they would lose no time in hiring another housekeeper once they were home.

Then one night, just as she was about to serve dinner, Jimmy burst through the back door to the kitchen, out of breath and glasses askew.

"Cy's tying up his boat down at our dock," he said. Gudrun rested the casserole she was removing from the oven on the butcher block and wiped her face on the towel she'd been using in place of potholders. Her hand touched her hair, and she was taking off her apron as Cy knocked on the screen door.

"Come in!" She opened the door wide in welcome and stepped aside for him to enter.

"I can't come in. Can you come out here for awhile?" She stepped outside and he stood stiffly close to her, speaking softly as if he didn't want the Gendrons to hear him or even know he was there. "I've decided to marry you, so you go ahead and make the arrangements and have Arne get ahold of me as soon as you know." There was no soft expression of love as in Gudrun's dreams. He didn't kiss her or even press a gentle hand to her cheek in affection. He stood awkwardly, poised for flight down the cliff stairs to the much maligned *Siren*, rocking in the waves and ready for a swift getaway at the touch of his hand to the ignition.

77

"But you need to plan the wedding with me. You're getting married too, and have some say in what happens." In spite of the absence of romantic words or gestures, her body relaxed in relief for the first time in weeks; and she smiled and tried to take his hand in a conciliatory gesture. But he pulled away and his voice was hard and determined.

"Look Gudrun, I'm marrying you to give the baby a name, but don't think I'm gonna be tied down to some play house bull shit. I'm willin' to do this, but then you go back with the Gendrons and let them take care of you. It's what we call a compromise."

"I didn't say I'd consider a compromise. Either you do the right thing and we're a family, or you take your consequences and I take mine." Gudrun was amazed at how strong she had become in the past couple weeks, but she was fighting, maybe not for her mortal life, but for a life she had glimpsed from the time she came to the Island: a couple living happily together, like Willow and Arne; love and life without the constant restraints of an angry God. Cy returned her calm gaze with incredulity and whispered back, spitting the words out with venom.

"What happened to the sweet, innocent, little Gudrun? You sure fooled me, lady!" He turned to go and spoke over his shoulder, "Make the arrangements and let me know." It hadn't happened in any of the ways she'd imagined, but the outcome was the same: they were getting married. Had she won? Things had to progress one hurtle at a time, and first and foremost, they had to be legally married, then she would go about winning him over by making him happier than he'd ever been. It may appear that she was forcing the issue in her own interests, but in the process she was also saving him from a life of bitterness and depravity. It was a happy rationalization and she grabbed it as if it were a lifeline. She did marvel at the assertiveness she'd just exhibited for the first time in her life. It had appeared out of desperation, but the feeling it produced was a power surge that she could easily come to crave, like a strong addiction to a drug.

She had forgotten all about Jimmy until she turned to the door and saw his perpetually startled face behind the screen. "What baby are you and Cy gonna name?" She knelt to his level and took both his shoulders in her hands.

"It was just grownup talk, but you can't tell anyone what you heard … not even your mother. It has to be our secret. Can you do that for me?"

"Sure, I can keep a secret real good." He looked proud at having an adult trust him with something obviously important. Gudrun gave him a quick hug.

"Now, wash your hands and get ready for dinner," she said, as she organized the casserole, salad, and bread basket for transport to the dining room. Later, as she did dishes, Mrs. Gendron came into the kitchen to fill her coffee cup, and Gudrun wiped her hands on her apron and asked, "Do you have time to sit down with me for a few minutes?"

"Of course. What can I do for you?" She sat on one side of the breakfast nook and Gudrun slid into the seat opposite.

"I didn't mean to be disrespectful to you the other day when you asked me to work for you permanently. You've been good to me. I've so enjoyed the summer here, and I'd go back to St. Paul with you in a minute, it's just … well, I'm getting married."

"I had no idea," she almost gasped. "Francis said you skated with a boy in Bayfield on Wednesday nights, but I didn't know it was anything serious. Have you only known him this summer? Are you sure? Oh, I don't mean to meddle, but you're so young and inexperienced, and I almost feel like your mother, in a way. And it isn't just that I want you to keep your job with us … well I do want that too, but I don't want you to make a serious mistake. I only want the best for you," she concluded as she took Gudrun's hands.

It was too much for Gudrun, and she wept freely, hoping that Mrs. Gendron would think they were tears of happiness or bridal nerves.

It was a beautiful September day. The weather had turned balmy and the further they drove south from the Big Lake the more evidence they saw of the changing seasons: leaves were turning and roadside stands displayed pumpkins and apples. Arne's rusty pickup was once again pressed into service. Willow and Gudrun sat next to him in the cab while Cy sat behind them in the truck bed, leaning against the cab, the back of his head visible in the window. Gudrun could see wisps of smoke from his cigarette as they curled backward in the wind. She was also aware of his frequently tipping his silver flask to his lips and wondered if he would be sober enough to get married once they got to Pine City.

Willow had contacted Island friends and acquaintances and learned that couples who wanted a hasty marriage went to Pine City, Minnesota where you could get a license and marry in the same day; since, for some reason, there wasn't a waiting period. Any more waiting was out of the question for Gudrun, and she opted for the trip even though it was a long day's ride down and back.

Actually, Gudrun had half expected that Cy wouldn't show up, and heaved a sigh of relief when they drove the truck off the ferry that morning in Bayfield and saw him leaning against a dock piling smoking a cigarette. He wore work pants, but they were clean with a sharp, if slightly crooked, crease in both legs. His sport coat looked a bit tight across the shoulders and arms, and he wore a knit shirt under it: one Gudrun had seen him wear for skating at the Pavilion. Emotion tugged at Gudrun's heart as she thought of how handsome he was, how he had made an effort to look presentable for the occasion, and how he would soon be her husband. *Let it all turn out in the end,* she silently prayed.

Her wedding dress was purchased on a trip she and Willow had made to The Vogue in Ashland. It was a lavender colored cotton printed with dark sprigs of violets. It was a happy, carefree day when the two friends had laughed and planned and dreamed. It was even more memorable when at lunch, Willow had presented her with a package containing a beautiful blue nightgown. "It's a wedding present," she said, "and don't get all weepy on me either," she added, even though her own dark eyes looked bright and moist with tears.

On her wedding day, Gudrun wore her mother's gold chain and cross around her neck and carried her blue sweater, Willow having used her alchemy to remove the wine stains from the front. Mrs. Gendron had insisted on giving her money for a new dress and an additional stipend for a celebration afterwards. Gudrun knew there would be expenses, and brought some of her saved wages in case Cy hadn't thought about it. Since he wasn't involved in the planning, she didn't know what she could expect of him.

They made gas and rest room stops where all four were unusually polite and spoke little. An onlooker would hardly identify them as a group off on a happy outing. However when they reached Pine City and located the courthouse, Cy, whether emboldened by whatever courage flowed from his flask or by at last his acceptance to do the right thing, was jovial and friendly, joking with clerks and winking at Gudrun when they were asked questions about the forthcoming marriage. For Gudrun the whole day was like a seesaw of emotions with Cy's moods: down one minute, up the next.

She gave Cy 25 dollars to pay for the license at the courthouse; and when the brief marriage ceremony, held in an adjoining office, was over, he inclined his head toward the justice of the peace indicating that more money was needed. Gudrun doled out another 10, at which he looked disgusted with her and whispered, "You have to give him at least 25." She was worried she wouldn't have enough for supper and gas, which she felt was the least she could do for Willow and Arne who had driven them and acted as witnesses. But Cy was busy being the benevolent bridegroom and when the justice tried to give him back some of the money, protesting that it was too much, Cy refused to accept it. "This is my wedding day. Let me be generous," he said as he put his arm around Gudrun's waist and pulled her close.

"Well, thanks so much, and good luck to you." He leaned towards Gudrun and in a loud stage whisper said, "You're one lucky little lady to get this one." Cy flashed a broad smile and shook his head modestly.

They stopped at a supper club for a meal on the way home. Cy said he wasn't hungry but ordered a couple drinks while the others ate. For the rest of the trip he slept in the back of the pickup, rousing himself only when they drove off the ferry in La Pointe and bumped down the road to the Gendron house, now dark and deserted with the family gone for the winter.

Gudrun had decided that they would stay in her room at the house for another week until she had finished the winterization, and planned to talk to Cy about other living arrangements as soon as she could. It was late and quite cold. Millions of stars made the night bright, and Gudrun wished on all of them as she stood thanking Willow and Arne. Willow looked sympathetically at her and hugged her tightly. They didn't speak. When she ran to open the door, she found Cy sitting on the back step drinking from his flask. He must have had it refilled at the supper club, Gudrun thought.

"Well, well, this is the first time I've ever been in here," he said. He turned around in the middle of the kitchen surveying everything in mock awe. "So this is the great house." He walked through to the living room, all the while pretending to be impressed with the décor and the grandness. He took the stairs two at a time, as Gudrun tried to direct him to her room next to the kitchen. When he finally did come into her room, he held his arms out in surprise. "Are we supposed to sleep in this narrow bed? It looks like a coffin. I may be trapped, but I ain't dead yet!" He laughed loudly at his joke as he took another swig of his flask. "There's a great big bed upstairs. Let's use that one."

"That's the Gendron's bedroom, and I don't have permission to use it." Gudrun was more than a little nervous and anxious to appease him. She was especially worried about his use of the term trapped. She was also reminded of the night on the *Siren*, and just wanted him to go to sleep. Tomorrow would be time enough to start the rehabilitation of Cy.

"There's nobody here to give permission. I give you permission, and I'm your husband. From now on you have to do things my way. You never thought of that, did you Goody?" He pretended to tickle her chin, then turned and walked out, forcing her to follow him upstairs where he fell on the bed propping pillows behind him so he could continue drinking. Gudrun managed to move him enough to pull away the fluffy chenille bedspread, then went downstairs to get her nightgown. She tied the blue ribbon at her throat and looked in her bathroom mirror. She stared at the reflection: the blue in the gown set off her eyes, but they had dark circles and looked tired. This was her wedding night, and all that came to her mind was, "Oh Lord, what have I done?"

When she got back upstairs, Cy appeared to be asleep, but he still held the flask upright in his hand, and when she entered the room he started. "Where the hell you been? You shouldn't keep your new husband waiting."

She pulled the bedding aside and began to put her feet under the covers, but he sprang up suddenly, startling her, and threw the bedding to the floor with one swipe. She cowered like a frightened animal, pulling her feet up under her nightgown, while he slowly undressed, dropping his clothes on the floor. He carefully replaced the cap on his flask, laid it on the bedside table, and grasping her feet, pulled her flat on the bed where he straddled her, breathing heavily. He fumbled with the blue ribbons. "Let's see what I bought here." But his fingers weren't working and he swore and grabbed the hem of her gown, thrusting it almost over her face and attempted to enter her with difficulty.

"What you bought?" Gudrun couldn't help but question the crude remark. He stopped then and took her head between his hands coming close to her face and expelling the smell of liquor with every word.

"You listen to me, Goody. You may have paid for everything today, but I have bought and paid for you with my freedom. And that's worth a lot more than you'll ever spend, and don't you forget it." The liquor and his emotional declaration had left him impotent, and to save face he feigned resignation and fell over onto the bed. "What's the use?" he muttered as he fell into a deep sleep.

Gudrun quietly replaced her gown, remade the bed, carefully covering her new husband's nakedness, and lay down. She thought she wouldn't be able to sleep, but she was so overcome with physical and mental exhaustion that she mercifully fell asleep immediately, telling herself that she'd deal with everything tomorrow.

Chapter 11

"Yet hasty marriage seldom proveth well!"
(HENRY VI) WILLIAM SHAKESPEARE

he sun didn't rise until nearly seven o'clock. The days were getting shorter and cooler on the big lake, and the wind was crisp—a forerunner of the gales to come. Gudrun had been up early baking: muffins bulging with apple slices and crusted with sugar cooled on the chopping block. She took a pan of bacon from the oven which rivaled the steaming coffee pot for the predominant aroma infusing the warm kitchen. *I'll bet he's never had a proper breakfast,* she thought as she transferred the crisp slices to a platter, *what better way to win him over than to start with showing him how good married life could be.*

She was engrossed in her preparations and didn't hear him come down the stairs until she looked up and saw him leaning against the kitchen door jam. His hair was a rumpled mass of dark curls and his eyes were surprisingly bright without the effects of liquor. She felt the familiar stirring in her chest at how handsome he was, and she suddenly realized that she had never seen him when he hadn't been drinking to some degree. *How little I know you; and yet, you are my husband,* she thought with a tinge of apprehension. "Good morning! You must be hungry. You didn't have much to eat yesterday."

"Morning." He scratched his head and looked around the room in an almost confused way, as if he didn't remember where he was or how he had gotten there. Gudrun poured a mug of coffee and brought it to him. He accepted it gratefully and slid onto the bench of the breakfast nook. His hand trembled slightly as he raised the cup to his lips.

"Sit still and I'll get you some breakfast."

"Coffee's enough. I don't eat much breakfast." But Gudrun ladled scrambled eggs and bacon and perched a muffin at the side of the plate. When she put it in front of him, he stared at it as if he'd never seen such food before but he found his fork and picked at the eggs, slowly becoming more interested, until he was eating with relish. Gudrun brought her own coffee to sit opposite him and watched with satisfaction.

This is going to work. I'll make him love me, she thought to herself with a small smile.

And so the week progressed. Gudrun would remember it as the most wonderful time of her life. They talked and laughed and got to know each other. She delighted in cooking for him and he became profuse in his compliments, causing her to blush and protest in the Scandinavian way.

The nights were Gudrun's fantasy life come true, as Cy proved to be the gentle and considerate lover she had always imagined in her daydreams. As the days passed Gudrun became so sexually aware that she found herself stopping in the midst of her winter preparations of the Gendron house to find her husband where he was fishing from the dock or clearing the vegetable garden and fall into his arms—with the expected result. They would hurry to the closest secluded spot, removing clothes as they ran, to once again consummate the marriage that had gotten off to such a bad start.

Once as they lay close and sated, Cy caressed her naked stomach and started, half sitting. "I think I feel the baby move!" he announced excitedly. Gudrun's eyes flew open. She was taken completely off guard.

"Oh, it can't be!" she said. Then to cover, she sat up and reached for her clothes. "It's way too early."

But he was suddenly intrigued and couldn't let it go. "No, I felt something. It's my kid, so it's gonna be strong and mature early, you'll see. I wonder if it's a boy. That'd be great, if it's a boy. Oh, a girl would be okay too, but I'd know more about how to treat a boy. Not like my father though, no sirree!" He kissed the back of Gudrun's neck as she sat to dress and pulled her back down beside him, once again cupping her stomach with his hand and smiling into her eyes with what she recognized for the first time as love.

Oh Lord, let me be pregnant, she prayed, *How can I disappoint him now? What have I done?* But the dye was cast, and her idyllic honeymoon week was now overshadowed by her approaching menses and the possible need to stage a miscarriage if it arrived on schedule.

Later that week, Cy took the ferry into Bayfield to pick up the *Siren* which had been parked at the town dock since the morning of their marriage. "I'm gonna do a little fishing, but I'll be back early," he said. "With the *Siren* here we can go picnic on some of the islands and really have some privacy." He leered suggestively at her, kissed her quickly, and bent to lay his ear against her stomach. "Take care, baby," he whispered. When he'd left, Gudrun sat down hard at the breakfast nook, laid her face on crossed arms and cried until she was weak.

True to his word, he returned late afternoon with a beautiful trout for their dinner. "I thought you could ask Willow and Arne for supper. We been kinda ignoring them all week," he said with a smile. "Oh, yeah! There was a package for you at the post office. It's a big one. Looks like it's from Mrs. Gendron." Gudrun opened the wrapping to find pairs of pillowcases, tea towels, luncheon cloths, and napkins. On top were skeins of every color embroidery thread you could imagine.

Gudrun read the letter. "My friends have all admired the beautiful things you've done for me and wondered if they could hire you to do the same for them. I've enclosed items that they want embroidered in the hope that this will fit into your new life. If not, just store the materials in the linen closet at the Island home, and I'll retrieve them next summer. If you decide to do this work, ship the finished products to me along with your bill. This could prove to be lucrative for you, but I'll surely understand if you choose not to take it on at this time. Every good wish to you, Gudrun."

"What do ya think?" Cy inquired when he read the letter. "You'll probably have lots of spare time. This afternoon I talked to this guy who has a cabin on Rocky. He said he'd rent it to us for a few weeks until the weather turns bad. It'll give me some good fishing time, so I can earn a little money before we have to move into Bayfield for the winter."

Gudrun threw her arms around him. She had wondered how she was going to broach the subject of where they'd live; they couldn't keep on staying at the Gendrons. He was acting responsibly, and she also noticed he hadn't had anything to drink. She half expected him to have stopped at Junior's Bar while he was in Bayfield. He hadn't had alcohol since the night of their wedding, when she had confiscated his flask and dumped the contents down the drain. He'd not asked her for it.

They had fun with Willow and Arne at dinner that night. Gudrun forgot her dilemma temporarily as the married couples talked and laughed, and she nodded enthusiastically when Willow, in the kitchen with her to get the coffee, had asked, "Are ya happy? You look like a cat that swallowed a whole nest full of canaries." They returned to the dining room just in time to hear Cy tell Arne,

"You wouldn't believe how it felt. It was just a flutter, but it really got to me. I mean to know that it's your kid and all. Well, I know it sounds corny, and you probably never thought you'd hear me say this, but, well, it just got to me." His voice broke with the strain of the unaccustomed display of emotion, and he jumped to his feet to help with the tray, bending to kiss her cheek when she sat. There was a long silence; then Arne reddened and cleared his throat, Willow looked stricken, and Gudrun burst into tears for the second time that day.

"She's just tired and overwrought," Willow quickly explained, as she led Gudrun back into the kitchen.

Toward the end of the month, they moved into their cabin on Rocky Island. Gudrun fell in love immediately with this small strip of vegetation that rode high on the waves of the Big Lake. The first thing she saw when the Siren docked at the pier was the large, handmade sign over the boathouse.

"Ya, we have it good here in North America" declared the Norwegian immigrants who had built the tiny cabins and earned their living as they had in Norway. Gudrun felt a kinship, although traditionally the Swedes and Norwegians didn't get along, and thought she had come home.

At first, life was good for Gudrun and Cy. She walked the beach adding to her collection of pretty stones and lake polished glass which she kept in a jar on the windowsill to catch the morning sun. She spent the long days sitting on the dock with her embroidery work while she waited for Cy. She gradually turned the unadorned materials Mrs. Gendron had sent into stacks of pillowcases with ivy entwined morning glories; luncheon cloths with delicate, spidery daisies and knotted blue forget-me-nots; and bureau runners that admonished in cross-stitch, Honor Thy Father and Thy Mother.

At the end of September, Gudrun waited apprehensively for her monthly period, elated when it was a couple days late. God had answered her prayers! Then in the middle of the night she was awakened by the familiar cramps and she felt the blood of betrayal between her thighs. She crept from bed and left the cabin for the outhouse, hoping not to waken Cy. She hadn't been there long, however, when he came looking for her. "You okay?" His eyes were swollen with sleep but worried.

It wasn't hard for Gudrun to cry since she was devastated, so she let it all out, rocking back and forth as she sat. "I'm losing the baby," she wailed, as Cy, now distraught, tried to help her rise.

"Get to the Siren, he said, "we'll go to the hospital in Washburn."

"I can't move. I've been out here a long time. The baby's gone. I had terrible pain and then I felt big lumps come out of me and now it's just blood."

"Why didn't you call me?"

"There's nothing anyone can do. It just happens sometimes. I'll be okay."

"That's all there is to it? It just happens sometimes?"

Gudrun realized she should be more hysterical. She was too composed, too matter-of-fact but she was worn out from the deception and eager to put the whole thing behind her. Maybe she could pass her lack of concern off with being a cold, unfeeling Scandinavian.

After awhile she allowed Cy to help her to the cabin, rejecting his offers to take her to Washburn, "At least for a checkup, so we know everything is okay." She didn't have to fake her instability; sitting so long on the hard wooden plank in the outhouse had temporarily paralyzed both her legs. Cy didn't go fishing the next day, in spite of her assurances that she was fine. He made her stay in bed and brought her cups of tea and toast.

He did go fishing the next day, though, and came home late. "I stopped to see Willow," he said. "I tried to get her to side with me that you should see a doctor, but she said there was no need. You'd be fine. They'd come out to see you soon." There was a familiar distant look in his eyes, and Gudrun realized that he'd been drinking. "What's wrong with you women? A baby dies and you act as if nothing has happened." He was shouting now and he pulled away when she tried to embrace him and ran out the door.

She found him sitting at the end of the dock with an open bottle of whiskey in one hand. He didn't look at her as she sat down beside him. He just stared at the horizon, occasionally tipping the bottle to his lips. "It's not easy for me to express my feelings, Cy. It's the way I was brought up. I could cry and scream and beat my chest if you want me to, but it wouldn't do any good. We just have to get on with life. We can have another baby. What can I do?"

"You can care," he shouted. "You just shit him out and left him up there in the outhouse like he was a bad meal. He was my little boy." Then he turned his face to her. Tears were streaming down his cheeks and he could only manage a strangled whisper, "I just want you to care."

Nothing was the same between them after that. All the love that had blossomed so briefly disappeared with that fictitious, originally unwanted baby that had taken hold of Cy's soul and had come to represent the good that was in him and his hope for the future. As for Gudrun, the burden of guilt became almost unbearable, and looking at her unhappy husband, not knowing what to do, was a constant reminder of her great sin and the wanton lechery that had instigated it.

She remembered the passion she had felt and tried to return to that place in her body that had yearned for her young, handsome husband—a yearning so insistent it became a sharp pain. But just when she thought she'd reached that place, she'd hear his voice again, "You don't care. I just want you to care."

"Oh, I care," she'd wanted to lash out at him, "I care for you and our life together, but you're throwing it all away over something that only existed in your mind: a gas bubble in my stomach, a tremor of a muscle." But of course she couldn't say any of that, because then the great deception would be revealed. So she read her Bible by the oil lamp. Cy would come in off the lake, smelling of fish, and now always of liquor, and wanted to make love quickly and hotly before he fell into a dead sleep. When he'd been satisfied, she'd sit at the tiny, wooden table in the cabin reading the verses that comforted her and allowed her to forget about the baseness of the human spirit and remind her of her wifely duties.

"I am my beloved's, and his desire is toward me." Isaiah 7:10. "Thy desire shall be to thy husband, and he shall rule over thee." Genesis 3:16
Now it froze hard every night, and the wild flowers and ferns were dead and brown. The wind off the lake would slam the waves across the sand and into the treeline, making it impossible to walk the beach and hunt for stones and glass. Mostly, Gudrun sat in the cabin and embroidered, so she was happy when Cy announced one night that they couldn't stay on Rocky much longer, and that he'd rented an apartment for them in Bayfield.

Maybe this change would be good for both of them. After all, this is where the baby and the dream had died. Maybe one or both could be regained. Gudrun still had hopes of getting pregnant, although she had come to suspect that God was punishing her. A phantom baby, who looked so much like Cy, plagued her dreams, always crying plaintively and wafting away when she reached out for him.

The hope of a happy change seemed bleak, however, when they climbed the stairs and opened the door to the furnished apartment that would be their winter home. The wallpaper had water stains from past leaks and the whole place smelled incredibly musty. Past tenants had left debris everywhere and the furniture was broken and dirty. Gudrun worked hard at scrubbing and shored up the furniture, where she could, with hammer and nails borrowed from the downstairs tenant. She cleaned the stove and icebox so their food could be kept clean and set traps for the infestation of mice she discovered when she began the massive housecleaning.

"So it ain't the Gendron's," Cy would remark sarcastically. "It's a roof over our heads, and it's all we can afford."

When the apartment was as good as she could get it, the days became long for her. She couldn't walk the beaches, embroider in the sun, or pick wild flowers. Her other domestic specialty was baking and she reasoned that as long as she was using heat in the wood stove to warm the apartment she may as well bake their bread. Eventually she fell into her old habit of keeping a supply of cookies in a jar in the kitchen. It was a good winter pastime, and she cooked savory fish stews and venison roasts, if some of Cy's drinking buddies were also hunters and shared their kill with him. Sometimes she would work all day on the evening meal only to eat alone, the food turning to dross in her mouth, as she sat waiting for Cy to drift home from the taverns.

When he came in he was most often belligerent at first, pushing away the heated food she offered, but finally eating in great gulps that didn't remain in his mouth but fell on his shirtfront or back on his plate. "What you been doing sitting around here all day," he would slur.

Tight-lipped, but dutifully, she would reply, "Same old thing; I baked and embroidered a little."

"You really lead the life of Riley, don't you?" he'd bellow.

"I thought I'd married a woman who knew how to work! Bake and embroider! You should have to work gutting stinkin' fish or pulling them half rotten out of the nets. Then you wouldn't have time for any baking and embroidering!" His fist hit the table, and the gravy boat turned, causing a greasy, brown stain to creep toward and obscure a delicate circle of pink French knots on the tablecloth. Gudrun wanted to lash out and ask how hard it was to sit on a barstool all day and swap stories with his cronies. She wanted to tell him the number of hours she spent cleaning, laundering, and cooking, on her feet all the while. But she didn't. Instead, she became stoic; her mouth drew into a thin, hard line, and her blue eyes became steely. She dabbed at the spilled gravy with a tea towel that proclaimed, GOD IS LOVE!

After the meal and a cup of coffee, Cy was still unsteady on his feet, but his mood turned amorous. He'd grope at Gudrun's breasts as she stood at the dishpan and pull her back against him where she could feel his crotch bulge through her house dress. She was completely disgusted and considered him an animal, but she knew that if she refused him, or even turned away, he'd become violent and eventually get his own way after she'd gotten a split lip.

Afterwards, she couldn't sleep with the dirty, smelly excuse for a man who snored wetly into a pillowcase edged with delicate seashells. She heated water in the teakettle, and without cooling it down, she stood at the washbasin and scrubbed, with scalding water, every part of her body he had touched. She then often sat at the kitchen table, reading the Bible until dawn.

"Woe unto them that rise up early in the morning, that they may follow strong drink; that continue until night, till wine inflame them!" Isaiah 5:11

The next morning, he would be sick, contrite, and whiny. He'd sit on the edge of their one bed with his head in his hands and belch softly. Noticing her straight back and silence, he'd complain, "It's the season, Gud," You know how worried I am about money; I just want to be able to support you and give you things, you know that." He'd try to pull her down by him or put his arm around her legs as she walked by. This time she knew he wasn't thinking about love but more of appeasement, and then being nurtured. But she knew she was in command now; he never hit her when he was sober, and if she showed any signs of last night's lovemaking, such as a swollen cheek or black eye, he'd cry and touch the afflicted area gently and swear it would never happen again. Sometimes Gudrun would look at him then and see the handsome, cocky sailor who had twirled her around the roller rink. She remembered his curly, black hair, his smile that expressed pure delight over everything, and the way his hard, tight body swayed when he walked like a top on a string, veering from side to side, but always remaining stable. Sometimes she wanted to take him in her arms and tell him she loved him. Always, better judgment prevailed, however; she felt she couldn't afford to lose the power in the game of marital struggle.

She didn't rail or accuse; she just gave him the cold shoulder and silent treatment, which usually lasted for several hours, depending on how contrite he was. The incidents, however, were never discussed.

Chapter 12

"Suspicion always haunts the guilty mind."
(HENRY IV) WILLIAM SHAKESPEARE

he fall of 1950 turned stormy in October and the ground had a thin covering of snow by Halloween. A couple nor'easters foretold a hard winter for those who weathered the season around the Big Lake. Willow came to visit whenever she was in Bayfield, and the friends would laugh and drink coffee and remember the summer picnics as they hugged their sweaters tightly to their bodies, sitting close to the kitchen wood stove in the drafty, cold apartment. Of course, during this season, you never knew when or where ice would make a difficult crossing from the Island, so these visits were all too few and far between. Gudrun often felt isolated, but it didn't really bother her, since it was a familiar feeling, regrettably, one she thought she'd put behind her when she fell into her new life on the Island.

Every day was full though: she sandwiched her "busy work" (as Mother had called it) around her preparation for Cy's evening homecoming. She kept the shabby apartment spotless; washed and neatly folded Cy's sparse wardrobe; and kept meals ready for heating. She took her wifely duties seriously and always put them first, even though she knew there was a good chance he would arrive home drunk and abusive.

As for Cy, fall was a fairly busy time for fishermen. They mended nets and worked on their boats, tackling projects postponed during the busy season. Cy kept the *Siren* in the water and ready for the late fall fishing and worked at odd jobs when he could find them: painting, shoveling snow, and hauling garbage. He complained constantly about these occasional duties, however, and always had to try to erase the memory of his degradation at Junior's Bar, swapping stories with his fishermen friends and usually spending any money he'd made in the process.

So aside from Cy's occasional bag of groceries or a five-dollar bill here and there, it was Gudrun who supported them with the money she made on her handiwork. Mrs. Gendron provided a steady flow of orders from the Cities; and as she'd predicted, the fledgling business did prove lucrative and expanded. Soon, in addition to the embroidery, Gudrun was knitting custom-made sweaters, hats, gloves, scarves, and socks for adults and babies. If Cy was aware of her contribution, he didn't acknowledge it. Sometimes she wondered how he thought they were living. She decided he would suppress anything to save face, and she understood that and kept her silence, as saving face always weighed heavily on her mind too, but sometimes she had to bite her tongue when he railed at her for "sittin' at home."

She walked to the post office with her securely-packaged products almost every day and included her grocery shopping in the outing. The short trip became a highlight, allowing a change of scene, human contact, and fresh air. Her route included one of Bayfield's steepest streets where, coming and going, she'd pass a small church tucked into the rise of the hill. Going home, she often stopped to catch her breath in front of its entryway, settling her grocery bags around her on the sidewalk.

The sign said, "Christ Episcopal Church." She loved looking at it, maybe because it reminded her of the churches pictured in her favorite childhood storybook, "Heidi." It had slanting gables and red, gingerbread trim. It was set back from the street in a well-kept, little yard where she'd seen a border of perennial flowers that fall and a variety of trees, all of which now, in winter, were beautiful, snow-covered adornments. It seemed sweet and approachable more than beautiful.

She'd seen beautiful cathedrals in the Cities, but found them cavernous, cold, and uninviting. She didn't know if common people really worshiped in them, or if they were meant for "grand people" who crowded the steps in elegant costumes: weddings, funerals, Christmas, Easter.

Her own religion frowned on ostentation in any form which came in handy, since the congregation of Gudrun and her mother's St. Paul church was comprised of people whose economic status was at or barely above the poverty level. They could hardly afford their weekly contribution, much less funds for trimmings. They met in a rented storefront, equipped with a makeshift pulpit and a crude, painted plywood cross suspended from the ceiling at the front of the room. Folding chairs allowed a perch but not comfort, since the metal backrest seemed to hit at an unfortunate spot, no matter how tall or short you were. Pastor Lundquist was fond of saying, "It doesn't matter where you meet as long as you meet in His name."

Gudrun thought this a noble sentiment, but couldn't help but notice their Church's shabby setting and mostly its smell: start with the lingering odor of decayed organic materials left from the days when the building had been a neighborhood grocery store; add to this the smell of a gradually deteriorating structure; of summer perspiration or wet winter, wool coats; and trap the smell of fear and desperation, which Gudrun recognized from an early age, and you had the incense that their congregation identified with worship.

Christ Church fascinated Gudrun, however, even though she knew the Episcopalians were practically Roman Catholics, a group her mother and their church had cautioned against "having anything to do with."

Walking by the church on her daily trek, Gudrun often saw a man sweeping the sidewalk, clearing snow, and doing general maintenance work. Their relationship started with a curt nod from both parties, progressed to "Good morning" or "Afternoon," and eventually settled into friendly comments on the weather or on Bayfield events or news. Gudrun figured him to be somewhere in his forties with slightly gray hair, blue eyes like her own and short in stature. He introduced himself. "I'm Einer Olson, just one among the hundred Olsons in this town." His being Scandinavian engendered an instant trust which grew with each subsequent meeting.

"Going to the big doin' at the Pavilion? It's an art fair or somethin'."

"I don't think so. I don't know anything about art and I don't know anyone here."

"Oh, I don't know nothin' either, about art that is, but I like to look at the paintings. What brings you to Bayfield?" And so began a general sharing of information. She learned that Einer had been a fisherman, like Cy, but sought other employment when he'd severely wrenched his back while hauling in a heavy net. "Can't say as I don't miss it sometimes but on cold, stormy days I'm just thankful I can pull up the covers and stay in bed." He had a self-deprecating way of talking about himself that was the Scandinavian way of sharing information and was familiar and welcome to Gudrun. She felt she was with her people again when she visited with him.

"Cy says he hates fishing," she blurted. She couldn't believe she was telling a stranger such personal information. "He'd like to do something else, but he only knows fishing, and I can't seem to come up with another plan that suits him."

"Maybe I'm nuts, but it seems to me that's his job," Einer commented dryly. "He probably likes fishing more than he's willing to admit and uses it as an excuse not to change. Change is hard and takes a lot a guts."

She thought about his words. *Did Cy have "the guts" to change?* He was always talking about how brave he was: going on the lake in the worst weather, or standing up to the biggest bully in the bar. *Did he want a new life enough to make sacrifices and move away from the familiar?*

One day when she stopped at the church, she felt a little dizzy and sat on the bottom step to regain her equilibrium. Einer was there immediately with a hand on her shoulder.

"You okay, Missus? You look awful white. Come on inside and I'll get you some water." He collected her bags in one arm and helped her to her feet with the other, and that was how Gudrun entered the little church for the first time.

It was exactly like the pictures in her storybook, and she half expected to see Heidi and her grandfather kneeling in the aisle. The altar had candles and a beautiful stained glass window above it. There was carved wood everywhere, even on the end of each pew. By far the most imposing feature, however, was the organ whose ornate and colorful pipes took up one third of the back wall. Gudrun wondered what sound would come out of something that looked that complicated.

Christ Church had a certain elegance, and yet it was cozy and comfortable, and it had its own smell: maybe a little musty but in a different way. It was the smell of melted candle wax and worn hymnbooks and the exotic fragrance of spent incense. No vestiges of previous lives lurked in its cracks; rather it seemed to represent tradition and stability and heritage. Although it was all so new to her, she had the strange feeling that she belonged and sank onto a back pew to drink in the ambiance, as Einer went through a door at the side to get water.

From then on, Gudrun stopped almost everyday to sit in a straight-backed pew and rest. Einer said he'd leave the door open during the day, and she could go in whenever she wanted. It became her private place to think, trying always to work out a solution to her problem with Cy and their dysfunctional marriage. Her conversations took place in her mind, never aloud, and gradually she began to think of them as talking to God, only they weren't like formal prayers but more like telling your troubles to a friend, just to be relieved of them if only for a few minutes.

Did she really deserve Cy's treatment of her because she'd lied and tricked him into marriage? He didn't know she'd lied, and still he punished her; or did she allow him to hurt her because she felt she deserved it? Sometimes she'd catch him looking at her with eyes that seemed full of unasked questions, and she thought he suspected her treachery. He often accused her of being cold and not caring, and then she hardened her reserve and refused to defend herself, further fueling his anger; but she was afraid of saying something in a fit of retaliation that would reveal the whole plot.

So the cycle continued, seemingly without end. Her head ached from mulling it over and over, and the only solution she ever found halfway plausible was to get pregnant but God seemed to be taking his revenge in that department too, and she remained barren in spite of her prayers. But then, maybe God didn't see fit to send a baby as a result of the angry, drunken coupling that their lovemaking had become.

One Sunday morning she paced their little apartment in agitation. It was cold. The wood stove had gone out during the night, and the morning fire she'd laid hadn't yet had a chance to produce any heat. Cold air blew in around the window frames and stirred the flimsy curtains she'd hung in her attempt to make a pleasant home. She'd been awake for hours, unable to sleep after a Saturday night confrontation with Cy. She saw a distraught face reflected in the bathroom mirror as she gingerly touched her swollen lip with trembling fingers and noticed a dark bruise forming beneath her eye.

Much of her unrest, she realized, was due to the growing anger which had fueled her courage, and she'd tried to wake Cy and have it out with him while he was sober. But he wouldn't waken and slapped her offending hands away as you'd shoo a bothersome insect. In frustration she had to walk and feel the cold, fresh air on her wounds. Without realizing it, she ended up in front of Christ Church just as people were filing in for the morning service. Forgetting how she must look, she followed on the heels of the last in line and sat at the end of the row nearest the door.

A small man in a black robe trimmed in red took the bench by the organ and elicited sounds from that instrument that filled the sanctuary. It felt as if the music rattled the windows in their frames and invaded the corners and crevices of the small room. The surging melodies seeped into Gudrun's body through every pore and filled her with a feeling of elation that transcended her physical and emotional condition.

She heard little of the sermon or readings, concentrating on the hymns … hymns so different from those she'd sung: "Jesus is fairer, Jesus is purer, who makes the woeful heart to sing." The lyrics and melodies conveyed hope and joy in the love of God. Surely this was allowed. Surely celebrating your religion was as important in worship as confessing sins and begging forgiveness. Surely she deserved to hear her heart sing. In spite of her rationalizations, however, she felt a tinge of betrayal at entering the camp of a group so close to the dreaded Catholics. She had best be on her guard lest they try to convert her, an act her mother would have considered tantamount to stealing her soul.

Once, when the organ swelled, two men took their positions at the front pew and gradually worked their way back, passing a collection plate at each row. Gudrun wondered what to do since she had no money and initially thought of heading for the door, only a few steps from where she sat. Then she noticed that the usher on her side of the church was her friend Einer, unfamiliar to her in a somewhat ill fitting suit and without his signature crumpled hat. He passed the plate directly to the person next to her, low and close in front of her so it appeared she had deposited her contribution.

After the service, she quickly exited before the minister walked down the aisle to greet his parishioners. But Einer caught her elbow before she'd made a complete getaway and drew her aside. "What happened to your face?" he whispered. "Did your husband do that?"

"It's nothing. I fell." She turned away and tried to walk on, but he detained her.

"I could be wrong, but those aren't the kind of injuries you get from a fall." He sounded angry and accusing, causing Gudrun to resort to her usual guilty assumptions..

"It was my own fault," she started, but he interrupted her.

"No one ever deserves to be hit! Ever!" he declared vehemently. "He should be locked up!"

"Just leave it alone. If you're my friend, you'll just leave it alone," Gudrun pleaded, and of course, Einer clamped his mouth shut and released her arm. In 1950, a marriage license still granted a man the right to forcibly discipline his wife and children. The "love, honor, and obey" clause in the contract was liberally interpreted but stringently enforced, both psychologically and physically. It was an area in the sanctity of marriage that no one questioned, even if that right was being abused. There were no shelters for women, and the law turned a deaf ear to complaints.

And so, Gudrun continued to find her rest in the little church and also regularly took to slipping into the back row on Sunday mornings, mostly to hear the music from that majestic organ. She'd save out a coin or two from her grocery money for the collection plate and gradually began to feel at home and comfortable.

She continued to be the first one out the door, however, and didn't wait to greet the minister or visit with the other worshipers. Then one Sunday Einer stopped her flight and said the minister (he called him Father, which was a Catholic red flag for sure) wanted to talk to her. "Okay, this is it," she thought. They're either going to try to convert me or ask me not to come to church any more." She waited with Einer, feeling trapped, until Father had shaken the last hand and exchanged the final pleasantry

"Well, here's our young sprinter. I've been wanting to meet you but you always race off before I can even get down the aisle." He held her hand in both of his and laughed at his joke. She couldn't help but stare at his hands: they rested like two soft, white doves over her own rough and reddened hand, but for all their softness, they felt strong and firm. These were the hands that summoned forth the voice of the great organ and caused it to thunder in exaltation or whisper a sweet melody in prayer. He held the emotions and responses of the congregation in his hands. It was as if, through his music, he could reach into people's hearts and open a flood of feelings and memories that they'd forgotten or maybe were experiencing for the first time.

She couldn't respond, but she felt her face redden under his attention. "I just wanted to meet you and invite you to our church suppers on Friday nights. We all bring whatever's left over in our cupboards to pass. You're a newcomer, so just bring yourself. We have some very nice people in our church. I'm sure you'd enjoy them."

She managed a "Thank you" and he hurried away, only to turn again and say,

"Oh, and bring your husband." How did he know she had a husband? Had Einer told him? Did he know Cy hit her? Her face was aflame, she knew, with shame and she was desperate to know what Einer had said. She was suddenly aware that she wanted this man who held the music in his hands to think well of her.

"What did you tell him?" she asked Einer, trying to keep her voice calm and unaccusing.

"Just that you were a friend of mine and new to Bayfield. Please come to the suppers, and do bring your husband, if he'll come. You need some friends and particularly other women friends that you can talk to. Anyway, that's the way it seems to me." Einer's voice trailed off at the end as if wondering if he'd gone too far and entered a forbidden territory in her life. Gudrun was touched that someone cared about her loneliness.

"I'll try," she said noncommittally as she turned up the hill to her apartment building, leaving Einer unmoving and looking after her for a few seconds before he too turned and started down the hill.

Cy usually went out on Friday nights, and Gudrun thought about going to the church supper without telling him. Then she decided to make an effort at getting him to come with her. She could tell he'd already been drinking early that week when she broached the subject with him. He looked at her suspiciously.

"How long you been goin' to that church?"

"Just sometimes on Sunday mornings while you're sleeping, I go to hear the organ. You should hear it Cy. It's like nothing you've ever heard, and … "

"How do you know what I've heard? You think I'm dumb or somethin'? You been talkin' to all them people over there in that fancy church?"

"No, no! Actually I've only talked to the minister once when he invited me to the suppers and to Einer who does the maintenance at the church. He sometimes leaves the door open so I can rest on my way up the hill." She realized too late that she shouldn't have mentioned Einer.

"Sounds like you're a little too friendly with this Einer. Is he your new boyfriend? Is that what's goin' on over there?" He spoke derisively, as if the idea of her having a boyfriend was out of the question but worth a little teasing.

"Don't talk silly. He's old enough to be my father, but he's been kind and we talk when I go by the church. I don't know anyone to talk to here in Bayfield."

"You can talk to me. How about talkin' to yer husband? Besides, you'd have some friends here if you weren't such a damn, cold Swede. All you do is sit in this damn dump and fiddle with all that junk for your fancy friends down in St. Paul. I wish you would find a boyfriend. Maybe he'd take you off my hands. Let him support you!" He slammed out the door to seek more balm for his guilt and disappointment, the issue of the church supper unresolved and completely forgotten for the time being.

The church suppers were not the only things on Gudrun's mind, however. One day as she was absentmindedly checking her mailings on the calendar, she suddenly realized that she hadn't had her period for at least one and possibly two months. She instantly came alert and strained at her memory. She hadn't been paying attention and had even given up hope. Now she remembered her bouts of dizziness and how, recently, she had felt sick to her stomach in the mornings, dismissing it as nerves. On her walk that day she asked to use the phone at the grocery store and called Willow on the Island.

"I'm sorry, but I need to get to that doctor in Washburn you took me to that time, remember?"

"Course I do, but ya ain't sick or nothin' are you?" Willow sounded genuinely worried, and Gudrun was instantly thankful for this good friend she had managed to make, in spite of all her social shortcomings.

"I'm not sure, but I think I might be pregnant. Oh, it would solve so many problems," She couldn't keep the excitement from her voice, and it proved contagious as she and Willow eagerly planned the outing to Washburn, once again in Arne's rusty, old truck.

"Oh please hold back the ice just a little longer, so Arne can get the truck over on the ferry," she prayed that night, "and please give us a second chance to do the right thing."

On Doing the Right Thing

And so, God had forgiven her, or so it seemed when the old doctor pronounced her definitely pregnant, laughing at her insistence that there be no mistake. She floated on a cloud for the next couple days, planning on how she would make the announcement to Cy. She decided on making a fine dinner celebration to accompany the news, and roasted pork with apple fritters, as it was one of Cy's favorites. She hoped he wouldn't be drunk when he came home that night, but her heart fell as he opened the door and leaned clumsily against the door frame, giggling. At least he was in a good mood. If she could get him to eat and watch what she said maybe she could keep him friendly long enough to give him the wonderful news that would save their marriage. As he finished his plate, she said,

"Cy, I've got something to talk to you about."

He eyed her warily, his fork suspended in midair. "I don't want to hear no more talk about that goddamned church, you hear." He pointed the tines of the fork close to her face.

"But this is important, and I know you'll want to hear it."

He threw down the fork and jumped to his feet so fast that his chair tipped over behind him and the table skidded forward against the sink. Gudrun jumped up too but not fast enough to escape, and that same strong arm that used to hold her so tightly and lovingly as they danced at the roller rink, now pinned her to the table, bending her backwards, the other arm raised with fist clenched as if to strike. "I don't want to hear nothin' about the church or the organ or the friendly people."

"But that's not what I ... " and her voice caught in her throat as she recognized the flick of his fist, like the cock of a gun, and knew it would explode in her face in seconds; but also in that split second, anger filled her heart and she thought of the spark of life that now lived inside her and vowed that from that moment on all her love and protection would be lavished on that miracle baby God had seen fit to give her. Maybe she did deserve punishment for lying, but her innocent baby didn't.

With all her strength, she strained against Cy's arm and her fingers curled around the handle of the heavy cast iron frying pan in the nearby sink. Used to fry the fritters, it now became a makeshift weapon which she swung as hard as she could against the once loving face so close to her's. It seemed to be happening in slow motion ... a ballet which could easily, without the threats and weapons, have been a tender moment between a husband and wife: an embrace with the promise of a kiss.

As Cy slowly sank to the floor, she managed to yell in a voice unaccustomed to being raised, "Not this time! I'm pregnant with your baby," she continued shakily; "and you will never lay a hand to me again." Cy sat on the floor leaning against a table leg, clearly dazed by the liquor, the heavy food, and the blow. Blood dripped from his forehead where the edge of the pan had made contact. He touched his head and looked incredulously at the blood on his fingers.

Gudrun remained above him with the pan in hand, fearing that he would now rise and beat her and the precious embryo to death. He rose, picked up his coat, and walked slowly and unsteadily out the door. He didn't come home that night; and when he came home the next day he said little. He didn't apologize and neither did Gudrun.

The episode was never mentioned again, but their relationship became even more strained, if possible. They were like two strangers who shared the same house and bed but led separate lives. At first Gudrun couldn't help but enjoy her newly found power. She didn't have to be careful of what she said to him. She was on equal footing, maybe even had the upper hand because of the pregnancy. He seemed almost frightened of her, giving her a wide berth when they passed each other. He also no longer sought to have sexual relations with her, giving her a wide berth in their only bed as well. Oh, it wasn't that he didn't come home drunk. But when he did he went quietly to bed, refusing the suppers she continued to prepare.

One night when he was sober, she tried to talk to him. "I know how disappointed you were that we lost that first baby, but now we have a second chance, like I told you, and we can work hard and make a nice home. Maybe it'll be that boy you wanted." She nudged him and smiled, hoping to stir some interest. "Oh Cy, we used to be in love. Remember how it used to be at the Gendron's? It was good then because you stayed sober, and it could be that way again. Don't you want to do the right thing?" Without meaning to, she had used that old cliché that she'd heard from her mother and friends when they talked about men and marriage. Doing the right thing was always so important to them and applied in a multiple of instances: marrying, earning money, and attending church.

"What's the right thing, 'Good'?" She brightened when she heard him respond and was even more hopeful when she heard him use his nickname for her. Maybe he'd come around. "Is the right thing always what you say it is? You've made all these conditions, and when I don't live up to them you turn on the silent, cold shoulder and punish me like I was a kid. You never want sex unless I get mad and force you into it, and you support us with that stuff that ordinary women only do as a hobby. You've taken away everything about me that was a man, and all I can do is drink to forget about what a failure I am."

Gudrun couldn't believe what she was hearing. It had never occurred to her that she was in any way responsible for his drinking. His defense was an oversimplification, to be sure, but suddenly she remembered how her mother had expected certain behavior from her and the looks and the silences that accompanied her lapses. Had she unwittingly become her mother? "Once I believed that you were right about everything," she started; but he interrupted her.

"Oh yeah, that was when you were sweet little 'Good,' always tellin' me how wonderful I was; but you were settin' the bait then and reelin' me in. You weren't so sweet when you brought the hammer down and forced me into marriage."

"But you weren't willing to do the right thing by me after we'd had relations," she flung the words at him like a slap, and only after they hung in the air did she realize that she was on the brink of having her lie uncovered. He looked at her for some time, and it felt to Gudrun as if he were peering right into her soul.

"You didn't care about that baby I loved, and now I'm supposed to care about another baby? Are you really pregnant, or is it part of another right thing I have to do? Tell me now, Gudrun, were you even pregnant when we got married?"

Panic boiled in her throat, but he remained calm and resolute, looking steadily into her eyes. There was no time to think or to plan. He'd caught her unawares. "Don't be silly," she said," then attempted to shift the blame. "That's water over the dam. Now we've got a chance to move on and do it right. Is there no talking to you?" Time crawled as Cy stood looking at her and she tried in vain to return the gaze without flinching, blinking or fidgeting. "Maybe now it's time for you to do the right thing, 'Good,' how about it?"

"Yes, of course I was pregnant when we married," she yelled in anger, "do you think I'd sign up for this if I didn't have to?" She indicated the small apartment with a sweep of her arm and collapsed in tears as she realized that she had failed to keep her promise to God and had just lied again. Jesus' words to Peter on the eve of the crucifixion instantly came to mind and seemed to apply to her situation.

"You will deny me three times before the cock crows," he had said. How many more lies, which were really denials of God, would cross her lips? Where would it all end?

Becoming a Herring Choker

From the minute Gudrun entered the post office she sensed an air of excitement among the regulars who came every morning to retrieve their mail from the grid of locked boxes. It wasn't that anyone expected important mail, but it did provide another excuse to meet and exchange news or just visit.

"I hear they're runnin' in the channel between Madeline and Long."

"It's a little early, but I've known it to happen this early."

A girl waved to Gudrun from across the room and headed towards her as she stood in line at the counter to mail her packages. "You're Cy's wife ain't you?" she asked. Gudrun nodded. "I'm Caro Miller. My husband, Dan, helps Cy on the *Siren* sometimes." Cy had mentioned Dan.

Damn good worker when he's sober," he'd laugh; but he'd not mentioned a wife. Gudrun wondered briefly if this thin, sober girl was subject to the same treatment as she. She hardly looked to be 16 or 17 years old.

"Are you gonna work the herring run? They say it'll start next week."

"I'm afraid I don't know what that is." Gudrun was again reddening in embarrassment.

"Oh, I forgot. You're not from around here are you?" She pulled Gudrun out of line and warmed to her story, speaking in a confidential tone as if what she was about to share was a secret. "Well, the herring are real little fish and they stick in the nets. Usually the guys just pick them out on the boats; but when the herring are running, they fill the nets so fast the guys don't have time to get them out. So they bring them into the herring sheds and they hire women to pick them out. They call them herring chokers. It's a chance to earn extra money, if you can stand the work. I'm surprised Cy ain't told you. Maybe he don't want you down there." She backed away a little when she realized she may have spoken out of turn. "Don't tell Cy I told you, okay?"

"How do I get hired? Will someone show me what to do? Will you help me?" Caro Miller was already going out the door, shaking her head as if she hadn't mentioned it.

That night when Cy came home he was, incredibly, sober and ravenous. He ate several bowls of the potato soup she'd fixed and finished off a loaf of freshly baked bread. He even commented on how good the food was and, for the first time in a long time, looked directly into Gudrun's eyes. Gudrun was encouraged to speak.

"Today someone at the post office told me about the herring run. They said it'll start next week."

"Ya, that's what I been doin' today. Gettin' the Siren dinged up and pullin' out the mesh nets." He poured a cup of coffee. "I guess I got pretty hungry, workin' out in the cold and all." He was almost apologetic, and Gudrun felt guilty that her husband had to justify eating in his own house.

"Oh Cy, you know I love to see you eat." She touched his arm. He pulled away. "I heard they hire women to be herring chokers." She spoke casually as if only slightly interested and laughed. "Do you think I could be a herring choker?"

He looked surprised then shook his head. "It's nothin' you'd be used to. It's hard work and it's hot and stinky, and with you bein' pregnant and all ... " His voice trailed off, but she could tell he was looking for her reaction to his mention of the pregnancy.

"Everything seems to be good with the baby," she touched her stomach, "and I've even quit having morning sickness. You know I'm used to hard work, and I'm not squeamish. It would be some extra money." It was a long speech, and she sat back and waited.

"Well, I guess you could try. If you can't do it, you can quit." He finished his coffee and carried his cup to the sink, then turned back to her. When he spoke, his voice was strong and his words carried the hint of a threat. "This is my thing, this fishing. Just make sure you don't choke more than the herring when you're in my territory."

Gudrun was used to responding to threats. She had learned early on that every action produces a reaction. She would do this job well, but take great care not to intrude in his business. She would make Cy proud of her. It was with these goals in mind that she reported for duty the next week outfitted in rubber overalls (oilers) and rubber boots.

The herring sheds abutted the docks and had doors opening directly onto them. When the fishermen came in with a load of herring, they would pull the fish laden nets off their boats, across the dock, and directly onto the long tables inside the sheds. Workers, men and women alike, untangled the small fish from the nets and deposited them in boxes for cleaning.

There were wood stoves in the sheds, since it was November, and the doors had to stand open to the elements when the boats came in. The resulting temperature in the sheds was either cold or sweltering; and when it was sweltering, the accumulated stench from years of herring runs was almost unbearable.

When Gudrun got to her shed, she spotted Caro Miller near the door and went to stand by her. Caro showed her how to quickly slip a finger between the twine of the net and the fish to pull them out. Caro also provided a steady stream of chatter that helped the time go by and made Gudrun feel accepted. She made many friends during her herring choker days and began to feel a part of the Bayfield community.

The run lasted about three weeks, and Gudrun saw little of Cy in the sheds during her working days. She saw him on the dock pulling nets, but he didn't speak or wave like some of the fisherman husbands did to their choker wives. At night they were both exhausted and usually fell into bed right after a hurried supper.

True to her resolve, Gudrun gave her best to the job, but stayed out of Cy's way. Her health remained good; but sometimes, when the doors were closed, she'd feel so sick at the smell of fish that she'd have to occasionally step to a large crack in the wall near her table and gulp in some fresh air.

"You look awful white today. Ain't you feelin' good?" Caro looked concerned, and as Gudrun turned to reassure her, she was aware that Cy was standing by her elbow with a steaming cup of coffee.

"You look like you could use this," he said quietly into her ear. Then louder, he flashed his white teeth in one of his signature smiles and said for the shed workers, "You Scandihoovians think your coffee cures everything." Then he was gone in the midst of smart replies from the rest of the chokers. That night he asked if she didn't think she should quit.

Gudrun was elated at his concern, but still determined to see the herring run through. Already it was slowing down, and in just a few days it would be over. "I'll be fine," she assured him, "only a couple days left. No sense quitting now." He shrugged and went to bed. As Gudrun lay beside him, she thought as how he must be watching her or he wouldn't have known to bring the coffee. Such a small ember from which to build a fire, but Gudrun fell asleep enveloped in a warm feeling and the hope that the ember would gradually turn into a flame of love and burn again in her husband.

The Church Supper

The herring run was over, and Gudrun felt a sense of accomplishment at having completed it, although it was a relief to return to the domestic duties she so enjoyed. On the first Friday morning after the run, Gudrun rose early to set yeast dough for her famous orange roll ring that had won her such praise at the Gendron dinner parties. Cy was out of the house all day, and she busied herself with her usual chores, taking time to check the rising dough until it had doubled in bulk, kneading and resting the sponge, and finally forming the rolls and piling them in the angel food pan for one more rising before baking. She tipped the glorious looking crown out of the tin at 4:30 and drizzled the final orange glaze over the top.

She walked in the cold evening air to the church, carrying the rolls, still warm, wrapped in a clean dishtowel sling. This would be the first supper she'd attended even though the Father had invited her several weeks back. The herring run had occupied her every waking moment for the past three weeks, and there hadn't been any time for going new places and meeting new people. She hadn't even had time for Sunday morning services, and wondered if they still wanted her to come. Einer kept the invitation open, however, and she finally decided to give it a try. She could always slip away if the company proved too difficult. She was good at that.

There was no turning back, however, once she opened the church basement door. A blast of warm air almost sucked her into the room where her senses were immediately assailed by a combination of delicious smells: brewing coffee, bubbling casseroles, sugary cakes and cookies. There was no chance of blending in unnoticed either, as several women hurried to her side to take her coat and welcome her. Her thoughts instantly traveled back to the church dinners with her mother in St. Paul. She saw the huge, speckled, blue enamel coffee pot filled with egg coffee, the mainstay of any church event from funeral to christening. Even the murmur of voices and laughter seemed familiar and a wave of nostalgia rolled over her. Recently, in retrospect, she had to admit that her life in St. Paul had not been all that bad. There were many good things about that tightly knit, Scandinavian, extended family of hers that time and distance had allowed her to appreciate and miss.

That night, Einer introduced her to so many people she couldn't possibly remember them all, but she ate supper with him and his older sister, Jenny Lundgren, a plump and jolly widow who adopted Gudrun from the first handshake. It was, altogether, a wonderful evening and it marked the beginning of a pleasant social life for Gudrun which would span many winters to come and reward her with lasting friendships. Her crown of rolls was received with near adulation and would be requested for many events in the future.

Gudrun walked home from that first supper, grateful for the cold air that cooled her cheeks which were blushing pink from all the unaccustomed compliments and attention. For the first time since she'd left the Gendrons last September, she felt happy and appreciated. Maybe she could regain her "born again life" that she'd so enjoyed when she first came to the Island. Maybe Cy would change his mind when she grew large with the baby and came to trust her again. She realized now, after much soul searching, that most of her trouble with him hinged on the matter of trust, and she had to admit that she hadn't given him many reasons to trust her. However, she still didn't dare reveal her deception for fear he would leave her, baby or no baby.

On nights like this in the northland, when it is clear and the sky is filled with billions of stars, you might think you have slipped into a cosmic geode and stand surrounded on all sides by sparkling crystals. There is a quality of magic in the air when a mere human, allowed to view this phenomenon, feels a peaceful sense of well being. "God's in his heaven, all's right with the world."

This was such a night for Gudrun. If only Cy could see her now as she walked home in the dark winter evening, pink cheeked, bright corn flower blue eyes and a tentative smile on her lips, he might remember the girl at the roller rink who caught his attention one soft summer night before the world moved in to spoil it all.

"Born Again" For The Second Time

That Sunday, after church, Gudrun wasn't allowed to hurry away after the service. All her new friends from the supper crowded around her to talk and exclaim again over what had come to be known as the crown of rolls. Jenny Lundgren was among them and invited Gudrun for coffee the following Wednesday afternoon. "It's just a few other Scandihoovians," she'd assured her with her ever-ready laugh. Gudrun remembered Willow's use of the same perversion of the word Scandinavian and found herself laughing with Jenny and, once again, feeling free to make good-natured fun of herself.

Jenny's apartment was in the second floor of a downtown Bayfield building. Its rooms were small and decorated in an old fashioned way: many lace doilies on overstuffed furniture; a lifetime of framed pictures arranged on every flat surface; colorful rag rugs and flourishing house plants that hung in corners or were tucked around the perimeter of the rooms. It was very clean and smelled of coffee and something decidedly sweet.

The other guests were all Jenny's age and similar in looks and personalities. They were slightly chubby from years of providing their families with the rich, Scandinavian dishes that in the old country, as well as in northern Wisconsin, sustained them through bitter, cold winters. Now graying, they were fair and blue-eyed, with hands that showed evidence of hard work; those hands all now busy as they sat with some form of handiwork: knitting, embroidery, crocheting.

Ida Torgerson seemed to laugh constantly and even when a shared tale or piece of news was very sad she'd shake her head in sympathy and then conclude with a smile and a twinkle in her eye, "Ya, but life goes on, ya?" It was clear that Ida loved life.

Alma Halvorson seemed to Gudrun to be more like the women from her St. Paul church. Her face was held in a tight expression and she looked very judgmental. However, even she had to succumb at times to Ida's merriment and her lips would twitch into a smile, then a modest laugh, and finally full enjoyment, which she tried to hide by putting a hand over her mouth. Gudrun never saw her without an apron, even in church. It was as if she never knew when she would need protection from something messy.

Ingrid Carlson, small and rather bird-like, was the historian of the group and the authority on the old country. She was constantly tracing people's lineage. A casual mention of someone would send her off on a family history search that usually ended in some obscure Swedish province on the North Sea. "Oh, you know her," she'd begin, "she's Snoose Swenson's daughter. The Swensons who lived out on the old Boe farm?" And she was off, sharing more knowledge about Snoose (who had the misfortune of forever being known by his bad habit) than anyone wanted to know.

The ladies set aside their omnipresent busy work when coffee with date-filled sugar cookies and a rich banana nut bread were served. "In the old country," Ingrid said as she laced her coffee with cream and sugar, "a Swedish hostess was expected to serve at least seven kinds of cookies if someone dropped by for coffee. "Oh, not that you should do that," she hastily assured Jenny, "It's just a bit of knowledge about the old country." She rolled her eyes innocently and so, established her role in the group for the newcomer.

At the end of the afternoon when the remaining coffee was divided among the ladies, Jenny held up her cup as if to make a toast and the others followed suit. "It's kind of silly, but we've gotten into the habit of singing this little song that old country Swedes used to sing when they got together for a sip or two. Maybe you know it, Gudrun." In unison with a singsong lilt to their voices they all sang a short verse in Swedish. Gudrun had never heard it, but Jenny translated for her, and she eventually sang along with them.

"A cup of coffee is the best drink in the whole world,

It braces the body and strengthens the soul,

And thrills one's whole being from the head

All the way down to one's toes."

"There are many customs from the old country we don't observe," laughed Ida, "like holding a cube, we called them sugar lumps, of sugar on your tongue while drinking coffee so you sugar it as you go, or pouring your coffee into your saucer to cool and slurping it up from there."

"Much too messy for me," said Alma.

"I'm sure that was more in the case of low people," said Ingrid, miffed at the attempt to usurp her historian's role.

"Oh, my mother used to do both those things," Ida persisted "but maybe she was low." She shook her head as if sad and looked up through her lashes at Ingrid. Then her laughter escaped again and she concluded with, "Ya, but life goes on, Ya?"

They all laughed and then busied themselves with their leave taking. When they had left, Jenny hugged Gudrun tightly and said, "Now you know all of us. I hope you weren't too bored. We're all so much older than you. We should really introduce you to some young women." Gudrun found herself returning the embrace.

When she walked by the church the next day, it seemed as if Einer had been waiting for her. He was smiling broadly as he spoke. "Pardon my asking, but how did you fare with the *tants*? He used the Swedish word for aunts and seemed so tickled with the whole subject that Gudrun couldn't help but smile her response right back at him.

"It was the best afternoon I've had in a long time. You were right when you said I needed a woman to talk to, and now I have four. Thank you for that." It was a long, but heartfelt speech for her, and she reddened in embarrassment and walked on, leaving Einer to stand watching as he let his smile slowly fade into a satisfied look.

Gudrun was overcome with the camaraderie of these well-meaning ladies and forever after would think of them as her family, sharing good and bad times alike. As years passed, she would be the one to make sure she visited Ida in the nursing home, trying to have a new Ole and Lena joke ready to coax a laugh. It was she who made sure that when Alma was laid in her casket she had a clean apron over her Sunday dress, just in case heaven proved messier than anyone imagined.

Winter Without End

The winter of 1950 deepened. Several periods of extreme cold were relieved by warm ups which, in turn, produced heavy snows. By Christmas, Gudrun had begun to show her pregnancy. The *tants* were beside themselves with the excitement of having a birth to anticipate. All their handiwork turned into items for the baby until Gudrun had to allow as how the baby would grow too fast to be able to wear all the tiny garments that were folded lovingly in a large clothes basket the *tants* had lined with a soft, flannel fabric printed with pink and blue hobby horses—good for both a boy or a girl.

As Gudrun had hoped, once a small protrusion appeared below her waist, Cy began to change towards her. He spent less time at the bar and became more solicitous, helping with the wood stove and carrying the pails of water needed for laundry or bathing. Money was a little easier; they both had earned extra during the herring run and Cy now contributed to the household budget.

One evening as she cleaned the supper away, Gudrun felt definite movement from the baby. She had felt life before, but this was like a rolling wave that started at one end of her belly and continued to the opposite side. She was so excited she forgot about the wall that separated she and her husband and rushed to where he sat drinking coffee at the table. Impulsively she grabbed his hand and laid it across where the proof of life had appeared; and lo and behold, it happened again as if on cue. His eyes widened and his fingers tightened on her stomach to feel more and further confirm the pregnancy that in his heart he had still doubted, until now. Gudrun could not contain herself. She threw her arms around her husband, hugging and laughing, until he finally returned the embrace and stood holding her, rocking back and forth in a soothing motion which she couldn't determine as being for her or the baby.

When she stepped back, he gave her a long but gentle kiss on the lips and she felt his whole body relax in her arms. From that moment on, they were husband and wife again. Oh, there were lapses, but they both tried to treat each other with respect and kindness because of the growing infant. That tiny embryo continued to exhibit so much vigor and assertiveness that Gudrun was often forced to stop what she was doing and soothe it by massaging the hard little ball below her stomach. It was like a symbol of endless possibilities and an exciting future.

That Christmas was like none Gudrun had experienced before. Cy was still not agreeable enough to accompany her to church; but he did go to Jenny Lundgren's with her for Christmas Eve, where he also met Einer. It was like another miracle for Gudrun. Cy and Einer immediately started sharing fishing stories and became friends even without the background of the bar and the beer. They gorged on meatballs, mashed potatoes, and an array of pastries, even laughing over their ability to enjoy the pickled herring that was traditionally on every Scandinavian holiday table. "Any of these guys look familiar to you?" Cy joked to Gudrun as he helped himself to a serving of the silvery little fillets.

He also unveiled his present to her on Christmas Eve. She went to midnight church services with Einer and Jenny, leaving him at their apartment with some mysterious work he said he had. When she came home, a little white crib stood in the kitchen assembled and ready for bedding and, eventually, baby. Gudrun sat down and cried, silently reciting a prayer of thanksgiving for all the recent miracles in her life.

Willow and Arne braved the windsled on Christmas Day and had a turkey dinner with Cy and Gudrun. Cy produced a couple bottles of wine and although Gudrun couldn't face drinking any herself, she didn't keep the others from partaking. She had to admit it made for a jolly time, and Cy didn't drink too much or exhibit any of the tendencies she associated from other bouts with alcohol.

"Ya got it made, kid," Willow said as Gudrun showed her the crib and all the little garments. "I don't mind tellin' ya, I'm jealous."

Gudrun took both Willow's hands. "Don't be, because you are going to be this baby's second mother. I don't want to be a mother like I had, always critical and strict. I know she loved me and had my best interests at heart but I want to be more open with my child. You can help me with that because you always tell me when I'm being too religious and strict for my own good. I want my baby to be more like you." They laughed then and shook hands, as if sealing a pact.

"Never had nobody say they wanted to be like me," Willow mused, "I'll be anxious to see a little blond, blue-eyed Sweetwillow runnin' around."

Hard Times

After Christmas the winter bore down with more snowstorms and temperatures that hovered well below zero. The herring run money was long gone, and even the handiwork orders from St. Paul tapered off. It was as if all activity was as sluggish and unyielding as the thermometers.

Gudrun often didn't have enough grocery money for basic items like flour for their bread or sugar and butter. Jenny Lundgren asked her to come to her apartment and bake bread for her. "I can't knead the dough with this arthritis in my hands. Bake four loaves and keep two for yourself as payment for your work. You'll be doing me a big favor." Gudrun suspected Jenny's motives but decided to say nothing, since she often literally did not know where their next loaf was coming from. Some of the churchwomen brought her bags of sugar and pounds of butter and requested baking as payment for sharing the ingredients. Their wood supply was also running low, and Einer brought logs and piled them with their own dwindling supply under the stairs, being careful to cover them with the tarp Cy had placed there.

Gone were the pork roasts and fresh stews of early winter. Sometimes Cy's ice fishing yielded a catch, but mostly their food supply was enriched with smoked chubs contributed by a buddy of his from the bar. They were small, heavily salted fish that were left so long in the smoker they were sometimes more leathery skin than flesh; but they did provide protein and tasted quite good with boiled potatoes.

So they weren't starving. Cy must have been aware of the help they received but chose not to make an issue of it, since his wife and the baby needed all these things to live. Only Gudrun could see how it lowered his self-esteem when she served a fresh loaf of bread or when he carried an armload of wood up the stairs from that self-replenishing woodpile. "Some people never get a break," he was fond of saying, as if there was some special luck involved in having a supply of wood and flour.

Gudrun didn't know where Cy got the money for beer, but he had taken to hanging out at Junior's Bar again. She suspected his cronies treated him for his camaraderie: he was well liked and always had stories and jokes. He made them laugh when there was no reason to laugh. Usually he came home a little tipsy and went directly to bed. Sometimes he was argumentative and asked, for instance, why she hadn't done any baking. It was as if he wanted her to accuse him of being a poor provider in order to defend himself. Gudrun would only comment that she hadn't felt well enough to bake, not that she didn't have the ingredients. Then he would look hard at her for a few seconds, shrug, and take himself off to bed. He didn't become violent with her any more; but Gudrun feared that if their fortunes didn't change, he might again hit that level of discouragement. If only the long winter would lessen its grip. If only the men had work.

Sometimes in the dark of night, Gudrun thought that if he had spent more time in the fall preparing for winter, they might not be in such dire straits. Sometimes she defended him in her mind thinking he couldn't have anticipated the long winter or her faltering money supply. Whichever way her thoughts veered, she kept them to herself, since she was insightful enough to not want to add to the guilt she could tell was already eating away at him.

With some amount of shame, she remembered his words when he had been trying to get out of marrying her and how now they sounded like a prophecy. "You don't want to marry me! I'm a heathen, a drunk! I barely make enough to keep myself alive. Just write me off to experience or damn me to hell or whatever you have to do; but for God's sake don't tie yourself to me or your life will be ruined worse than you can ever imagine." But when all was said and done, one fact remained: she loved him.

CHAPTER THIRTEEN

Chapter 13

"Give sorrow words; the grief that does not speak
Whispers the o'er fraught heart and bids it break."
(MACBETH) WILLIAM SHAKESPEARE

O ne afternoon, Gudrun came back to the apartment to find Cy sober, cheerful, and busy pulling sweaters and jackets out of the cardboard boxes that served as storage for their clothing. "I've got a job," he announced proudly, "ice harvesting for a guy in Ashland who wants to ship a load of ice by train to a brewery in Milwaukee. Have you ever heard of such a thing? They want ice from Lake Superior because the water's not polluted."

She knew nothing about ice harvesting. It was, once again, like the herring choking. They used to get chunks of ice for their icebox in St. Paul. She remembered her mother putting a card in the window which would tell the ice truck driver how many pounds she thought she would need in order to last until his next round. She also remembered how she and all the neighborhood kids used to wait until the driver had rinsed the sawdust off the ice with a little hose on the side of his truck and with huge tongs, taken a chunk into the house. Then they would run from hiding places and fill containers with ice chips from the bottom of the truck. They acted swiftly, thrilled with the prospect of having ice to suck on in the hot summer. Once she thought he knew what they were doing and didn't care. He might have even given them the chips, but it was more fun to think you were getting away with something. Mother, on the other hand, might have considered it stealing, so Gudrun kept her mouth shut and took her stash to a shady spot in back of their apartment building to enjoy. She had not once wondered about the origin of the ice.

121

Now she listened in fascination as Cy proudly explained the operation, prefacing his explanation with the wonderful news that he was going to be making eight dollars a day for the duration of the job. "You score the blocks with an ice plow, then you saw through the scores with a machine that looks like a big mower. They'll set a conveyor belt up from the lake bank to trucks, and we'll pile the ice in and take it to the railroad car for loading. We'll pack it into the car with lots of sawdust and tarps to keep it from thawing. This guy came into Junior's and recruited a whole bunch of us. Seems funny, don't it? Maybe we'll eventually be drinkin' it in some of that beer they're makin' down there." He paused briefly, contemplating the irony of the situation.

He continued to pull long underwear and flannel shirts from the boxes as he talked and was in such good spirits that Gudrun couldn't help but catch his mood. "When do you start?" she asked. "Do I have time to knit some wool socks and mitts for inside your choppers? It's going to be cold work. What about food when you're on the job? Where will you be working?" The questions came fast and furiously as she too began to make lists and pile clothes.

"I start in two days," he replied, "so you better knit fast if you're gonna." He grabbed her and executed a slower version of a skating maneuver around the kitchen table, holding her body firmly but gently. "By next week we won't be eatin' smoked chubs," he promised gaily; and they both laughed and moved slowly until, once again, their dance became an embrace and then a kiss.

Cy put in several weeks dawn to dusk on the lake, working in the coldest weather, coming home half frozen and ravenous, but so happy to be earning money. One night he said he wouldn't be home the following night after work, as it was his turn to row a boat around the one acre of open water to keep it from freezing over night. Gudrun laid out a blanket for him to take and packed extra food for this difficult duty. Dan Miller, one of his cronies from the bar, came by just as he was leaving, and Gudrun saw him give Cy a bottle which he stuck in the blanket roll, casting a quick look back at the apartment stairway to see if Gudrun was watching. "It's just to keep the cold away on night duty, missus," the Dan called to her, and the two left without another word.

It was around six the next morning that Gudrun heard footsteps on their stairs. She was awake but lying in bed, unwilling to leave the warmth for the cold apartment and the chore of the wood stove. She rose instantly and drew her blue sweater over her nightgown. She thought it was Cy returning from his night shift and opened the door before the two men from the ice harvesting crew had time to knock. They had picked up Einer and Jenny, and the small delegation stood with stone faces in the freezing cold; the grim reality spread into Gudrun's heart like the sub zero air entering the room.

"Is he dead?" she asked tonelessly; and as Jenny with tear-stained face and in wordless confirmation stepped forward to embrace her, Gudrun was allowed to escape that cruel reality for an instant as she fainted into several pairs of arms that shielded her and the baby from bodily trauma and gently carried her back to her bed, still warm from the last carefree night's sleep she would have in a very long time.

She regained consciousness almost immediately and laid her hand on Cy's pillow, smooth and unwrinkled. "He didn't have a chance to sleep," she said, "he must have been so tired." She scanned the faces that surrounded her bed and years of conditioning prevailed as she steeled herself against making a scene. Under no circumstances would she embarrass others and herself by losing control, no matter what the situation. She sat up. "Thank you for your trouble, but I'll be fine now. Please don't feel you have to stay."

"But we have to get you to a doctor."

"I'm fine. I don't need a doctor. There are things that have to be done." "You have to think of the baby now, Gudrun. You've had a bad shock, and it may have affected the baby. Please let us get you checked over before we do anything else." Jenny was almost pleading with her.

"Would God be that cruel?" Her voice caught in her throat and threatened to produce tears, as she struggled for control.

"You're right. Nothing can happen to the baby now." Jenny talked to the men and they all left, Einer lingering by the door as Jenny instructed him to have Doc Olson from Washburn make an emergency house call and also to call Willow to come.

Jenny busied herself making coffee, as Gudrun sat staring ahead, trying to absorb the situation and its many implications. "Do you know what happened?"

she asked as Jenny brought her a cup and pulled a kitchen chair over to her bedside.

"The men said when they came to work this morning they found him floating close to the boat. They figured he'd fallen and knocked himself out, as he had a cut on his temple. Being as cold as it is and with him falling into the water, they thought he was probably dead before he could come to."

Gudrun's eyes were brimming with tears as she listened, but none spilled over onto her cheeks. "I have to go see him. Where is he?" She threw the blankets aside to rise.

Jenny restrained her and replaced the blankets. "They've taken him to the undertaker. You'll see him later. First you have to see the doctor." And so they sat and drank coffee. Gudrun's mind drifted to the many times recently they'd sat together drinking coffee … happy times. Now the Scandinavian comfort would have to see them through bad times. Would anything ever be the same?

It must have been an hour or more before they heard footsteps on the stairs and Gudrun heard Willow call to her from the door. Gudrun could hear Jenny's brief whispering, then she left as Willow rushed to take her friend into her arms and sit beside her on the bed, gently rocking. Gudrun responded to this much as she had on the first morning the friends had met, when Gudrun allowed herself to express grief over her mother's death for the first time. She cried until her sobs became merely painful hiccoughs and there were no tears left.

The next few days would become a blur in Gudrun's mind: the doctor who declared all to be well with the baby and the funeral arrangements made so difficult by Cy's lack of affiliation with a church. Over and over, Gudrun thought of how lucky she was to have friends who comforted her and made things happen for her, assuring her that any financial arrangements had been handled.

Cy's funeral was like a dream sequence. It seemed to move in slow motion: everyone whispered and tiptoed around as if literally in fear of waking the dead. Christ Episcopal agreed to bury him because of Gudrun's connection with the church, however, Father apologized for having to exclude parts of the service because they weren't members. She didn't care. Nothing mattered to her: the coffin, the flowers, and the rituals that were the same in every church.

People from church attended and some of the local fishermen were there. She even noticed a few of Cy's buddies from the bar, standing awkwardly self-conscious by the door as she followed Einer into the church on Willow's arm. Mrs. Gendron reached from a pew to take her hand, and Gudrun was so surprised and gratified that she had made the trip from St. Paul to attend. "Isn't it strange," she thought, "that in death Cy was in 'that goddamned church' that he had spurned in life."

When she was led to the coffin for one last viewing before the lid was closed, she took his cold hand and cried silently with her other hand pressed against her lips so she wouldn't make a sound. He wore the same sport coat he had worn to their wedding, and she saw him again as in those few months past, the coat too tight across his shoulders, smoking a cigarette as he leaned against a dock piling waiting for the wedding party to alight from the ferry.

His face in death, usually so lively whether in happiness, anger, or love, was without expression. His hair was slicked back with some sort of dressing into a pompadour effect that straightened his black curls. She touched the site of the wound on his temple, now concealed with makeup. It wasn't him, but it didn't matter. This cold stranger wasn't him.

After the funeral, she tried to spend time withdrawing into her parallel universe with Cy now the man of her fantasies. It had been a long time since she'd made use of this coping device; but after a few days, she decided it was no longer comforting to her; every time she left her dreams for the real world she had to once again painfully accept the agony that he was gone forever.

Einer had moved a folding cot into her apartment, and for the first couple weeks after Cy's death her friends took turns spending nights. She felt guilty at causing them so much trouble but knew that she needed someone near in case anything went wrong with the baby.

One night she went to bed early. She was tired and thought that maybe she could sleep the night through. A blizzard was howling around the house and when she opened the door to let Tant Alma in for night duty, the stairs were completely covered with new snow. Even Alma's footprints were filling in behind her as the wind whirled and whipped. The women shared a cup of cocoa, visited a while, then banked the wood fire and crawled beneath the covers.

Gudrun fell into a deep sleep, but came instantly wide awake when she felt Cy's kiss on her lips. She turned to respond before she remembered that he was gone. It was so real. She felt the softness and warmth of his lips and pressed her fingers over her own lips as if to keep the kiss from drifting away. The clock said three a.m. She hadn't managed a full night's sleep.

She rose to check the progress of the storm and opened the door to see the depth of the snow. What she saw was mysterious, and she stood in the icy wind a long time trying to formulate an explanation. Tant Alma's footprints were obliterated. The stairs were a sheet of fresh snow except for the clear trail of footprints which she recognized as a man's by the size of the imprint and the tread of the boot and which stopped outside the door. Whose were they? No one had come by after Alma had entered. And why hadn't the wind filled in this set of prints as it had Alma's?

She crawled back into bed and lay for a long time, imagining several scenarios. Maybe Einer had come by to check and, finding no lights, gone back home without waking them. Who else would have been out walking in the storm? The soft kiss lingered on her lips and in the back of her mind, as she lay in the cold darkness listening to the wind shooting up the stairs as if it were in a tunnel, she decided the footprints were Cy's and that he had come one last time to bid her goodbye. It was a comforting thought which allowed her to fall asleep for several hours until she heard Tant Alma struggling with the stove and making morning coffee.

Of course, the last thing on her mind before sleep became the first thing she thought of in the morning. "It was all a dream," she decided in the light of day. She drew her sweater tightly around herself and greeted Tant Alma on her way through the kitchen. The wind was still fierce and almost whipped the door out of her grasp when she opened it; there on the clear expanse of snow were the footprints intact in spite of the windy night.

Gudrun knew she would sound crazy if she shared this experience with anyone; so she decided to keep it filed in her mind like a favorite story that she could remember and tell herself when she felt alone or unloved. As she drank her coffee and mused on this decision, she suddenly became aware of a scraping sound on the stairs and realized someone was shoveling the snow away. She jumped up and flung open the door to a red-nosed Einer who was just clearing the doorway. "Oh no, you've destroyed them," she yelled into the wind."

Einer looked at the distraught woman, leaned his shovel against the wall, and ushered Gudrun into the apartment. "I'm sorry," he said. "Did I do something wrong? I just thought I'd get you shoveled in case you needed to get out." Gudrun calmed herself, now sure that keeping her secret was the right thing to do.

"No, no, it's okay. I just thought there were some footprints on the stairs. Did you come over late last night to check on us?"

"No, that's why I came early this morning. Figured you'd be snowed in. We got about a foot last night, and it's still snowing." He stamped his feet and shook his cap in preparation for the cup Tant Alma offered him. "You feel okay, Gudrun?"

"I'm fine. You didn't notice any footprints on the stairs?"

"Can't say as I did. You want me to look around outside? You think someone was here?"

"No. I think I had a silly dream is all."

"Wind probably made you edgy. It'll do that."

"I expect you're right.

Born Again for the Third Time

The weeks after Cy's death were a time of contemplation, of guilt, and finally, of resolution. Dan Miller had stopped by the apartment to return the blanket Gudrun had sent with Cy for his night duty. After he left, she held it in her arms almost in an embrace. "Is this the last thing on earth he had touched? She wondered. Would his smell linger on it?" She pressed her nose into the fabric and inhaled deeply. Immediately the strong smell of liquor caused her to turn her head and cough. She'd forgotten, until now, the episode with the bottle as Cy was leaving for work that fateful morning. As she shook the blanket loose from its folds, the origin of the smell, a dark brown stain, bloomed like a frightful, asymmetrical flower across the front.

It was more a splash than a dribble, caused by impact more than by a bottle tipping over. For Gudrun, it told the story of his death. Alcohol had taken his life as surely as a fatal disease. She could imagine the scenario: he had drunk enough to impair his faculties, stood unsteadily, and dropped the bottle onto the blanket. In an effort to right the bottle and save the remaining liquid, he had tripped, knocked himself out, and succumbed to the freezing waters of Lake Superior. In the end, whiskey was more important than life itself.

Why hadn't she intervened that morning and demanded that the bottle be left behind? Did Cy's buddy now grapple with the fact that he was the cause of her husband's death? She doubted that. But then again, Cy was alone that night on the water. No one forced him to drink too much. That was his decision.

Then she remembered the funeral and her discovery of the concealed lesion on Cy's temple and a similar image flashed across her mind: the wound she had caused in the same spot when she hit him with the frying pan. Maybe the previous wound had weakened the spot and she really had caused her husband's death. Or maybe it was her insistence that he marry her because he had taken her virginity. If Cy hadn't met and skated with her, he'd be alive today, she sometimes concluded.

Over and over, she reviewed this list of perpetrators—hoping to conclusively pin one down as the guilty party. Somehow it seemed so important to be able to lay blame. Was it Cy himself and his addiction to alcohol, his friends at Junior's Bar, his forced marriage and ensuing responsibilities? Back and forth went the arguments in her mind.

The denouement of the whole situation occurred one afternoon as she sat alone, once again mulling over the mess. Suddenly the baby did one of its now familiar, all-encompassing rolls across her stomach. As she gently stroked and rubbed the rising bulges it occurred to her that she must be strong for the next 18 years in order to raise this child. She also knew that if she were burdened with the guilt of Cy's death, she would be a damaged person incapable of being a good parent. Of course it was silly to blame Cy's friends, because he had acted of his own free will. And that's how it was resolved. *In the final analysis, how convenient it is for us humans to rationalize our actions, especially when it involves the dead who can no longer speak for themselves,* she mused. And in Cy's case, in the end, didn't he only have himself to blame?

Of immediate concern to Gudrun during these post-funeral weeks, however, was how she and her child would live now that they were alone. She had lain awake nights trying to decide. She could keep her apartment and live on her handiwork money and maybe a domestic job of some sort. Having the support group of Einer, Jenny, the church, and the *tants* was very tempting. But would she be depending on them too much? Going back to St. Paul seemed tantamount to recreating the second generation of her mother and herself, and that thought made her shiver. She couldn't let doubts spoil her newly-found contentment; and so she put the familiar fears out of her mind, lowered her head and proceeded with her thanks to God.

Reincarnation

The winter of 1951 did eventually turn into spring and with it came the much-awaited baby, a girl born in the shabby, upstairs apartment in Bayfield. Old Doc Olson, Jenny Lundgren, and Willow attended Gudrun. The *tants* had equipped the apartment with all that would be needed for the home birth and Gudrun, true to her character, had obligingly proceeded through each stage of delivery with no drama or complications. The baby had come early but still weighed a good five pounds and was screamingly healthy.

That night, when all the paraphernalia had been cleared away and everyone had gone home, Gudrun and Willow sat alone by the little white crib and watched the infant's every move with fascination. She was the most beautiful thing either of them had ever seen: long, black hair that curled as it dried from the amniotic fluid; small, perfect features; eyes so dark they almost looked black. Cy hadn't gotten his boy, but he'd been reincarnated so completely that it was a little scary.

"What's her name?" Willow asked as if it were an afterthought.

"Well, I wanted to name her Lupine after the flowers that are so strong and beautiful." Willow screwed her face in distaste.

"I don't think she'd ever thank you for that moniker."

"I know. I know! So I came up with a combination. My mother's name was Anna, and if you put that with Lu, you get LuAnn. Isn't that pretty?" Willow nodded thoughtfully.

"LuAnn. Very nice. What about a middle name?"

"Oh, that's no problem. It's Willow. LuAnn Willow Gaudette. What do you think?"

Willow touched the baby's palm and watched and felt the tiny fingers close over her finger and heart simultaneously.

Chapter 14

"Sorrow concealed, like an oven stopp'd
Doth burn the heart to cinders where it is."
(TITUS ANDRONICUS) WILLIAM SHAKESPEARE

The first summer after Cy's death was a time of bittersweet remembrances for Gudrun. Each sunrise over the lake, each wild flower that bloomed in its season, each thunderstorm took her back to the summer before and the whirlwind romance which had spun out of control, settled to short-lived happiness, and then to tragedy. It was almost as if she'd lived a whole lifetime in a few short months.

Over that first year without him, she often felt as if she were enclosed in a thin membrane which kept all the parts of her body from flying off in opposite directions and she worked hard at keeping anything from piercing that thin covering for fear that, once it was torn, she could never gather herself together again. When she felt tears stinging the inside of her eyelids, she willed them to dry; when her heart twisted slowly over a chance remark or sudden recollection, she laid her palm across her chest and calmed it; when she was tempted to speak out in grief or bitterness over her plight, she swallowed her words before they found a voice.

At that time, staying whole for LuAnn was the reason for Gudrun's existence, and was, of course, a 24-hour job. The tiny, helpless mite who curled her tentacle-like hands around any proffered finger proved to be a creature of many and varied moods. In sleep she was a beautiful angel, with her black curls framing a placid face, the long, black eyelashes lying peacefully against her pink cheeks. Awake it was a different story: she cried with a fury that was astounding in one so new. Her face transformed into a swollen red fist and her dark eyes snapped with anger but didn't produce one tear.

At first Gudrun, like any new mother, thought something must be physically wrong and many times wrapped her in blankets and ran to Jenny's apartment, thinking they must get her to a doctor. Jenny, having raised three children of her own, first made coffee, then took the writhing bundle over her shoulder and walked back and forth until the screams lessened and gradually stopped. "She might sometimes have colic which causes some pretty bad stomach aches," she said. "Put her over your shoulder or on her stomach over your lap, pat her back, and always speak softly into her ear"

And so, this became a relentless routine for Gudrun. Many a night was spent walking, jiggling, patting, and crooning to the little tyrant of the shabby apartment and like all tyrants, she came to know when she had the upper hand and pressed her advantage. It was a pattern that, established early, would guide their mother-daughter relationship for life.

LuAnn could also be engaging, however, and had many eager babysitters in the *tants*, who vied to care for her, dressing her as if they were playing with a doll and brushing her curls around their fingers. All this was lucky for Gudrun since she had to spend a good deal of time on her handiwork inventory and her newly-launched baking business.

Lucille Gendron not only kept the orders for embroidery and knitting at a steady pace but was instrumental in starting a gift shop through her church. Named "Beatitudes," it specialized in Gudrun's items: runners, pillowcases, and napkins, all adorned with beautifully-worked flower designs and Bible verses. All the proceeds from Beatitudes went to support the church's missions, which made Gudrun feel as if she were not only earning a living but also doing the Lord's work.

As for the baking, many people had sampled her breads and pastries at church events, and word of mouth resulted in a growing number of orders. That first summer after LuAnn's birth, the days weren't long enough for Gudrun. She rose early to set her bread dough before the baby's six o'clock feeding. When LuAnn's little stomach was full and she was changed, Gudrun propped her with pillows on the kitchen table near her workspace as she started her cookies and cakes, all the while keeping up a steady stream of talking and singing. Two dark eyes followed her every move, and LuAnn soon learned that she could control this attention with the slightest sound; no need to tire herself with screaming and crying. A crumpled face and plaintive whimper would send Gudrun to her side with a shaking rattle or crooning voice.

As the day wore on, "Grandpa Einer" would stop by to pick up and deliver the baked goods. Often "Grandma Jenny" or one of the *tants* would appear to take LuAnn for an outing and give Gudrun a chance to catch her breath.

The summer sped by. There were no boat trips or picnics on the Island. Gudrun didn't even have time to take the ferry over to pay a social visit to Willow or the Gendrons. Willow was particularly upset with this state of affairs, and her nose was seriously "out of joint" at not spending time with LuAnn while her adopted Bayfield family did.

"I thought we was best friends," Willow complained one afternoon when she visited the apartment. She tried to hold LuAnn, but the baby drew away and cried in a display of recent temperament, which the *tants* called, "making strange."

"She doesn't see you enough to know you," Gudrun defended, "She doesn't know you're Mommy's best friend." As she held and comforted the baby, Gudrun hoped her words would also comfort Willow.

Perhaps it was good that she had no time to worry about hurt feelings and few moments to formulate regrets, however, her obsession with repressing her feelings and "soldiering on" (as her mother used to say) resulted in a stony, cold demeanor that caused many in Bayfield to dismiss her as unfriendly or even snobbish. Consequently, she had no friends her own age and few social outlets beyond the church.

Early in her widowhood, Jenny had sought to console Gudrun with the thought of a new husband someday but Gudrun immediately shut the door to that possibility. "I am spoiled for a good Christian husband," she had declared, "and I have no time or stomach to promote any other kind." Jenny and the *tants* gave up arguing with her and hoped silently that someone would come along to spark her interest.

The next spring Gudrun received a long letter from Mrs. Gendron.

My Dear Gudrun,

I so admire your ambition and skill. Your handiwork has made our little gift shop very profitable for the church; and I understand your bakery business prospers as well. I know you are working hard to support yourself and your child and hesitate to interfere with success. I do want to make a new position available to you however, on the off chance it would appeal to you.

The woman who replaced you as cook and housekeeper has found other employment. I shouldn't say "replaced you" because she was far from doing that, but I wondered if you would want to have your old job back this summer with several enhancements:

1. Willow and Arne have bought a little farm in the country, which means their cottage would be available for you and LuAnn, providing lodging separate from the main house.

2. It is expected, of course, that you would keep LuAnn with you during your working hours.

3. In the fall, if you desire, we would like to have you move with us to St. Paul and continue to work at our home there with similar accommodations

If this arrangement is not to your liking, we understand and will continue to be of support to you in any way. Please think on it, and let us know.

Your Friend,

Lucille Gendron

Gudrun was flattered and overcome by the continued kindness Mrs. Gendron had shown her. That night she sat down with Jenny and Einer to weigh the pros and cons of the proposed arrangement. A steady job would provide economic security and the living arrangements simulated the family situation Gudrun wished for LuAnn. Whatever the cons were—mostly that her Bayfield family hated to see her leave—they seemed unimportant when compared to the prospect of a perfect job with caring people.

And so it was decided that Gudrun and LuAnn would caste their lot with the Gendron family, an alliance that would last for the next fifteen years.

BOOK
TWO

Chapter 15

"There are many events in the womb of time which will be delivered."
(OTHELLO) WILLIAM SHAKESPEARE

Once again, Gudrun stood on the shore of Lake Superior peering into the fog and mist of an early, May morning. There was no sign of the ferry, and she pulled her coat tighter to her body, feeling a damp presence which hadn't emanated from the weather but seemed to invade from within. The northern spring had been unusually warm and pleasant, and she fought to resist the thought that this gloomy day, springing out of a month of sun and fair breezes, was a portent of things to come.

It was 1966, and Gudrun and LuAnn, surrounded by suitcases and boxes, were waiting to be carried to another summer on the Island, just as they had for the last fifteen years since Cy's death and LuAnn's birth.

Gudrun sat on the upturned end of a suitcase and, using her well-developed gift for reverie, allowed herself to travel into the past, returning to the first time she had sat waiting for the ferry to take her to a new adventure. How young she had been! How vulnerable! How stupid! She had learned much in the last fifteen years, but how had she changed?

Oh, that first year had left her with such a weight of unresolved grief which gradually turned into bitterness and a wariness and caused her to turn aside proffered friendships or respond to acts of kindness. She remained lonely. She thought of herself as fearful and indecisive, a feeling that influenced the raising of her strong-willed daughter, often causing her to wonder which of them was the adult and certainly, who was in charge.

When first she looked on that tiny newborn, she vowed not to subject her to the kind of childhood she'd had: isolated, strict, and overly obsessed with religion. She wanted friends, and fun, and loving relationships for her. She even hoped one day she'd go to college and have a career that didn't involve serving other people. Then she heard a voice from the past:

"You'll laugh, but I'd like to go to college. But why think of such things? It ain't never gonna happen, and it just makes you crazy thinkin' about it!" These were Cy's words from a time long ago when they were in love (when she was in love anyway) which wafted across her mind like an errant breeze. She forced them out. It was possible for their daughter to succeed! Gudrun would make it happen.

"Like you made Cy marry you?" It was Willow's voice now. "Animals don't think kindly of the ones who trapped them."

Then it was her mother. "Be careful what you wish for ..."

Gudrun shook her head to clear her brain of these unwanted memories. This day was really playing havoc with her mind. She sighed with relief as the ferry approached the dock and called over her shoulder for LuAnn. When she turned, she saw LuAnn kissing Danny Miller as they said goodbye on the dock. The kiss ended with a long embrace as the two hugged each other so tightly their bodies became one: two skinny teenagers, children really, who seemed the embodiment of love. For an instant, Gudrun thought it beautiful and her heart went out to them. Then she remembered they were on the public dock and that she considered Danny Miller a bad influence on LuAnn.

"LuAnn!" This time her voice was angry, and the couple parted immediately but purposefully slow, their arms disentangling, their bodies parting and, lastly, their fingertips still touching and their eyes locked as they stepped backwards from each other in leave taking.

LuAnn and Danny had walked away from Gudrun and the other passengers who were waiting for the ferry. They probably would see each other in another week or so, but because they were young and in love, the separation was cause for anguish and drama. Danny was yelling at her, but she knew he wasn't mad, just frustrated. "Why can't you stay in Bayfield with your aunts?"

"She wants me on "The Rock" so she can keep an eye on me. There was more than a tinge of sarcasm in her voice which belied any chance of her remark being a defense of her mother. "You know how she gets. Usually I can control her, but when it comes to the Island she won't back down."

"It's just so damn hard to get over there all the time, and I don't really trust you with all those summer guys." He'd become pouty now, but she knew she could talk him out of it. She knew him better than anyone, even his mother. Perhaps it was because she loved him more than anyone else.

LuAnn was strangely attracted to the strong, bad-boy persona he had developed. Other Bayfield boys her age seemed like babies in comparison. She'd challenge them to do something daring: "Let's get some beer and drink it on the beach." To which most would usually reply,

"Naw, my dad would kill me!"

"Let's go!" would be Danny's reply. Even the summer guys fell short of her challenges, since their parents' money represented a strong enough reason to comply with the rules rather than succumb to the wiles of this beautiful, wild girl, no matter how desirable she was.

"C'mon," she coaxed, "I'll come over on Wednesday nights, and you get over when you can in between. It'll work out. It always does."

"I just wish we could leave. Let's run away from this crappy town where everyone thinks we're losers. We could get jobs and even get married." His voice sounded light and hopeful as he gave voice to his dream.

"Get real!" She brought him down hard. "We don't even have enough gas money to get out of town, and in what? Your dad's old truck? It wouldn't get us to Duluth. We're not old enough to get married or even get jobs that would support us." She immediately softened when she saw the devastated look on his face. She took his hand in both of hers. "Let me think about it though; there might be a way."

Danny knew from experience that when LuAnn put her mind to anything there was a good chance she could make it happen. With this reassuring thought in mind, he pulled her to him for a long goodbye kiss, which lasted until they heard Gudrun's voice calling them as the Nichevo docked.

Once again, Arne was at the ferry on the Island with yet another beat-up old truck, ready to drive Gudrun and LuAnn to their little cottage by the Gendron's.

"Come for supper," he said when he'd finished hauling their personal effects and the traditional cleaning supplies for the yearly opening of the big house.

"Gladly," Gudrun responded as she eyed the boxes and remembered the amount of work they represented.

"I'll come pick you up about five." They were easy with each other now, old friends; and Gudrun was anxious to see Willow. Willow and Arne were happy with their little hobby farm out by Big Bay, and Gudrun remained happy that she had inherited their former cottage for the summers. It was good to be back on the Island!

She'd been wintering in Bayfield for the past thirteen years. The original plan was to have her move to Minneapolis every fall with the Gendrons; but after one winter in the Cities, Gudrun spent a lot of time thinking about how she could move back to Bayfield without offending her employers.

The family was kind, although Frances and Mr. Gendron remained aloof. Gudrun and LuAnn had their own room and bath and were told to use the kitchen or living room when they wanted; but Gudrun noticed how surprised Mr. Gendron seemed when he chanced to encounter her in the living room, or how disappointed Frances looked when she'd stumble upon Gudrun in the kitchen late at night having a cup of tea. Both would flee after an awkward exchange.

Gudrun's biggest concern, however, was sharing her baby with Mrs. Gendron. At first she was flattered that LuAnn was so admired. Lucille Gendron often stopped in the kitchen when Gudrun was working and took LuAnn out of her baby seat, keeping her for hours until Gudrun had finished her work. Sometimes she'd ask to take her out for the day and carried her, all "dolled-up," to lunch with her lady friends. She brought her gifts of little dresses and coats to wear on such outings, and fussed with hair bows and matching socks. LuAnn held her arms out to this honorary mother whenever she saw her and took to jabbering something that resembled "mama." Gudrun knew she shouldn't be jealous of a baby, but swallowed resentment behind a forced smile, while Mrs. Gendron eagerly accepted the attention, her eyes welling with tears.

When their conversations turned to what was best for her daughter whether future schools, toilet training, or schedules, Mrs. Gendron became the leader by virtue of having two children of her own. Gudrun could see that gradually the raising of LuAnn would fall, by superior qualifications, to Lucille Gendron.

Maybe if Gudrun had a life of her own it would have been different. Well, she had tried to take up her city life again but realized she didn't feel nostalgic about her hometown, not knowing anything but life with Mother in their small apartment, and the church. She had gone to her old church one Sunday where she felt even more the outsider. There was a new minister and few of the people she had known as a child and young lady were still there. During the service she found the outbursts of "amen" and "yes, Jesus" from the congregation disconcerting and compared it unfavorably with the dignified responses and booming organ of the Episcopal service she had come to know back in Bayfield. Guilt followed and she heard again her mother's voice, "Pride goeth before a fall." She was not going to find a home there.

Then too, she missed Jenny and Einer and the *tants*, and she missed the visits from Willow and Arne. She began to think that coming to the Cities was but another stupid decision on her part. LuAnn was her life, and she alone wanted to make the decisions and be called mama.

One night towards the end of March, Mrs. Gendron knocked on her door to say there was a telephone call. Gudrun had never gotten a call at the house and couldn't imagine who it would be. It was a distraught Einer who told her that Jenny had suffered a stroke and was in the Ashland hospital. Once again it was Mrs. Gendron to the rescue, arranging transportation for Gudrun and assuring her to take as much time as she needed.

"We'll keep the baby here," she said firmly. "You don't know what you'll be getting into or how long you'll be, and it's best not to uproot her." Gudrun saw the wisdom in that but was torn about leaving her. Why were the older woman's ideas always unarguably the best?

She wept when she saw her friend Jenny, always so cheerful and full of life, now so white and still in her hospital bed. Einer rushed to embrace her when she entered and breathed a sigh of relief. "At least they need me," Gudrun thought, and she felt as if she'd come home after a long time. And they did need her, as much as she had needed them when they first met. Gudrun felt pride at being able to repay her friends for their kindness. Surely that kind of pride couldn't be labeled a sin.

Jenny would live but would require care: a great deal at first and then help in making a recovery. Gudrun, Einer and the *tants* sat in Einer and Jenny's small apartment that night working out a plan of action over cups of coffee. In the end, it was decided that Gudrun and LuAnn would occupy Jenny's sewing room. The *tants* would help with the care and would also mind the baby when Gudrun needed to be with Jenny. Einer would take care of his usual plus the marketing and other household chores. It seemed workable. The *tants* were older, but loved taking care of the baby and were able to do some cooking and cleaning if needed.

Of course when Mrs. Gendron heard the plan, she immediately said that LuAnn should remain with them in Minneapolis. "A sickroom is no place for a baby," she said and looked horrified that Gudrun should even suggest it.

I'm sorry to leave you in the lurch, you've been so good to me," she answered, "but they're like my parents and I must help them. Of course LuAnn must go with her mother." Gudrun was surprised at her own strength in opposing this determined authority figure. At first the relationship was strained, to be sure, but after Gudrun had left, gradually she began to hear from her former employer: first with orders for sewing, and then with friendly inquiries about Jenny's health and LuAnn's welfare.

Over the next summer, Gudrun saw Jenny take her first wavering steps after her stroke and saw LuAnn pull herself to her feet and strike out on a wobbly journey of her own. It was as if the two most important people in her life were progressing at the same rate. Gudrun would look back on that summer as one of the most rewarding times of her life. Her child grew while her friend recovered, and both needed Gudrun to survive. Suddenly her life seemed so much more important than it had been when she cooked meals for the family or planned fancy dinner parties for their friends.

The Gendrons returned to the Island and hired a new housekeeper and cook, of course, and Gudrun saw her occasionally in Bayfield. She was much older than Gudrun and wore an indifferent expression which didn't encourage friendship. Gudrun knew her own countenance left much to be desired in the way of warmth, so she didn't judge, but neither did she approach her to introduce herself.

She saw very little of the Island that summer. She was too busy with Jenny and LuAnn, and the three months flew by until one day when she was doing errands, she happened to see the family at the ferry dock, amidst a sea of luggage, and realized that Labor Day was near, and it was time for their exodus to St. Paul. She approached warily, not sure of what reception she'd get, and was immediately almost bowled over by Jimmy, who flung his arms around her waist and hugged her with genuine feeling. Mrs. Gendron also seemed genuinely happy to see her and inquired about LuAnn first of all. Then she drew her away from the group and lowered her voice.

"Our housekeeper, Mrs. Lindahl, has proven to be quite satisfactory for the city house, but she's been miserable all summer out here on the Island. She misses her family back in St. Paul. I know you're busy with Jenny, but if she's better in the spring, would you consider working next summer for us in La Pointe? I've been going to ask you, but didn't quite know how."

Gudrun was surprised and taken completely off guard. Suddenly the tables were turned, and she was thrust into the position of authority. Now she was being asked to do a favor and her compliance would change the two women's relationship forever. From now on it would be more of a partnership than that of a kind employer and an ever grateful servant.

Over winter the details of the arrangement were decided. The dour Mrs. Lindahl was pleased to have the summers off instead of being exiled to The Rock; and Gudrun was equally as happy not to have to winter in the Cities.

Chapter 16

"Alas, how love can trifle with itself!"
(TWO GENTLEMEN OF VERONA) WILLIAM SHAKESPEARE

air weather returned with Gudrun's arrival on the Island, and she soon finished the duties required to open the house for the summer. She worked quickly, familiar with the routine she had established over the years. She was happy with her double life in Bayfield and the Island and looked forward to the next three months. Oh, it would be work, to be sure, but she loved the cooking and planning the parties.

Under Mrs. Gendron's tutelage she had learned what to serve and when. On her own she had studied magazines and cookbooks and had become quite the expert on gourmet cooking and presentation. She smiled to herself when she remembered the first time she had served a tossed salad liberally sprinkled with nasturtiums from the kitchen garden. Mrs. Gendron was about to take it back and question Gudrun's sanity when one of her guests said, "Oh, I just read about edible flowers in *Gourmet* magazine. How clever of you, Lucille."

Of course much of her summer pleasure would be her proximity to her best friends, Willow and Arne, and the many excursions on their boat, the camaraderie of dinners and picnics, or just the daily coffee visits with Willow.

From Lupine season to the autumn storms, that small rock and the vast lake that cradled it continued to hold her respect and admiration. When she prayed, she often gave thanks that she had found her true home.

LuAnn

LuAnn wasn't much help with the household preparations. Gudrun worried about her recent listlessness and irritability but when she tried to talk to her about it she would lash out,

"I'm fine! Can't you ever quit with the questions? My God!"

"LuAnn! Don't take the name of the Lord in vain!"

"Oh, don't start with all that religious stuff. I'm not in the mood!"

"Well, maybe you're in the mood to be grounded for a couple weeks. I won't have you swearing!" Gudrun knew from past experience that it was useless to get angry and make threats. LuAnn would either just ignore any pronounced punishment, giving Gudrun the silent treatment in the process, or coax her way out of it. Either way, Gudrun would always end up giving in just to be back in the good graces of the person she loved the most. It was the basis upon which their relationship was founded.

"I'm sorry, Mom! It's just so hard to leave everything and come over here for the summer. It's fine for you, 'cause you love it and you have Willow and all. But I have nobody and I'm just bored most of the time."

"You always make friends with the summer people. You're invited to all their parties. Some weeks you're gone every night to a beach picnic or something." Too late, Gudrun knew she had been lured into this seasonal discussion. It was an old battle, this wanting to stay on the mainland in the summer, and it was the only battle that LuAnn had, to date, not won.

Gudrun was adamant that her daughter should remain with her. From the time Mrs. Gendron had seemed to be taking over the raising of the baby to the present time, when LuAnn preferred to be with friends, Gudrun's resolve had remained firm: "I am her mother, and she stays with me." So, she may never be able to enforce hours, dictate dress, or deliver talks on appropriate behavior, but she would always have the dubious pleasure of her daughter's company for the summer months.

As after every confrontation, Gudrun thought back to where the pattern had begun. This time her memory landed on a time when LuAnn was about four; she had tried her mother's patience to the point that Gudrun had turned her over her knee and raised her hand to spank. Then a calmer feeling prevailed. Feeling guilty, she had taken the crying child in her arms and apologized profusely. The crying stopped almost immediately, and Gudrun marveled at what could only be described as a triumphant look that came into those brown eyes.

When next they visited the *tants*, LuAnn immediately informed them, "Mama hurt Annie." Gudrun blushed.

"Not really," she attempted to defend, but LuAnn's little face remained solemn as she nodded her head and hit herself on the backside, simulating a wince.

"Well," Alma said, "they do say, spare the rod and spoil the child, but not our Annie. She's such a good girl." She held the bowl of sugar lumps out and smiled lovingly while LuAnn daintily selected one and smiled up at her.

As with most problems, Gudrun consulted Jenny, whose opinions she respected above all others. "You don't have to spank, but give her punishments like sitting in the corner or not being able to go on a particular outing. Surely your mother must have had ways to control you."

She had only one way," Gudrun said, "staying in the house and reading the Bible. I'm not going to do that to LuAnn. I don't want her always afraid of sinning, and lonely. I guess what I'm saying is I don't want to break her spirit, but I do want to teach her to behave."

"Ah yes," Jenny laughed, "it's what we all want for our kids, but it requires nerves of steel and a will to stick by what you've said. It's so easy to give in, and they'll try you harder than God tried Job. Wait until she's a teenager!"

Willow alone saw through the many faces of LuAnn but tended to ignore the bad behavior and admire the control she had with her smile or a strategically delivered hug. "She's spoiled, and she knows how to get what she wants. I just hope she learns what's worth wanting early on, so she don't make some bad mistakes," she confided to Arne.

Jimmy

Gudrun thought, and worried a lot, about why LuAnn was so difficult when Jimmy had remained the sweet, respectful, compliant boy she had met that first summer on the Island. They had bonded then over some strange mutual need to be noticed, the origin of which Gudrun couldn't identify. After all, Jimmy had his family and she had been overly watched by her mother and the church. Maybe it was because they always responded to what others expected of them, whereas with each other they were free to explore likes and dislikes and express opinions without being reprimanded.

She thought she had encouraged her daughter to express herself, but LuAnn's expressions took the form of tantrums, and she would refuse reason or compromise. What could she have done differently with LuAnn? Sometimes, after a particularly bad blow up, Gudrun would conclude that she should have let Lucille Gendron raise her when she had wanted to take her as a baby. Then again, she wondered if Lucille would still want LuAnn now.

Gudrun couldn't help but smile when she thought of Jimmy. Over the years they had become best friends, or maybe it was a second mother-son relationship. Lucile Gendron loved her son but was so preoccupied with her social life that in the summertime she often left his care to Gudrun.

Each summer would be devoted to whatever book or classes at school had sparked Jimmy's interest. Consequently, they would become Gudrun's interests also. Jimmy told her all about the different rocks and their characteristics, as, during one summer they combed the beaches for concretions or for agates which they polished in the rock tumbler. Jimmy said he'd like to be a geologist and even had a list of places all over the world where he'd like to rock hunt. "And you could come with me," he'd magnanimously offer.

One summer was devoted to wildlife and Jimmy's Christmas camera. Many an early morning or twilight hour found them sitting quietly in bushes near the lakeshore waiting for deer or raccoons to come and drink or for songbirds to alight, engaged in their sunrise chatter. "I think I'd like to be a photographer," would be the resulting dream when his pictures were developed and lay spread on the kitchen counter for evaluation.

Many a hurt rabbit or bird with a broken wing would occupy Jimmy's back yard hospital, with Gudrun helping to apply splints and supply suitable food for each patient. "Maybe you'll be an animal doctor," Gudrun said one day, as they worked to feed a baby squirrel from a tiny bottle.

"Maybe," he said, and then his eyes turned thoughtful. "I think my father wants me to be a lawyer."

"But surely he wants you to do what you want," Gudrun said.

"He thinks he knows what's best for me, and I guess he does."

One day when Jimmy was about ten, he came into the kitchen when Gudrun was getting out the beater and mixing bowl in preparation for a cake. "What you making?" he asked.

"I thought I'd make a chocolate cake for dinner. We haven't had one in a long time."

"Can I help?" His eyes lit with interest.

"Sure! Here, you beat this butter until it's soft and creamy, and then you can beat this sugar into it. It's called creaming." She gave him the technical term, because she knew that was the way he liked to learn something.

She tied an apron around his waist as she handed him the melted chocolate. They went on through the sifting of the dry ingredients and the addition of eggs; he pausing after each step for her inspection of the batter. For once Gudrun was the expert, and he followed her directions to the letter, looking at her in admiration. It was almost like baking with mother ... one pleasant memory of her childhood.

They laughed and licked their fingers when all the ingredients had been added and they had taken the beater out of the bowl. Neither of them had noticed Mr. Gendron standing in the doorway.

"What do you think you're doing?" He was angry, and he came across the kitchen in two strides, pulling Jimmy off the kitchen stool and ripping the apron off. "My son doesn't bake, and if you need help with your duties, we'll get some."

Gudrun was shocked into silence and wondered if Jimmy would get a spanking or if she had lost her job. She was sorry she hadn't defended Jimmy; she couldn't think of anything wrong or questionable about baking a cake and letting a child help.

Mr. Gendron never mentioned the offending episode again, but Mrs. Gendron came in after dinner that night and, with considerable embarrassment, attempted to explain. "Mr. Gendron has some old-fashioned ideas about men's and women's work. He thinks a boy ought to engage in masculine things. You're so good to Jimmy, and he loves you so much, and he told us he asked you to let him help." And so it was left, but from then on, Gudrun gave a second thought to what Jimmy wanted to do, especially when she knew his father was in the house.

As LuAnn grew, Jimmy was her favorite person. He played endless games with her and was everything a big brother should be. He was good at calming her when she had her tantrums and often took her off to swing or walk on the beach to give Gudrun time to calm herself.

As Jimmy grew older, he didn't need Gudrun's companionship in the same way. He often came into the kitchen, however, to sit in the breakfast nook talking about books he was reading or movies he'd seen. Even during the winter months when he was in the Cities, occasionally a note would arrive in the mail telling her what he was doing and inquiring after her Bayfield family.

It was with great disappointment then, when in the last couple summers, he and LuAnn ceased to be brother and sister, or even friends. The animosity started when she began having invitations to beach parties and boat trips from the summer young people. Of course she was wild to go, but Jimmy screened her party groups, telling Gudrun she shouldn't go with certain people, or when he thought there was apt to be alcohol served.

LuAnn eventually got wind of who was influencing her mother's decisions and threw a monumental fit. "You're not the boss of me," she screamed childishly. "You're just jealous because you don't get invited, because you're such a weirdo! Everybody knows it!" The insults and accusations flew from her mouth like barbed darts, and because Gudrun was so attuned to Jimmy's feelings, she knew the barbs were reaching their mark, and she felt for her dear boy, now almost a man.

"Stop it LuAnn! You don't know what you're saying. We're just trying to protect you."

"I want to have fun. I don't want to read, or collect rocks, or look at the stars."

"You've loved doing that with us, LuAnn!"

"Ya, when I was little. I've grown up now, and Jimmy hasn't." She glared at her mother. "Oh, go ahead, take his side. You've always liked him better anyway," she concluded with the time-worn cliché used by siblings throughout the ages.

After that, Jimmy didn't consult with Gudrun about the invitations, and LuAnn found a way to go to the parties whether Gudrun gave her permission or not. Gradually Gudrun had to admit she didn't know where her daughter was at any given time, and it was easier to leave it that way, hoping that God or some of Willow's Native American spirits, or fate would keep her from harm.

Chapter 17

"Who can control his fate"
(OTHELLO) WILLIAM SHAKESPEARE

he weather was hot and humid during the summer of 1966, but produced fewer storms and generally less rain than previous years. For Gudrun, however, it seemed as if a storm was always brewing. Oh, not by the looks of the sky over Lake Superior, but by the feel of her surroundings: the people, the house. A dark aura, or cloud, had fallen over her immediate spaces, and she couldn't put her finger on any one cause. She spent her time off in Bayfield with Einer and Jenny or biked out to Willow and Arne's farm. It helped to get away from the source of the malaise, yet it proved to be hard to return. It saddened her, because she had always loved the old house, her little cottage, and the people who shared it with her. How strange that she could only find peace away from them.

Gudrun thought initially that her constant conflict with LuAnn was coloring her Island time; but with the arrival of the Gendrons, the cloud expanded to include their family dysfunctions. She had been aware in the past of tensions between Mr. Gendron and Jimmy, and Francis and Mrs. Gendron, but up until this year, Mr. Gendron was only a weekend visitor to the Island, and any problems with Francis had disappeared a couple years ago when she had grown and quit spending time on Madeline.

This summer, however, Mr. Gendron was in permanent residence, except for the odd overnight excursion to St. Paul. He spent most of the day in his office which was off limits to everyone, even Gudrun who was told he would take care of his own cleaning. She often heard him arguing with his wife or Jimmy while she was working in the kitchen or cleaning the living room. He seemed particularly angry with Jimmy, and often looked for him, inquiring of Gudrun if she knew where he had gone and eying her suspiciously, as if she were lying, when she said she hadn't seen him.

This summer the three members of the family seemed at cross purposes, and although Gudrun tried to stay out of their affairs, sometimes the disagreements spilled over onto her, often resulting in explanations and apologies that were awkward for all of them.

Gudrun's heart went out to Mrs. Gendron when she heard her crying in her room after a shouting session with her husband. She had been cleaning the upstairs bathroom and couldn't help but hear.

"You've made a goddamned baby out of him. He's in college, and he still runs to his mommy with everything: What should I do? How should I act? He's pitiful!"

"He's kind and considerate. He doesn't trample over a person's feelings like you do. I'm sorry if that's not masculine enough for you, but I think he's going to be a fine man."

"A fine man! They'll eat him alive at college. Have you ever thought that he might be a homo?"

"Oh for God's sake, why are you suddenly carrying on this vendetta against your own son. He's done nothing his whole life but honor your wishes. I don't even think he's interested in law; he's just trying again to please you; and now you're calling him a homosexual?" Gudrun stepped behind the bathroom door as Mrs. Gendron ran past into her room. Mr. Gendron stomped down the stairs and slammed his office door.

Gudrun was shocked! Of course she knew what a homosexual was, but she had never known one nor had she thought much about what that might mean. And Jimmy—why was his father singling him out for such unwarranted criticism?

Jimmy had seemed different this summer. Of course, he no longer offered any information to Gudrun about LuAnn's social life, and that had resulted in a certain coolness between them, which she regretted greatly. But it was even more than that. He seemed unusually nervous and quiet. Where was he the many times his father would come looking for him? She could understand it if it were LuAnn. She'd disappear for hours at a time and Gudrun had gotten used to it. But Jimmy was always close at hand: in the garden or down on the beach. He seldom even rode his bike into La Pointe without telling Gudrun or his mother.

LuAnn, herself, was presenting a whole new set of problems. Gudrun had steeled herself for June and the coming of the summer people when she expected her daughter to pick up the whirlwind social life of the privileged younger set. She had invitations right from the first; but, to Gudrun's surprise, she no longer seemed interested. LuAnn was always at hand whenever Danny Miller showed up, of course, and it worried Gudrun that they disappeared often together.

This summer LuAnn had become friendly with James Gendron, of all people. Gudrun was putting fresh flowers in the living room one afternoon when LuAnn came out of his office. "What are you doing in the office? What if Mr. Gendron came in? You know he doesn't want anyone in there?"

"He is in there. Relax, for God's sake!"

"LuAnn!"

"I know, I know, don't 'take the name of the Lord, blah, blah, blah. Listen, he just wanted to show me his new typewriter. He heard me say I was going to take typing in school next year. It's really nice. Do you think I could get one, when I learn to type, that is?" She was talking rapidly; obviously changing the subject. Gudrun could tell she was making the story up as she went, all the while walking away.

"When did you strike up a friendship with him?"

"Really? I've known him all my life. We've lived in the same house. He's practically like my dad. He's a nice guy. You've just never gotten to know him, because you're afraid of him. You're afraid of everyone. Well, I'm not like you! I'm like my dad; I'm not afraid of anyone." She chose the moment to stalk away in righteous anger.

After dealing with LuAnn for years, Gudrun recognized another one of her ploys to keep from answering questions: talk fast, go on the offensive, and try to work in a mention of her dead father, just to throw in a little guilt.

Gudrun couldn't help but wonder over this new relationship. She wanted to think of it as a good thing. Maybe LuAnn was missing a father figure, and James Gendron would prove to be a stabilizing influence on her. But why now? He had known her for all her 16 years. Maybe he related to her more now that she was a young woman. Some men just felt uncomfortable with children or babies. Maybe he hadn't been friendly before because he was so pre-occupied with his work. There were a lot of "maybes," as Gudrun tried to explain this new development to her satisfaction.

As the summer wore on, she gradually got used to seeing them together and willed herself to acceptance. One night, Gudrun came in the back door of the main house in the evening. Walking by the door to the widow's walk, she was startled by voices on the stairs and even more surprised when LuAnn and Mr. Gendron opened the door and came into the hallway.

"Mom, what are you doing here? You said you were tired and going to bed early."

"I wanted to make some changes on the planner, but I'd left it in the kitchen. Why were you up on the walk?" She turned to Mr. Gendron. "I thought you said it wasn't safe and no one should go up there"

"LuAnn said she'd never seen the view from there, and I wanted her to see the stars from the walk. The view is spectacular, and I remembered you used to take her and Jimmy out to star gaze. Don't worry, I didn't let her go near the bad spots in the floor." With uncharacteristic kindness, he put his hand on Gudrun's shoulder. "Hey, you work hard enough around here without putting in time after hours. Forget that planner until tomorrow, and get some rest." While he talked, LuAnn had made her getaway, and Gudrun saw her ride her bike by the door. Once again she wouldn't see her until much later, and then the time for questions would have passed.

One late afternoon Gudrun was in the kitchen garden cutting some parsley to garnish the dinner roast with when Jimmy and LuAnn rode down the driveway on their bikes. She was happy to see them together. Maybe one strained relationship in this house would heal itself over the summer, she thought. But they acted embarrassed, as if they'd been caught misbehaving. Gudrun smiled and waved.

"Hi, where have you two been off to?"

"Just around," LuAnn replied with a sarcastic tone.

"We took the road out to Big Bay, just for the ride." Jimmy was always respectful, even though Gudrun had a sneaking suspicion that this wasn't the truth. Why did he feel the need to lie?

"Oh well," she thought, "at least they're together again. I'm glad for that."

When Gudrun thought back over that time, she remembered many instances that, in retrospect, seemed odd. Mr. Gendron came into the kitchen one morning searching in the contents of the tool drawer for a screwdriver, which he took to the widow's walk with him. He was up there a long time and eventually found Gudrun where she was cleaning. He was sweating profusely, often wiping his face with a hanky. His clothing was covered in dust, and the knees of his trousers were particularly dirty, as if he had been kneeling

"I've just inspected the widow's walk and found the railing to be dangerously loose," he told her. "Please make sure no one goes up there for any reason. It isn't safe."

"Oh, I know," Gudrun replied, "I tell everyone, and I don't have a key, so I couldn't let anyone up there."

"I know, I know, I just wanted to make it clear again." Mr. Gendron spent a lot of time that hot summer up on the widow's walk.

"I think he's assessing the damage in preparation for repair," Mrs. Gendron told Gudrun. But no carpenters ever came to consult, nor did building supplies arrive.

Chapter 18

"One sorrow never comes but brings an heir."
(PERICLES) WILLIAM SHAKESPEARE

he moon was full, but even so it was a black night as the wind gusted and sent clouds scudding across the sky to cause sudden and frequent eclipses. Strangely, the gale hadn't produced rhythmic waves, but rather the surf seemed a confused boil responding not so much to the wind as to unknown forces beneath its surface.

Two Island policemen walked the beach with flashlights and tapes cordoning off an area from the foot of the cliff descending stairs to the woods on either side of the beach and back to the shore, the lake itself providing the fourth side of a rectangle. A crowd, standing motionless, had gathered along the edge of the cliff some 100 feet above; the squad cars parked behind them captured their shapes in spinning lights and silhouetted an eerie, ghost-like audience.

The object of attention was a person sprawled in the sand about 10 feet from the last stair. It was hard to identify as a person: no human form was discernible. It looked more like a shirt and jeans carelessly cast aside by some impetuous swimmer in a hurry to take an impulsive midnight dip in Lake Superior. A woman and a man struggled down the stairs with a folded stretcher and rushed to kneel by the body.

"You can't do this one any good," the officer in charge said. "You'd best see if you can take care of Gudrun over there." He pointed to a middle-aged woman slumped in the sand. Her graying hair had blown wild in the wind, and she held her arms clasped tightly around her body, her hands on opposite shoulders in what was more like a lover's embrace than the usual tightly folded arms denoting withdrawal or protection. She stared straight ahead and rocked back and forth slightly. "I think she's in shock," Nelson said as he returned to measuring distances from stairs to body, from body to shore line, and from body to woods, all of which he was carefully recording in a small notebook.

"You okay, Gudrun? Are you hurt? What happened? Where does it hurt?" There were no responses, and the medics settled for laying a blanket across her shoulders and trying to convince her to stand. But Gudrun had mentally retreated from the grim scene into her fantasy world, which somehow would keep reality at bay until she could absorb what had happened. She was unwilling or physically incapable of answering questions, explaining events, or even getting to her feet.

"Keep everybody off the beach. We don't want every yahoo and his maiden aunt down here stirring up this sand." Arvid Nelson was uncharacteristically upset to the point of lashing out angrily at anyone who came near him. He struggled inwardly to remember and follow the proper procedures he had learned, years ago now, at a week-long law enforcement workshop; procedures he hadn't been called upon to use until now. "Don't come down those stairs," he barked at a quickly descending figure.

"Hey Arvid, it's me!" A short, chunky woman entered the circle of his flashlight beam. "What happened? Does Gudrun need me?" He recognized Willow Peterson, Gudrun's friend, and immediately directed a path of light across the sand to where Gudrun sat rocking. "Hey, honey it's me. What have we gotten into now? Come on up to the cottage. I'll make us some tea." She looked at Arvid Nelson for approval, and he just nodded and once again shone the light to the stairs for them. Gudrun seemed to sigh in relief at the sight of her friend, and released her self-embrace as she maneuvered to stand, almost fall into Willow's outstretched arms, and leaned heavily as the two slowly made their way up the steep stairway.

Nelson paused for a moment to follow their ascent, shaking his head. He'd known Gudrun ever since she first came to the Island and started keeping house for the Gendrons, and he liked her. He'd often stop for a visit at the Gendron house on his rounds, and she always had fresh coffee and some of that Swedish baking she was so famous for with the summer people. "She's had a tough life, he mused, why do these things happen to good people? She was always so damn quiet, though, almost as if nothing ever touched her, kinda cold in a way. He shook his head again and returned to pace the beach, his eyes following the scanning trajectory of his flashlight.

The cabin was warm to the point of being stuffy, but Gudrun shivered with shock and her teeth chattered. She sat at the kitchen table, the blanket still draped across her shoulders. Her arms now lay across the oilcloth surface, the palms of her hands turned upward, almost in supplication. "What have I done?" she whispered. Willow saw her friend's face in agony as she turned from the teakettle in response to Gudrun's voice.

"You haven't done nothin'! Now don't be saying that! Who fell?" Willow's immediate response was to defend her friend. "Who's down on the beach?" Gudrun raised her eyes in surprise, having assumed everyone knew.

"It's LuAnn, Willow, our baby is dead, and it's my fault. I killed her." The last was but whispered. Willow reacted as if she'd been struck across the face.

"Nooo," she wailed. "What do you mean, you killed her? Did you push her? Did you push her on purpose?" Willow was hysterical, but the questions went unanswered as Gudrun cradled her head in her folded arms on the table. Arne walked in at this point to view the two women silent and frozen in a momentary tableau of horror.

"No, she didn't push her! It was a terrible accident. The railing came loose," Arne explained.

"You can't be saying you did it then." Willow was immediately coherent. "People remember the first things you say when there's trouble, and you're in no shape to be answering questions."

"She leaned against the railing, it gave way, she fell," Gudrun had raised her head from the table, crying uncontrollably now and shaking with shock. Willow threw her body over the back of her friend holding her in her arms, and they rocked each other for a long time until the initial outpouring of grief had subsided.

"We have to talk this out, and get our stories straight, and you're in no shape to do that right now. Best you just keep quiet. Do you understand me?" Gudrun nodded and let her eyes drop. One finger traced the outline of a flower on the tablecloth and as if having been granted permission, Gudrun again lapsed into her fantasy world where she had spent so many hours of her life. But a new and exciting story didn't reveal itself across the private screen of her mind. Instead, she found herself returning to the day she had first come to the Island at the age of 20. A day she often referred to as, "the day my life began."

Chapter 19

"Fortune brings in some boats that are not steer'd."
(PISANIO) WILLIAM SHAKESPEARE

A rvid Nelson squatted by the body sprawled in the sand, one knee elevated to provide an elbow rest. He had asked the ambulance crew to leave it unmoved after they had determined for themselves the loss of life and had gone back to their vehicle to complete reports and wait for a signal to transport. He sat looking long and hard, his chin in his hand, as his assistant, Billy LaDuke, fidgeted and sighed audibly in the background. He knew he had the reputation of being slow and tedious, but throughout his 20-year law enforcement career on The Rock, he had noticed that most mistakes, big or small, occurred when snap judgments were made.

The victim lay in the sand on her back, face up, with the lower torso twisted slightly sideways due either to the force of the landing, broken bones, or both. The face was fully visible, the head turned a little to the side. He had seen lots of dead bodies, mostly as a result of natural causes and some occasional accidents, but it never ceased to amaze him how once the soul had departed, the remains appeared two-dimensional like a wrinkled, deflated balloon. Narrow spaces between the closed eyelids looked dark and empty; it was a mere shell that once had lived and moved.

The sight of this dead girl, whom he had known since she was a toddler, filled him with more regret than he had ever felt. She was so young, just 15, and beautiful. Even in death the black curls, her crowning glory, made a halo in the sand around her head. He used to stop at the Gendrons occasionally for a cup of coffee with Gudrun and recalled what a sweet, friendly child she could be. Then too, he had witnessed temper tantrums where she had lashed out at everyone and everything around her, causing him to recall, because of the close physical resemblance, her father in one of his famous bar fights.

It wasn't until her teenage years, however, that Arvid saw her on a regular basis. She had become wild and willful. She was always in some trouble on the Island: illegal drinking, use of drugs, vandalism, and other inappropriate misdemeanors. Consequently, he saw more of Gudrun then also, and observed her inability to admit to, much less cope with, her daughter's infractions. LuAnn came to consider Arvid an enemy, and once again he saw that derisive smile that had served her father so well.

He allowed himself to think about Cy Gaudette and his tragic story. The wild, young fisherman had been Arvid's nemesis when he had first taken the job as the Island's policeman. Cy preferred Morty's or Junior's Bars in Bayfield, but a Saturday night often found him at Leona's Bar outside La Pointe. If Arvid saw the Siren moored at the town dock, he knew that almost surely he'd eventually get a bar fight call from Leona's. Wrestling that young buck out the door and into the squad car was no small accomplishment, and he could still feel the many pummelings he'd had to endure in order to make arrests. Arvid always knew that if it hadn't been for the amount of alcohol Cy had ingested on any particular night, he could not have taken him.

Although The Rock didn't have an official jail house, Arvid used to take his prisoner back to a room they used in the back of the firehouse where he could sleep off his drunk and be released in the morning. Arvid never wanted to put him aboard the Siren and turn him loose in the darkness to a capricious Lake Superior. His thoughtfulness in this resulted in a feeling of responsibility and concern on Arvid's part and a somewhat grudging indebtedness on Cy's. Although both would deny any such feelings, they formed a mutual respect which eventually made their encounters less physical.

"All right! All right!" Cy would shout when Arvid appeared at the bar. "The big, bad copper is here. I'm so afraid!" With a derisive smile, Cy would cower and hide behind the person nearest him until everyone was laughing at Arvid; only when the cop had been made a fool of would Cy submit to being led away. Arvid didn't mind, if it saved him a fight.

Now, as if suddenly arousing from a dream, Arvid finally broke his reverie and his scrutiny of the body and rose to find his backpack on the beach. He withdrew his trusty 35 millimeter Minolta, a tripod and a telescoping yard stick. He extended the yardstick to its full length and laid it in the sand perpendicular to the body, one end pointing to the middle of the body, the other the spot where the tripod with camera was placed. He took many shots, sometimes folding the stick to various lengths and measuring the placement of limbs, head, and clothing in relation to the body. His assistant paced and ground another cigarette into the sand with the toe of his boot. After what seemed an endless length of time for the medics, he motioned to them and gave instructions to transport the body to Trinity Hospital in Ashland. They looked surprised. "Shouldn't she go to the funeral home?"

"I just need to check a few more things before that happens," he said quietly, nodding to assure them that all was normal, and he was just being his stodgy self. He hung a twined length of rope on his arm, put his notebook and pencil in his shirt pocket, and took his flashlight in hand.

Lights were ablaze in the Gendron house and in Gudrun's little cottage. Although it was late, Arvid decided the questioning shouldn't wait until morning. The door was opened by Willow whose swollen eyes and grief-stricken face told him that she knew the victim to be her godchild, the light of her life. Gudrun sat dry-eyed and motionless at the table, her hands cradling a full cup of tea which showed no signs of heat.

"I hate to bother you now," Arvid said, "but I need to know what happened before LuAnn fell." He had put a name to the tragedy, and it hung in the air like an apparition. Willow keened softly to herself and her body shook with the effort of controlling her sobs. Gudrun turned with a face that looked as if she had seen the depths of hell.

"She leaned against the railing and it gave way. She fell." The coldness of the monotone delivery chilled Arvid to the bone.

"Who was up there on the widow's walk?"

"Me, Jimmy, and LuAnn." Her voice wavered with her daughter's name.

"Why were you up there?"

"The kids were up there, and I went up to tell them to come down, that it wasn't safe."

"Why do you say it wasn't safe?"

"It was old and some of the floorboards were rotten. The Gendrons talked about repairing it and told everybody not to use it."

"So why would they go up there?"

"I don't know why. They were just being kids."

"Did you try to catch her when she fell?"

"I was too far back, by the door, she leaned against the railing and it gave way." Arvid noticed, maybe unnecessarily, the repetition in her story and the slight irritation in her voice.

"Were they arguing about something?"

"I don't think so—I don't know."

"Do you know if they'd gone up there before?"

"I don't know—I don't think so."

"Were Jimmy and LuAnn good friends?"

Willow rose as if to defend Gudrun and almost shouted, "For God's sake, Arvid, can't you see she's in shock? Of course they were friends. They were raised together, like brother and sister. Now can't this wait?"

"I'm sorry! Please believe me I am so sorry for your loss." His words came out with more emotion than he was used to expressing, and he felt strangely embarrassed. "I'll come back another time."

"Why do you need to come back? It was an accident. She fell." Gudrun was beginning to sound a little hysterical, and Willow put an arm around her shoulders, pointing with her free hand toward the door and motioning for Arvid to go. He closed his notebook, nodded and let himself out. He had a feeling that something wasn't right, but what could it be? He had known these people for years. Were they lying? Why would they lie about an accident? What was at stake that required a lie?

He walked the few feet to the main house and knocked on the Gendron's kitchen door. James Gendron answered immediately, as if he'd expected him. They shook hands formally, although Arvid had known him for years. Now that he thought about it, though, he seldom dealt with him. He wasn't around much, and the women were usually in charge of any business he had with them

"Sorry to bother you so late … " He was in the middle of his opening statement when he noticed Jimmy sitting in the breakfast nook with his mother. When he saw him, Arvid thought he should recommend a trip to the emergency room of the Ashland hospital; he was shaking uncontrollably with shock and crying. His head was buried in his folded arms on the table. The thick glasses that were his trademark were lying, the frames twisted, on the table. His mother had wrapped him in a thick afghan, a cup of steaming liquid sat in front of him, and a bottle of brandy stood close to the cup. Arvid guessed a hospital couldn't do much better for him.

"I don't know that he'll be able to answer any questions yet," Gendron offered. "He's pretty overwrought."

"I can see that. I'll try not to upset him any more. It's just for the accident report." But before he had even stopped talking Mrs. Gendron started crying and stood up.

"It's all our own fault. Why didn't we have that railing repaired, or block off the stairs to the walk or something?"

"So, you say you knew the railing was bad? Had you noticed it wobble?"

"No, but it must have, if that poor girl leaned on it and it broke."

"I think we'll have to have this conversation tomorrow when we've all had a chance to calm down," Gendron quickly said, and he rose and put a hand on Arvid's arm, as if to see him out the door.

At that point, Jimmy raised his head from the table, and Arvid was again concerned for him: he was deathly white, his eyes were almost swollen shut from crying, and one cheek was fiery red with an oddly striped mark. "She leaned against the railing and it gave way. She fell," he recited weakly.

"Had you noticed the railing was loose?" But Gendron was applying pressure to Arvid's arm now.

"She leaned against the railing and it gave way. She fell," Jimmy repeated.

"Would you mind if I looked at the widow's walk?" Arvid said.

"Tomorrow will be time enough for that," Mr. Gendron said with irritation.

"Actually sir, this is an accident scene, and I need to look it over and secure it before I complete this report tonight."

"I just meant that it will be hard to see without a light up there." His tone had changed slightly, but he was still opposed to a trip to the walk.

"I have my flashlight," Arvid answered, "if you could show me the way please."

They walked through the large kitchen to the back hall where there was a door on one side. It opened to two flights of stairs with a door at the top, which was the entry to the widow's walk. Gendron started to follow, but Arvid stopped ahead of him. "I'm kind of a slow poke," he said, "so there's no need for you to stand around in the dark. I'll be down shortly as soon as I assess the damage to the railing."

As Arvid opened the door to the widow's walk, he turned his flashlight to the floorboards first. Hadn't Gudrun said there were rotten floorboards? But he saw no sign of rot, or broken boards. The wrought iron railing hung half in midair, the other half still firmly fastened to the floorboards. He had to admit Gendron was right, however, it was hard to make any careful observance without light. Arvid was still happy he'd insisted on coming up to the walk, though, because he wanted to firmly establish with Gendron that he was in charge of the investigation. It wasn't his ego at work, but years of experience with how easy it is to let family members and friends influence— or attempt to influence—evidence.

He stepped back out onto the stairs and knotted the rope across the stair railings close to the door. At first he busied himself writing in his notebook and didn't say anything to Gendron, who stood on the first landing with anticipation in his eyes. Then he slipped the notebook back into his shirt pocket, looked up and said, "You were right, Mr. Gendron. it's too dark to see much up there tonight." Gendron almost physically relaxed in relief but quickly recovered and assumed an irritated look of resignation as he led the way down the stairs.

Arvid knew he should go home, but he was too keyed up to sleep. Instead he went to his favorite thinking spot: back to the room he thought of as a sort of headquarters where he kept a beat-up desk that had once belonged to his predecessor, Old Jack. He poured coffee from the everlasting pot and threw his notebook down on the desk in front of him. He began to mull over his notes interspersed with random thoughts about the night. A terrible accident had occurred, made worse by the fact that the victim was a child. Why did he have the feeling that there was something missing and that those involved were trying to hide something?

Foremost in his mind were the identical explanations of what had happened. Both Gudrun and Jimmy had twice repeated, word for word, "She leaned against the railing and it gave way. She fell." They didn't say,

"The railing was loose. The railing was broken. She lost her balance."

Then there was the position of the body. Arvid had learned at some time in his training that bodies fall straight down. They don't fly off in any direction unless they jump or launch themselves—as you would in a dive, for instance—or have been pushed with some amount of force. He further knew that falling bodies tend to turn upside-down and land on their heads, since the upper portions of their bodies weigh more than the lower portions. The position of her body led him to believe that she had fallen forward and landed on her head with the impact causing her body to topple forward, exposing the front of her torso. But if she were on the widow's walk with her mother and Jimmy, wouldn't she have been facing them with her back to the railing when she leaned on it, causing her to land the opposite way, face down in the sand? Arvid turned to a new page in his notebook and made a list of questions that he would use the next day to interrogate those involved.

He was just finishing when the telephone rang. A female voice identified herself, "This is Trinity Hospital in Ashland," she said. "What do you want done with the body we just received? As you know, we don't have a full-time coroner and the one we have is out of town. We don't have the facilities to store the body, so I assume you want me to ship it to Minneapolis for autopsy." Arvid had anticipated some of the problem, so he was able to suggest a quick alternative.

"What if I had our own doctor perform the autopsy there in Ashland? He's semi-retired but still has hospital privileges at Trinity." And so it was that Doc Olson from Washburn, the same Doc Olson who had initially disappointed Gudrun by finding her not pregnant; who later had tended Gudrun during her true pregnancy and successfully delivered her daughter; and who had declared her husband dead of hypothermia; would be called upon to add another chapter to the story of the young fisherman and his ill-fated family.

Chapter 20

"Death lies on her like an untimely frost."
(ROMEO AND JULIET) WILLIAM SHAKESPEARE

he next day dawned cool and windy. Arvid left a sign on the headquarters door as to when he'd be back. It was only eight o'clock, but he wanted to catch everyone off guard before they might have a chance to prepare for him. The Island's opinion of him: honest, but slow, lacking in imagination and not overly inquisitive, had served him well in the past and usually resulted in people talking freely to him, often unburdening themselves.

When he knocked at the Gendron's kitchen door, he heard loud voices before James Gendron opened and stood resolutely in the doorway, as if blocking entry. Even at this early hour he was dressed in suit pants, white shirt, and tie. Lucille Gendron, standing behind him, was still in her robe. Tousled hair and a wan, puffy face showed the ravages of her sleepless night.

"I wanted to get an early start on inspecting the widow's walk, sir."

"I'm about to catch the 8:30 ferry. Come back tonight after 5, and I'll be glad to talk with you."

"Oh, I won't need you, sir, I just have some measuring to do and some pictures to take. Mrs. Gendron can see me in and out. I have some routine questions for her and Jimmy anyway."

"I can't allow you to question my family without my being present." He kept his cool, but Arvid could see that he was more than a little agitated.

"All right, sir, you just go catch the ferry, and I'll be back tonight. In the meantime, the widow's walk is an accident scene, and since last night I couldn't do all the investigating that my report requires, I'll have to do it today. You know how paper work is sir, I'm sure." Arvid could almost see the train of thought that passed before the lawyer's eyes: At this point it would be more suspicious to deny the cop access. Besides, it seemed as if the only thing on his mind was his damn report.

"Okay, but you understand I have to protect the members of my family, as their father and lawyer."

"Oh, of course, and I respect that."

As Arvid climbed the stairs to the widow's walk, he was able to hear the whispered exchange between Mr. and Mrs. Gendron. The whispering was excessively loud in Gendron's need to emphasize his instructions to his wife.

"Don't say one thing to him about the accident."

"What is there to tell? I don't know why you're so secretive. Shouldn't we cooperate?" Arvid sensed a lack of respect in the way the instructions were delivered.

"If you've ever understood anything I've ever told you, just do this."

Arvid got on his hands and knees at the door of the widow's walk and crawled the length of the walk back and forth as he examined the floor with his large magnifying glass. He was glad nobody was around to see him; he could imagine the stories comparing him to the literary Sherlock Holmes. He just wanted to be sure to find any patch on that floor that showed signs of rot; there were none. Even the strip of wood the railing was fastened to was solid and intact. So why did the railing come loose?

Measuring the whole railing he found it to be comprised of five even lengths: two on either side of the door and one across the far end of the rectangular walk. Holding his glass close he started inspecting the end of the railing still fastened. Each section was attached to the floor with five screws and a metal mounting. As he moved along, he found all securely in place and, in fact, had been that way for some time, since they were all heavily rusted around the mountings. When he came to the section that hung in the air, he sat back on the floor with his glass resting in his lap and stared out onto that wonderful view of Lake Superior that the builders of this grand old house had wanted to capture. He had come upon something that needed further thought.

Out came the Minolta for pictures of both intact screws and those ripped from the floor when the railing "gave way." It appeared that they had just unscrewed themselves from the mountings and hung from the railing undamaged. They weren't bent or broken off. The only way they differed from those still holding a portion of the railing securely in place was that the heads of each dislocated screw had striation marks in the heavy rust that still covered them. Someone had worked on those screws with a screwdriver. Had the accident scene just turned into a crime scene? But who would have tampered with the railing? And why? Who wanted a child dead? Or had the wrong person leaned on the damaged railing? Arvid sat with these questions and more racing across his mind.

As he came down the stairs he had a sudden thought and turned into the kitchen where he found Lucille Gendron, still in her robe, nursing a cup of coffee.

"Have some coffee, Arvid," she said. It was so natural. He'd had coffee with her many times before. More often he shared a cup with Gudrun, but sometimes she sat down with both of them. She mumbled on about how grieved they were as she got him a cup and filled it from the coffee pot. Unlike her husband, she didn't seem eager to get rid of him. In fact, she seemed comforted to have someone with her.

"How is Jimmy this morning?"

"He's sleeping. He finally fell asleep about five o'clock. He was so hysterical last night. I was afraid he'd have a heart attack or stroke or something. He was positively wild. James had to slap him to shock him into calming down." Check one question off the list, and he hadn't even had to ask her. He felt a little guilty as if he'd broken her trust, but then he remembered the dead girl.

"Have you had any work done up there on the walk lately?"

"No. As I said before, we should have, but we just didn't get around to it."

"Did the kids often go up on the walk?"

"I don't think so. Why would they? There are plenty of other places if they wanted to be alone." Then her eyes changed and she looked at Arvid differently. He could see that she had suddenly remembered her husband's admonition, and she became guarded and withdrawn. "Not that there would be any reason for them to be alone," her voice trailed off, and she kept her eyes riveted on the black liquid in her cup, suddenly roiled in response to a visible tremor in her right hand. " … or want to be alone," she finished.

"Well, thanks for the coffee. I'll be back tonight, as your husband suggested." He started out the door but turned, as if he'd just remembered something. "I hate to bother you, but do you suppose I could borrow a screw driver? I left mine back at the station."

She went immediately to a kitchen drawer and looked inside, viewing the contents as if nothing there made any sense to her. Arvid went to look in the drawer himself. "This'll do," he said, as he chose a fairly large tool that lay on top of an assortment of kitchen apparatuses. Back in his truck, he carefully placed the screwdriver in a plastic bag, but not before he had given it a cursory examination with his glass. He thought he saw flecks of rust. He could more definitely identify these small particles if he viewed them under his old, but trusty, microscope. Could he have been so lucky as to have found a murder weapon this easily? And was he calling it a murder now?"

The day wore on with not much time for Arvid to have a "good think" about all he had discovered. People sought him out with various problems, and Billy LaDuke pottered about on his duties, occasionally interrupting Arvid with a question about the accident.

"What you think the doc will find at the autopsy?"

"I mainly want him to determine the direct cause of death, so I can finish my damn report," he said, not wanting to arouse any suspicion.

"She died from falling, I guess," Billy offered as if that cause might not have occurred to Arvid.

"So, did she die of a broken arm? Or a brain concussion? Maybe she had a heart attack and died before she fell!"

"Or was pushed!" Billy blurted out the latter as he had failed to hear the sarcasm in Arvid's voice and had honestly thought the two of them were brainstorming. At first Arvid was stunned, but he regained his calm when he realized it had been just a chance remark. He felt a prick of conscience, though, when he acknowledged to himself that he had become condescending to Billy. What if Old Jack had treated him that way? He made a mental note to be more patient with Billy but before he could give another thought to him, Gudrun and Willow came through the door.

Both women were grim, and gray looking. He arranged chairs for them in front of his desk. "Thank you for coming in," he said, "I was going to call you and arrange this myself; just hadn't gotten to it. There are a few questions I still need to ask."

"We want to know when we can get the body. We need to make funeral arrangements."

"The body is in Ashland waiting for an autopsy. Doc Olson is going to perform it this afternoon. At that point we will transport it to whatever funeral home you want and you'll be free to make your arrangements."

"Why an autopsy? Why do we need an autopsy?" Both women had suddenly become animated, Gudrun even starting out of her chair.

"Don't you have to notify and get permission from relatives for this?" Gudrun was now standing in front of the desk, leaning forward.

"Which is what I'm doing right now," Arvid answered. "No one was in any shape to discuss this last night; and as the investigating officer, I felt we had to have a definite cause of death."

"She fell from over 100 feet. Isn't that enough of an explanation?" Gudrun's voice had begun to shake and she was crying. Willow jumped up and embraced her, casting a disgusted look at Arvid.

I hope you're happy! It took me all night to calm her down." To Gudrun she spoke in a conciliatory voice, "Relax, honey, they're just going to give her an exam and they'll be done by tonight."

"They're going to cut my baby up," she insisted. "I won't have it! You leave her alone. What does it matter now? She's dead and can't harm anyone ever again. She was just a little girl, and it wasn't her fault."

"Shh, shh, shh, of course it wasn't anyone's fault. No one is saying that," Willow soothed.

"I have no intention of causing you any more grief than you already have," Arvid said, "but I have to do my job the way I see fit, even when it involves friends." He paused then, as an afterthought, "Anything we do or find is confidential." That seemed to placate Gudrun some, and she sat down again, her hand shielding her face that was distorted with heartache.

Arvid motioned for Billy to run for a glass of water, which he presented in a formal manner. Gudrun drank a little and withdrew back into the shell that Arvid had seen last night after the accident. He decided to press on.

"Were you talking to LuAnn and Jimmy just before she fell?"

"Of course."

Was she facing you or facing out towards the lake?"

"Well, I guess she would have been facing us if we were talking."

"So, she leaned backward against the railing?"

"What difference does it make? It gave way and she fell."

"Was she arguing with you or Jimmy?"

"No! I just told them to come down because it wasn't safe."

"Why do you say it wasn't safe?"

"The floorboards are rotten and the railing is loose."

"Did you see this yourself?" She looked up at him confused and somewhat interested.

"I haven't been up there in years, but Mr. Gendron kept telling me that it was rotten and unsafe, and I shouldn't let anyone go up there."

"So, you say you haven't been up to the widow's walk in years, not even to clean or look out over the lake?"

"No one cleaned up there. Besides, it was locked most of the time, and I didn't have a key."

"Was the key with the other household keys?"

"No, it was on Mr. Gendron's personal chain."

"So, who unlocked the door for you and Jimmy and LuAnn?" Gudrun looked confused.

"I don't know. I heard LuAnn and Jimmy talking and went up to tell them to come down. I didn't think about it being locked. I guess Jimmy got the key from his dad."

Arvid made a note to look for the key. The door to the widow's walk hadn't been locked when he made his initial investigation last night. It wasn't locked this morning. Why hadn't Gendron immediately locked it after the accident; and why would he give the key to Jimmy if he felt so strongly about the safety issue? Or, if he did give it to him, why hadn't Gendron retrieved it and locked the door? Arvid pressed on.

"Were LuAnn and Jimmy upset about something?" The question hung in the air. Now Arvid was an avid hunter, not so much for the thrill of the sport, but because of his northwoods upbringing. As soon as he was old enough to walk in the woods, he had followed along on his dad's or uncles' hunting forays, learning to walk stealthily and to cut the chatter.

The old gravel pit frequently resounded with the sound of shattering glass as he and his brothers, even the youngest, engaged in target practice using empty beer bottles liberated from the bin behind The Beach Club. And so, already accomplished at an early age, it was a rite of passage for every Nelson man to receive his first hunting rifle around the age of 12 and become a member of "the party."

With this experience and his analytical mind, Arvid developed an affinity for reading his prey. There seemed to be a split second when his scope would find the chest of an animal and also reveal a look in their eyes of final resignation when they realized that neither fight nor flight was an option. In Arvid's case, that split second often caused his rifle to lower.

Such were the eyes that Gudrun turned to him now. She stuck to her story, but Arvid knew in that instant that she was hiding something, and it had to be something important to cause her to lie at a time like this. "I don't think they were upset," she muttered lamely and sank her head between her shoulder blades, spreading her fingers and inspecting each hand alternately as they lay in her lap.

"I'll call you as soon as the autopsy is over." He rose and came around the desk to see her and Willow out the door.

Arvid waited 15 minutes after the 5:30 ferry had landed in order to give Gendron time to get home. He didn't want to appear too eager, but he did want to pursue the investigation vigorously and in a timely fashion. He knocked on the kitchen door, it being his normal point of entry at their home. Mr. Gendron opened the door, still in his business suit and looking irritated. Mrs. Gendron and Jimmy sat quietly together on the same side of the breakfast nook.

Jimmy's condition seemed much improved over his hysteria of the previous night. He wore repaired, or a second pair, of glasses which restored his normal appearance. He was still deathly white, however, and the mark on his cheek had turned to purple displaying four distinct phantom fingers. Arvid fleetingly wondered at the force of that slap, supposedly used to restore Jimmy's sanity; but which now more clearly seemed to express the anger or desperation of the person who dealt the blow. He decided to start there. He took Jimmy's chin in his hand and turned his bruised cheek toward the light.

"Wow, this must have knocked you off your pins, Jim!"

"Not really, it looks worse than it feels."

"How did you get this?"

"I don't exactly remember. Everything is very confused in my mind."

"I told you before, his father slapped him to shock him out of his babbling and crying." Mrs. Gendron spoke defensively and covered her son's hand with her own, pressing strongly for support but also to suppress the trembling, which Arvid had already noticed.

"Oh, that's right, you did tell me that this morning. Sorry!"

Gendron directed a darting look at his wife and cleared his throat. "Now he's wondering what else she told me this morning," Arvid thought to himself: advantage number one. He sat down in the nook opposite Jimmy as if to shoot the breeze for a while.

"I haven't talked to you in a while, Jim. How old are you now?"

"Twenty." Jimmy managed a slight smile and seemed to relax a little.

"What are you up to these days? I remember hearing that you'd graduated from high school."

"I'm at Yale. It's summer vacation now."

"Yale, wow! I can't imagine what that's like. What are you going for, for a career I mean?"

"Law, eventually."

"Law, like your dad. Good for you! You must be a very proud father." The last was directed at Gendron who stood to the side, looking wary.

"Now Jim, I know you say you don't remember about last night, but maybe if you talk about it something will just pop out. Why did you and LuAnn decide to go up to the widow's walk?"

"It was a clear night and there were so many stars. We just wanted to get a better view."

"You go up there a lot … to look at the stars?"

"No, not a lot." His voice became almost a whisper, "just sometimes."

"How many times this summer you think you went up there, four or five?"

"Maybe four or five." He had averted his eyes.

"Weren't you warned about the rotted floorboards and the loose railing?"

"I guess so."

"Who told you the floor had rotted?"

"I don't remember."

"Gudrun told me that Mr. Gendron told her the floor was rotten. Do you think your dad may have told you?"

"I guess so. What difference does it make?" He shouted the last question directly in Arvid's face. His dead-white complexion worried Arvid, but he had to press on in a calm, quiet voice.

"In the four or five times you've been up there this summer, has it ever been in the daylight?"

"I suppose so."

"Did you ever see, in the four or five times you've been up there, that the floor had rotted?"

"No."

"Why do you think your dad would tell you that if it weren't so?"

Before he could answer, a frustrated Gendron stood and glared at Arvid. "I don't know who you think you are … Colombo or Perry Mason or some other TV hero of yours, but you can't put words in my son's mouth to complete your little scenario."

"Oh, I don't mean to offend you Mr. Gendron, but this isn't the courtroom. You can object, but I still am authorized to ask any question I think is relevant to the case."

"Very well, it's a stupid question with an obvious answer: so the kids would be too scared to go up there. It was a preventive measure."

"With all respect, sir, I'll be questioning you in a minute, but I have just a few more questions for Jimmy." Gendron stared daggers at Arvid but squeezed in beside his wife and son.

"So you and LuAnn went up to the widow's walk to see the stars. How did you get in?"

Jimmy looked surprised at first then decided to take a derisive tone, looking to his father for approval in his display of disdain for the local authority. It was uncharacteristic of him, however, and the answer came across weak.

"We opened the door."

"Wasn't it locked?"

"Not that I remember."

"So, you didn't have a key?"

"No! I've never had a key."

"Where is the key kept?"

Gendron rose and faced Arvid. "I think this has gone on long enough. The boy obviously doesn't know what you're talking about, and I must admit that I'm at a loss as to where this is heading."

"I understand, sir. I know you're concerned for your son, so maybe I can have you clear things up for me. Where do you keep the key for the widow's walk? Is it with the kitchen keys?"

"No, it's with my personal keys, for safety's sake."

"Did you give it to Jimmy or Gudrun or LuAnn the other night?"

"No, one of them must have taken it off my key ring in the office." The strain of his trying to remain calm and offhand was evident in the drops of perspiration that had formed on his upper lip. "Everyone is in and out of my office all the time. It's not as if there's any reason for it to be a secure area."

"Did you lock the widow's walk after the accident?"

"You know I didn't. You've been up there a couple times since then."
He answered loudly, as if he knew he was on safe ground and wanted
to emphasize the veracity of his responses.

"So, as far as you know, the key to the widow's walk is on your personal
ring in your office?"

"Of course not! I thought I told you. I wanted to lock the door after the
accident and couldn't find the key. I don't know who took it."

"Do you have it, Jim?" Jimmy looked startled when the questioning
turned to him and blurted out,

"No! I'm not allowed in my dad's office!"

"So, is Gudrun allowed in your office?" But before he could answer, both
Jim and Mrs. Gendron, in a word that wasn't meant to be heard aloud, shook
their heads simultaneously and replied almost in unison,

"No!" Gendron's face registered panic, then anger. When he spoke it was
more to his family than to Arvid.

"My office isn't off limits to anyone. Why would you say that?"

"Well, LuAnn must have taken the key then. Would you think that
possible?"

"Yes, it's possible. She was always some place she shouldn't be."

"Why do you say that? Was she troublesome?" Gendron was looking
visibly sick now but still managed to backtrack skillfully.

"No, not troublesome, just a little mischievous as kids will be. You know
how they question everything."

"Why would she question you?" Gendron completely lost his composure
and jumped to his feet.

"What are you getting at? Do you think one of us pushed her? Unless
you can come up with some way to charge us, I say this interview is over. I've
wanted to cooperate, but you're making it impossible with your imaginative
innuendo." He rose, walked to the door and opened it, gesturing for Arvid
to leave.

Chapter 21

"If the great Gods be just, they shall assist
The deeds of justest men."
(ANTONY AND CLEOPATRA) WILLIAM SHAKESPEARE

Arvid wasn't upset by his unfriendly expulsion from the Gendron's kitchen door. He was the type of guy who seemed impervious to slights or abuse. He had been born and raised on the Island, smack in the middle of the five Nelson boys. His mother had always admonished him to, "follow your older and take care of your younger brothers." This was no easy task, because each of the four, older and younger, was bent on making his own particular brand of trouble. Their father might have been a calming influence on what some on the Island referred to as "the tribe," but he was always away to far-flung corners of the earth: he worked on offshore oil rigs in Texas, Venezuela, Saudi Arabia or wherever the company sent him. This absentee father supported his family well but was not around to discipline them, leaving that monstrous task to their tired, little mother.

"I can't do a thing with them," was her excuse to neighbors, teachers, or policemen.

For some reason, known only to the fickle fates of the universe, Arvid was the only one of the five brothers who had escaped the warrior gene and early on, displayed the characteristics of an easy-going, respectful young man. Maybe he allowed his mind to advance a step further when he observed his brothers in action and decided the consequences were not worth the deeds. Maybe he was just an old soul from birth.

As he grew, he was often sent to the Island policeman, Old Jack Johnson, to pay fines or plead for leniency on behalf of the current vandal. His older brothers jokingly called him Loophole because he had become so adept at pleading their cases; he almost sounded like a lawyer. Of course the name caught on as his teenage nickname, sometimes shortened to Loop or Loopie. He often heard it even as an adult, although most everyone called him Arvid, to his face anyway.

In high school he thought briefly about actually becoming a lawyer; but he wasn't a very good student, usually resenting classes and mooning the time away looking out the window, as he imagined himself fishing or walking in the woods. How could he think of signing up for years more of what amounted to self-inflicted torture? Maybe he just wanted to be able to earn a living on The Rock he loved, where he could fish and hunt and lead a quiet life. And so it was that he became too often the victim of jokes or teasing, but also the one to call when there was trouble.

Then one day, as he was filling out some paperwork on behalf of a sibling, the Island cop, Old Jack, approached him. "You interested in a part-time job here, Loop? I just got the go ahead to hire some help. It'd be cleaning and answering the phone, taking messages—stuff like that." And so it was that Arvid's career was born, and as for Old Jack, he recognized a quick learner who, when not hampered by the tedium of the classroom, took the advantage of learning when it applied to something that interested him. Before long he was helping with reports and assisting on calls of all types.

Mostly the duo responded to fender benders or alcohol-related incidents, and Arvid watched Old Jack carefully, as he always presented a calm demeanor and spoke softly and with respect. Even when the perpetrators were shouting angrily, he seemed to be able to defuse the situations. Accidents, particularly drownings, were tough, and the young, aspiring lawman learned to steel himself in the face of death and never show his feelings to those around him. It was a hard lesson.

He started out thinking Old Jack devoid of any emotion. Then came the night when one of the Island boys was pulled from the lake after hours of a rescue mission turned to a recovery and their search lights showed a body floating face down in choppy storm waters. Afterwards, Arvid, shaken with horror and exhaustion, tried to calm himself by becoming immediately busy with the incident report, his fingers clumsily maneuvering the old, manual typewriter. As his thoughts traveled back over the events of the night, he became aware that Old Jack hadn't come in. A group of men who had been part of the search party stood talking outside the door and pointed around the building when Arvid asked about his boss.

The blackness was complete but Arvid was able to locate Old Jack by the disembodied point of light that glowed from his cigarette. When he raised it to his lips to draw that calming smoke into his lungs, the increased illumination provided just enough light to see the tears that streaked his face. Arvid never forgot that night or the lesson: never let them see you cry, but for your own sake, cry.

Aside from wondering why James Gendron was so uncooperative, Arvid had many other questions, and his mind methodically reviewed the whole scene as he drove away from that imposing house with the all-important widow's walk perched atop the roof. When he got back to his desk, he was very surprised to find Doc Olson waiting in his visitor's chair, Billy having supplied him with coffee and small talk while he waited. "Geez, Doc," he greeted, "I didn't mean to get you clear over here tonight." He motioned for a disappointed Billy to leave them alone.

"Well, ordinarily I'd have called or even waited 'til morning, but I'm fond of this family. I delivered LuAnn and been her doctor since then. You try to remain objective in these situations, but sometimes you just can't." He stopped to clear his throat and drank from his coffee cup … .

"What did you find, Doc?"

"She died from the fall; her neck was broken and some of her organs had just exploded from the impact of the landing. What makes it doubly sad is that LuAnn was pregnant, about three months I'd say, and I just can't bear the thought of the gossipers getting hold of that and desecrating her memory. And what about Gudrun? What I want to know from you is if we can keep this to ourselves? There's no need for anyone to know but the two of us."

"Were there any bruises or signs of violence on the body?"

"None, any more than the usual signs of lividity from the fall. Why would you ask about bruises? Do you think she may have been pushed or beaten? Or would she have committed suicide? I can't imagine a young, beautiful girl like her doing that unless she was distraught about the pregnancy. In any case, why does anyone have to know?"

"I understand your feelings and share many of them; but if someone planned the accident or pushed her in anger, it becomes a murder. Maybe it will turn out to be just the tragedy it appears to be, but some things don't add up. People are lying, and I want to know why. That little girl deserves that much, and so does Gudrun."

"I'm not trying to tell you how to do your job, I'm asking you to be discreet is all. I know you will be, and I didn't want to blab everything over the phone. Now I've got to get back on that ferry before I get stuck on this rock overnight." He started out the door, pulling his coat on as he hurried. "Wait up," he stepped back to Arvid and handed him a key from his coat pocket, "I found this in one of her inside pockets. Would you give it to Gudrun?"

He sat holding the key, an old fashioned skeleton key; the kind of key that would open a door in an old house; the kind of key that would open a door to a stairway leading to a widow's walk.

Arvid sat at his desk after Doc had left and worked for some time; he cut sheets of paper into four equal pieces. The names of those involved in the tragedy were written on separate pieces: Gendron, Mrs. Gendron, Jimmy, LuAnn, Gudrun, and the baby's father. Facts already determined about the case were written on the remaining sheets.

1. Jimmy lied about the reason for going to the widow's walk. "It was a clear night, and there were so many stars. We went up to get a better view." Arvid recalled the night. There was a full moon and there wouldn't have been many stars visible. Besides, he also remembered it as being partly cloudy, with the moon being obscured at times by clouds.

2. The missing key turned up in the victim's pocket, either stolen from Gendron's office or given to the victim, but by whom?

3. Someone had tampered with the railing before the accident. A section of

the screws fastening the railing to the flooring had been loosened with
a screwdriver.

4. Why was everyone led to believe the widow's walk had rotting boards and
was in a state of disrepair?

5. Gendron generally uncooperative.

6. What prompted the vicious slap to Jimmy's face?

7. Gudrun's hiding something.

8. Jimmy's hiding something.

9. Gendron's hiding something.

10. LuAnn's pregnancy enters the equation somewhere. If that's the secret,
who wants it hidden and why?

11. Both Jimmy and Gudrun used the exact same phrase when describing the
accident. Significance?

12. Gudrun said, "She was just a little girl, it wasn't her fault." Significance?

Arvid laid out the pieces like a storyboard and arranged them under each
name, sometimes rearranging the columns with additions or subtractions.
After a while, he gathered them together and put them in his desk drawer
out of Billy's inquiring eyes. He would take this homemade outline out many
times during the course of the investigation, making new slips of paper
as information came to light. By the time he was finally able to relegate it to the
wastebasket, it would be tattered and coffee-stained with use.

He decided to call it a day at that point but made one last entry in his
notebook which stated his focus for the next day: find the baby's father.

Danny Miller

The Miller family of Bayfield had drifted in and out of Gudrun's life over
the years. Caro Miller had been instrumental in getting Gudrun a job at the
herring run during her first winter in Bayfield. Of course Gudrun could not
forget, or forgive, the fact that Dan Miller had been a drinking buddy of Cy's
and, indeed, had been the one to furnish the bottle of whiskey that caused his
fall into the icy waters of Superior and his subsequent death.

The Millers lived from hand to mouth, Dan finding jobs with local fishermen or doing odd jobs, just as Cy had done during the long, Bayfield winters. Gudrun saw Caro occasionally in the stores or waiting outside Morty's. At that time, she seemed reluctant to go into the tavern, but waited outside to intercept her husband when he exited. Gudrun noticed Caro's advanced pregnancy quite a while before she was aware of her own, and she knew of their baby boy, born about six months before LuAnn.

Gudrun could have been a friend to Caro but chose to keep her distance. At first she didn't want to encourage any friendship between Cy and Dan, especially in the months before his death when Cy, as an expectant father, had become a loving husband. After the accident, when Dan tried to be helpful to her, she had uncharacteristically lashed out at him, accusing him of supplying the cause of the drowning. This thought had never occurred to Dan, and he was stunned at first, then defensive, and finally steadfast in his resolve that his gift of a bottle had only been an offering of comfort to a friend.

And so, the animosity grew with each slight on Gudrun's part and each feeling of guilt for the Millers. Caro referred to Gudrun as snooty, and Dan told his fellow drinkers at the bar that, "Cy had to put up with a crazy woman."

Danny grew up unattended for the most part. As a baby, he often cried himself to sleep in a beat-up old truck parked outside a bar. Caro had decided it was easier to join her husband in his pastime than to oppose him. Consequently, Danny was often tucked into the front seat of the pickup with a bottle in hand and a soothing promise that, "Mama's gonna check on you once in awhile." Of course, as the night wore on and if someone at the bar was buying, Caro and Dan often forgot that promise and at closing time, looked with surprise at the sleeping baby who had dropped his bottle, kicked his covers loose, and lay in an exhausted sleep, his face stiff with dried tears.

As he grew, little Danny was like a tramp, fending for himself and often depending on the kindness of Bayfield housewives for meals and clean clothes. Once Ray the barber encountered the young boy outside his shop and, having no business at the time, plopped him into his chair and proceeded to cut and style his unruly, long shock of hair. However, when Ray stood back to admire his work, he noticed that the new, short look had revealed an incredibly dirty neck. So, with the help of a neighbor woman, he pulled the old galvanized tub into the back yard, filled it with warm water, and gave Danny a good scrubbing. The boy protested at the time, but it must have been to his liking, because from that time on he started showing up periodically asking for odd jobs in return for haircuts.

When he was old enough, he started working on the boats for fishermen, or washing dishes at local restaurants. He was a good worker and earned his own money, which he learned early on to hide carefully for fear his parents would take it for liquor. Neither Dan nor Caro displayed much for him to respect, so he gradually formed a cynical, sarcastic attitude which was not endearing and certainly didn't foster trust. He was a thorn in the side of the Bayfield police, as well as for Arvid Nelson on the Island.

Gudrun thought they were morally beneath her, and over the years, cautioned LuAnn to steer clear of the Miller boy. The children paid no attention to their parents' feud or warnings, however, and often found it amusing to be friends just to, "piss them off," as Danny laughingly confided to his buddies. Danny wasn't laughing when Arvid showed up that morning at the fishing boat where he was currently working.

"You got Danny Miller working here?" A couple men were standing on the dock by a moored fishing boat.

"Yeah, he's below, but he's not feelin' too swell today, been pukin'. I told him to go on home, but he's stickin' around. What did he do? Whatever it was, I had nothin' to do with it. He just works for me some."

"As far as I know, he hasn't done anything. I just want to talk to him." At that point Danny appeared on deck, and in spite of all the past, ugly encounters he's had with the boy, Arvid felt a surge of compassion for this old child who was barely 16. He had always been skinny, but in the throws of nausea he held himself like a crippled old man, his thin arms cradling his stomach and his shirt falling open to reveal a spindly chest. His eyes were swollen and red.

"Hey Danny, you're not doin' too well? Come on the dock and sit on the bench with me. Can I get you a 7Up or something? They say that's good for stomach problems."

"I ain't got no problems. It's just that goddamn fish smell."

"Well then, I guess you chose the wrong kind of work, if it bothers you that much." Danny leaned over and grimaced. Suddenly a comparison popped into Arvid's mind. Danny looked much the same as Jimmy had when Arvid first tried to question him on the night of the accident. "Let's see if he has something to hide," Arvid thought.

"I suppose you heard about the accident with LuAnn and all? You two were friends weren't you? Seems to me I've seen you together many times over the years." Arvid refrained from saying he had arrested them together many times. Danny audibly caught his breath, and tears began to roll down his cheeks, but he managed to maintain a sarcastic tone.

"Is it a crime to have friends, now?"

"No, no it's not, but I just have to clear up some loose ends, and you are someone who was in her life. Is that a fair statement?"

"Not any more. She was getting married." The later statement was garbled, since Danny was now sobbing. Arvid involuntarily laid his hand on Danny's back; and for an instant it seemed as if he might lean into Arvid's arms for solace; but he pulled away and turned his back, unable to comment through his tears.

"Getting married? Gosh, she was pretty young for that wasn't she? Who's the guy?"

"Well, it's not me! I guess that's obvious! So, what do you want? I wasn't even on the Island that night."

"It kinda seems as if you wish you were the one she was marrying." This triggered an outburst of animosity.

"Okay, yes! I loved her and she loved me, but I can't compete with money and Yale, and everyone telling her what to do." Arvid wanted to ask Danny outright if he was the father of LuAnn's baby, but he remembered Doc's wish to keep the information between the two of them. Arvid wasn't going to let the leak come from him.

Women and love can do strange things to a man, he mused. He hoped that putting the conversation on a man-to-man basis would cause Danny to relax into the subject. "I guess by money and Yale you're talking about Jimmy. Am I right? Was LuAnn planning on marrying Jimmy?"

"She didn't love him!" Danny stood up and shouted, and the men on the dock looked their way, then turned back to their conversation quickly, as if embarrassed. "We used to make fun of him, call him the four-eyed freak. She was just going to lead him on, tell him she'd marry him until she could get some money, and then the two of us were going to run away together. We had it all planned, but now she's dead." Danny sat down heavily, and his voice was very small as he questioned of no one in particular, "Why didn't we just run away together? We could have worked for money."

"Was Jimmy in love with LuAnn? Was that why she thought your plan might work?"

"No, he's too big a freak for that, but LuAnn was going to work on him. She was pretty good at getting guys to fall for her."

"Oh yeah, how's that?"

"Well, she's, was, so damn pretty, and then she made a guy feel so important." Danny displayed a faint smile in remembrance, which faded into the trails of tears. This boy was clearly in grief, and Arvid felt guilty at exploiting his vulnerability.

"Any other reason you two thought the plan might work?"

"No, it was just crazy talk when we'd get together under the dock. Then all of a sudden she was working on him, and then she said she was really going to marry him. I was against it, but she said she could get more out of him in a divorce. She had her mind made up; you couldn't talk to her then." That was a long recitation and Danny grimaced again and hugged his stomach tighter. In his mind Arvid concluded that Danny didn't know LuAnn was pregnant, although he was undoubtedly the father.

"Listen Danny, let me give you a ride home and we'll stop and get some 7Up and crackers or something, and you can go to bed. You're in no shape to work." He rose and put his hand on Danny's arm. Surprisingly, he let himself be led away, seeming almost too exhausted to walk, much less protest.

Chapter 22

"Eyes, look your last! Arms, take your last embrace!"
(ROMEO AND JULIET) WILLIAM SHAKESPEARE

he afternoon of LuAnn Willow Gaudette's funeral was warm and sunny, with a fair breeze to just ripple the surface of the lake. It was the kind of day that a young girl might bike out to Big Bay on the Island to spread a towel on the clean, warm sand and let the sun turn her skin golden; or maybe it was the kind of day a young girl would share a picnic with someone she loved at the Bayfield town park, watching the ferry come and go with its crowds of happy, brightly-clad people. It was a beautiful summer day, not meant to be spoiled by the tolling funeral bell and the line of grim-faced mourners who filed into Christ Episcopal Church.

The small church had quickly filled, and so had the folding chairs set up on the lawn; and still people came to stand in the street. Many who knew LuAnn and Gudrun were heartsick. Many came almost in protest that this young girl had been taken before her time. Some looked with empathy, secretly relieved and thanking a deity of their choice that it hadn't been their son or daughter. Then, of course, there were the curious, come to hear the latest news of what had happened ... what had really happened?

Arvid Nelson came as a friend who was truly heartsick. But he was also angry at the selfish group of adults who had allowed a sequence of events to spiral into tragedy. Over his many years in law enforcement he had gotten used to human failings: the secrets kept that really weren't important—usually forgotten a few days after disclosure; the importance of saving face in the avoidance of scandal; the need for power and control; the failure to talk to each other.

He knew that the rumors were rampant in both Bayfield and on the Island, he knew this mostly from Billy LaDuke who had enjoyed a bit of popularity since people figured they could pump him for anything he may have heard around Arvid. "People are sayin' that LuAnn was gonna marry Jimmy Gendron," Billy told him yesterday.

"Oh, I hadn't heard that," he said, "Why would they get married? Isn't he still in college?" Billy looked sheepish.

"Ya, but they say she was pregnant or somethin'. He looked at the floor, avoiding Arvid's eyes, for fear he would be angry with him for repeating a rumor. So it had gotten out, and the only one who knew it besides him was Doc. He was pretty sure it was another case of people putting two and two together and getting five, but sometimes a rumor swirls around and around and hits the truth right on the head.

Actually, Arvid was pretty sure he knew what had really happened, and just had to lean hard on some of the parties involved to get an admission. He already knew that Danny was the father of LuAnn's baby. Doc had said that LuAnn was about three months pregnant which put her pregnant when she came to the Island in May. Jimmy would not have arrived on the scene until June. Besides, he believed Danny's story of their plan to trap Jimmy and extract money for their getaway.

Did Gudrun know her daughter was pregnant? Was that what the big discussion was all about when she fell from the widow's walk? Arvid could understand why Gudrun was eager to keep the information under wraps; she was so religious and overly concerned about what ruined reputations. He thought that now he could coax the truth out of her, especially if he stressed that what she told him was confidential.

He thought Jimmy would have been more forthcoming, since he was innocent. But something was holding him back ... loyalty to Gudrun? It had been Arvid's experience that sometimes the real brainy ones were devoid of common sense. That could be Jimmy also.

Of course there were still some unanswered questions, and they seemed to center around James Gendron. What was he hiding and why? Why did he lie about the condition of the widow's walk, and why did he give the key to LuAnn? He thought Gendron had loosened the railing on the walk, but why?

Arvid knew that it was just a matter of time before all would be made clear. He had waited out of respect for Gudrun until after the funeral. Then he expected to get them all together or maybe he would talk to them separately.

The crowd from the church filed out and into waiting cars to be taken to the cemetery where LuAnn was lowered into the ground beside her father. Gudrun looked like an old, old woman with Einer Olson and Arne Peterson helping her, followed by Willow helping Jenny. Just as they walked past Arvid, James and Lucille Gendron stepped forward and stopped Gudrun.

Lucille Gendron was in bad shape herself and attempted to embrace Gudrun, the tears rolling down her cheeks; but when Gudrun saw James Gendron her body straightened; and she spoke softly but distinctly.

"I know what you did, and I never want to see you again. I hope you rot in hell!"

The day after the funeral dawned on a complete change of weather: a brisk wind was blowing across the lake from the north and heavy clouds held the promise of rain. Arvid was anxious to wrap up the investigation. He still wasn't sure if someone would be charged, if only for negligence. He phoned the Gendron's, asked for Jimmy and arranged to pick him up in half an hour. Next he phoned Willow and Arne's farm where Gudrun was staying and talked to Gudrun.

"We need to have an end to this, and I'm on my way with Jimmy to talk to you." He didn't wait for an argument but hung up. Jimmy was waiting outside for him when he pulled into the driveway. They were passing through La Pointe before either of them spoke. "Do you have anything to say to me before we meet with Gudrun—something that you want to tell me privately?

"I guess I think the time for keeping secrets is over. Everyone involved has already been hurt and pretty much knows the whole story now, everyone but you that is."

"I have a version of the story which you all need to confirm with your testimony. I'll be talking to your father separately."

Arne was outside when they arrived. He shook hands awkwardly with both of them, acting almost as if they were all meeting for the first time. Arvid had the feeling that the three men who stood outside the farm house were united in thinking that this confrontation was necessary and that they hoped it would put an end to the tragic drama that had consumed their lives for the past weeks. Arvid laid a hand on Arne's shoulder as he walked past him into the house.

Gudrun and Willow stood behind the kitchen table where mugs had been set in preparation for the brewed coffee; the fragrant smell permeated the warm air. They nodded to each other in greeting. Arvid thought fleetingly how women always seemed to pull together the amenities in time of crisis. Maybe it was part of their nurturing aspect; anyway it always made bad situations a little easier. He pulled out a chair and sat, and the others followed suit.

"Gudrun, I hope you know how sorry I am for you loss and how terrible I feel to make you go through it again. I just have to put the whole story together and to make sure everyone's part in this comes to light."

"I want everything to come out. I'm not keeping anything hidden any longer. I want everything to come out." She repeated herself, but seemed fairly composed.

"Let's start with the three of you up on the widow's walk. Why don't you start, Jim? Why were you up there?"

"LuAnn stopped me when I came into the back hall after dinner. She said she needed to talk to me privately and wanted to go up to the walk where we wouldn't be bothered. She had the key. I didn't want to go up there with her, because she'd been acting really strange with me all summer." He stopped and looked nervously at Gudrun.

"What do you mean by strange?"

"Well, she hasn't wanted to have much to do with me since she was about 12, but suddenly this summer she kept wanting to go places with me, wanting to get me alone." His face flushed red and he looked at the floor.

"What happened when you were alone?" Arvid knew Jimmy didn't want to sully LuAnn's memory, but her plan was part of the whole sordid story, and it had to come out.

"She tried to kiss me, or sit in my lap. She even asked me if I'd ever made love to a woman, and did I want to make love to her?" Gudrun didn't make a sound, but she seemed to stiffen her body, as if to take blows.

"What was your response to all this?" Jimmy looked straight at Gudrun, and answered in a clear and steady voice.

"I told her I thought of her as my little sister, and I had no thoughts like that about her. I told her to stop. I finally just tried to stay out of her way and never be alone with her."

"Go back to the night on the widow's walk."

"Well, right away she started saying she loved me and wanted to kiss me, so I started to leave, but then she sort of changed her voice and she began pleading with me to help her. She said she was pregnant and she was scared; she wanted me to marry her and say the baby was mine. She said I'd do it if I really loved her and Gudrun, like I always said I did."

"What did you say to that?"

"I just kept telling her it was a crazy idea. I told her to talk to her mother, but she just kept arguing until Gudrun finally came up there."

"Okay Gudrun, why did you go up there?"

At Arvid's question, Gudrun's mind became clear, and with Jimmy's contribution of his part in that fateful confrontation, she forced herself to relive it again.

The Night of Retribution

It was the hottest and most humid day of the summer. It was almost unbearable, even on the Island where the surrounding water and Big Lake breezes usually provided relief from the occasional heat wave. Everyone talked about wishing for a good thunder storm to cool everything off; indeed it looked as if that might happen when, around twilight, lightning flashed intermittently across the horizon.

Gudrun was in the hallway, having just finished cleaning the kitchen after dinner, when she heard talking that was loud enough to carry through the door to the widow's walk. At first she thought Mr. Gendron must be up there, but then she heard a woman's voice; it was LuAnn's. Remembering the unsafe warning, she opened the door and walked up the stairs. They were too engrossed in their conversation to hear her. She stopped near the top and listened.

"LuAnn, I would never do that! You're like my little sister. I would never betray your mother like that, and I would never betray my mother!" It was Jimmy and he was very upset.

"Listen Jimmy, I thought you of all people would help me out of this jam; you've always protected me and my mom. Think of what this is going to do to her." LuAnn's voice had gotten low and convincing.

"If I do what you want, it's going to kill both our families. Please, tell your mom everything and ask for her help. She'll take care of you and we'll help too."

"What, I'm not good enough for you? You won't be hooked up with this Island trash?"

"That's not it at all! It's practically incest! You're under age! It's against the law! It's a marriage that would never last!" Gudrun stepped onto the walk at that point, and they both looked startled, then ashamed.

"What are you talking about? What marriage? What kind of trouble are you in, LuAnn?"

"Oh, Mom! I've wanted to tell you, but I'm so scared!" She threw herself into Gudrun's arms and sobbed into her shoulder. "I'm pregnant, and it's Jimmy's baby, and he won't marry me."

"Gudrun, I swear to you; I have never touched LuAnn in that way. I wouldn't do that! You know that don't you?" LuAnn broke free of her mother's arms and went to stand by the far end of the railing, her back to them, sobbing and looking straight ahead, as if she couldn't bear to face them.

"All right, I'll tell you the truth. It's your father's baby, Jimmy. He's been coming on to me all summer and he forced me several times. He told me not to tell anyone or he'd fire Mom and kick us out. He said nobody would believe me over him anyway. I thought it would be easier on everyone if you and I decided to get married. Mom loves you so much, and the Gendrons would make the best of it. Please Jim, this way your mom won't ever have to know."

CHAPTER TWENTY TWO

She grasped the railing, lowering her head as if exhausted from her confession.

Gudrun stood rooted to the spot, but finally spoke. "First we must see if you're really pregnant. You're so young, you may not know." She was grasping for words and thoughts that made any sense. "Then, we must find out what really happened. It's no good to accuse. You can't just trick someone into marrying you to hide the fact that you're pregnant!"

"Why not? You did it! Danny's mom told me all about how you tricked my Dad!" The minute Gudrun heard LuAnn's venomous attack, she had a flashback, and she was numb and speechless in the face of the cruel truth.

LuAnn gripped the railing and started to wrench her body around quickly to face them again, when that movement caused the railing to pull loose from the floorboards, and she toppled headfirst out into the lightning-filled sky and fell to the beach below.

Both Jimmy and Gudrun ran to catch her, but they were too far back, and Jimmy only managed to grab her foot which slipped out of his hand as her body gained momentum. Jim Gendron had stepped out on the walk at that point; and when they shouted that she had fallen, he joined them in stumbling down the stairs and running, almost falling, down the stairs to the beach.

They knelt around her body, which lay unnaturally twisted, and Gudrun caressed her cheek and held her face close to her daughter's.

"How did this happen?" Gendron demanded. Gudrun and Jimmy were crying uncontrollably, but Gendron had gone into his lawyer mode. "Exactly how did she fall?" He got no response from either of them, so he grabbed Jimmy by the shoulders and shook him into attention. "Exactly how did she fall?"

"She leaned against the railing and it gave way. She fell," Jimmy sobbed.

"Okay, both of you, don't say anything to anyone other than that: she leaned against the railing and it gave way. She fell. No matter who asks you, police or whoever. You got it?" Neither of them responded, so he turned each of their faces to him and held them until they repeated the tragic mantra.

"Now, let's go get help," he said. But Gudrun wouldn't leave, and Jimmy wanted to stay with her, but his dad forced him up the stairs toward the house, leaving Gudrun alone with LuAnn. "What started all this? Were you arguing?"

"She wanted me to marry her because she's pregnant, but I said I wouldn't. Then she said it's your baby."

"Oh, my God!" By now they had reached the house and Lucille Gendron stood at the door.

"What's the matter? Is someone hurt?"

"LuAnn's hurt real bad!" Jimmy was hysterical. "She wanted me to marry her because she's pregnant, then she said it's Da ... " but before he could complete his sentence, Gendron whipped him around and, bringing his arm as far behind him as he could, slapped him hard across the face. The force of the blow knocked Jimmy to his knees.

"For God's sake what's wrong with you?" Mrs. Gendron directed at her husband as she helped Jimmy to his feet.

"He's hysterical! It was the only way to bring him out of it. See, he's calmer now." And, indeed, Jimmy was calmer. In that short interval, he had thought of what it would have meant had he revealed LuAnn's accusations to his mother, but on the other hand, was torn between protecting her and not betraying Gudrun.

After Gudrun and Jimmy had finished their account of the night of LuAnn's death, Arvid couldn't find his voice for several seconds. The room was completely silent, and the only movement was from the steam that still curled from the coffee pot on the stove.

Now Gudrun was on her feet, leaning across the table and shaking a finger in Arvid's face. "It's all Gendron's fault! He forced LuAnn, and she got pregnant. That's a crime against a child isn't it? He needs to be put in jail! Are you going to charge him?" Willow put an arm around Gudrun's waist and attempted to calm her, putting her fingers around the shaking finger and whispering softly.

Arvid replied, "That's a fair question; but according to the autopsy, LuAnn was pregnant when you moved to the Island in May. That leaves both Jimmy and his dad off the hook, since neither of them was here until the first of June. Remember too that LuAnn falsely accused Jimmy, settling on his dad when that didn't appear to be working. Don't get me wrong, Gendron has been anything but forthcoming about this accident; and when I leave here, I intend to have a long session with him as well." He stood and spoke to Gudrun.

"I mean to have justice for LuAnn if anyone had anything whatsoever to do with her fall." He took a step toward the door, then turned back to face Gudrun again. "One last question for you and Jim: Did either of you loosen the segment of railing that gave way when LuAnn leaned on it?"

Both their faces registered shock as they shook their heads.

"I didn't know it had been loosened! I thought it was just old and rotten."

"Who could have done that and for what reason?"

"That's my remaining question, and I will have it answered." He touched Gudrun's shoulder as he passed by her and went out into the yard. He stood for a minute, breathing deeply of the chilly breeze that blew off the lake, grateful to escape the oppressively warm little kitchen so full of sorrow and regret and hate. "Let's go back to your house, Jim. You think your dad will be there?"

Arvid was silent on the way back to La Pointe, trying to absorb the news of Gendron's involvement in LuAnn's plot. Could it possibly be that he had come on to her, as she had said? He was like her father. He had known her since she was a baby. He was a lawyer who knew the consequences of seducing a minor. No, most likely he too was a victim of LuAnn's plot but not quite as innocent as Jimmy. Why had he and LuAnn suddenly become friends this summer? Why did he give her the key to the widow's walk and encourage her to go up there? Why had he loosened the railing? Arvid stepped on the gas in his frustration to talk to the final witness and have this whole sordid mess resolved.

He found Gendron in his office. The door stood open, and he walked in unannounced and took the one chair available for a guest.

"I've just talked to the others involved in this tragedy; and I want to get your testimony before I decide if anyone will be charged in the death of LuAnn Gaudette." He fished his notebook from his jacket pocket and proceeded to read in detail what had been said out at the farm. When he had finished, Gendron leaned back in his chair and threw his pen down on his desk.

"I was never inappropriate with that girl! For whatever reason, to extract money I guess, she did suggest a liaison between the two of us, which

I immediately rejected. I didn't know she was pregnant. I wouldn't have suggested what I did if I'd known. I'm not proud of my part, but it seemed to be a way for me to get a question answered that was consuming my life." He rubbed his face with the palms of both hands and rose to pace before Arvid, who was about to ask, "What question?"

"You don't have a son, Arvid. You don't know what it's like to look at that small baby in your arms and dream of all the things that he could do or be, things you'd never had the chance to do. I had so many dreams for Jimmy, and they could all come true: he was smart and ambitious. But as he grew, I saw him becoming soft. Maybe it was because he was being raised by women: my wife and Gudrun. I tried to exert some influence, but it always came out as anger and criticism. I threw myself into my practice, but the suspicion gnawed at me like a chronic pain: maybe my only son was a homosexual."

"It sounds selfish and obsessive, I know; but I'm used to getting my own way, and I thought maybe I could sort of lead him down another road. It was a last resort. It might already have been too late. He was in college, and my time of influence was running out. So when LuAnn started making advances, I sat her down and first I admonished her for her actions, then I suggested that if it was money she wanted, I could supply that if she would see if she could interest Jimmy romantically. As I said, I didn't know she was pregnant and planning extortion. I just thought it would give Jimmy a chance to pick a side, you might say. My wife and I had already heard that LuAnn was promiscuous with the summer crowd. I didn't think I was ruining a young girl." He sat down by his desk again and leaned over, putting his head in his hands.

It was Arvid's turn to rise, and he stood in front of Gendron's desk. "So you thought you could find out the answer to your question by turning her loose on Jimmy? Did you encourage her to meet him on the widow's walk?

"She tried, but he wasn't cooperative."

"Did you give her the key on the night she fell?"

"Yes, oh God, yes!" He looked at the floor, and the tears rolled down his cheeks.

"But you told everyone not to go up there, that it wasn't safe. Why did you say that?"

"Well, I wanted to provide a meeting place for them. I even went up there myself and checked everything out. A part of the railing seemed wobbly, so I got a screwdriver and tightened the screws on the loose part. My God, I guess I didn't tighten them enough because it gave way and she fell." Arvid noticed his use of the same statement he'd drilled into Gudrun and Jimmy's heads after the accident.

"So you didn't loosen the screws on the railing, but tightened them instead?" Gendron looked up inquisitively and answered readily,

"Yes, the railing seemed wobbly on one side."

"Why didn't you screw it tightly? Didn't you test it to see if it was still wobbly?"

"Of course I did. I thought I did." His tone had become defensive, and he lapsed into his usual cold, calculating lawyer voice. "I'm not a carpenter or a handyman. I fixed the railing to the best of my ability. I wasn't expecting anyone to lean against it. Look, as I said, I'm not proud of what I did, but I just couldn't stand the idea of my son being a fairy. He seemed to spit out the disparaging term as if he were ridding himself of a bad taste in his mouth. I'm guilty of bad judgment; but, as God is my witness, I didn't want anyone to get hurt."

"Except for Jimmy, that is." Gendron looked surprised and then guilty.

"I thought it would make a man of him. Aside from the shame and disappointment, you must know how difficult life is for a homosexual. I didn't want that kind of life for him."

His tone had become defensive, and Arvid decided it was useless to argue with him. Besides it wasn't his judgment to make.

"I guess that will be all for now. I'll get back to you if I decide on any charges." Gendron stood and started to speak, but decided to leave well enough alone.

Arvid drove to La Pointe and decided to stop at The Beach Club. It had been a tough morning and he needed lunch and maybe a good, stiff drink, even though he was technically on duty. When he entered he was more than happy to see Doc Olson sitting at a table reading a menu.

"Mind if I join you? He didn't wait for an answer, but pulled up a chair.

"I need someone to bounce a few things off, and I can't think of anyone better than you."

"Sit. Join me in a drink? I'm kinda curious about a few things myself, so have at me. I'm all done with a few calls I had over here, so my time is yours." They ordered, exchanged some talk about the weather and the lake, then Arvid started. He took Doc back to the beginning after the accident when he had made that list of questions that had to be answered, and brought him to the present with the morning's revelations.

"I guess all my questions have been answered, and everyone seemed truthful enough except for Gendron and aside from being a son-of-a-bitch as a father, he was able to explain everything, even the loosened railing."

"So what don't you believe?"

"I'm not sure. Maybe I believe everything. But if he tightened the screws on the railing, why didn't he tighten them all the way? And if the screws had been tightened, would they have pulled out clean and whole the way they did and not be broken or bent from the weight of a body?"

"Seems to me the disposition of the screws is going to be difficult to prove, and in the end it doesn't bring LuAnn back. What would be his reason to loosen them, if he did? He couldn't be sure who would lean on the railing. If he wanted to get rid of someone, there would be smarter ways; and James Gendron strikes me as a smart man."

"I know, I know … I just want justice for Gudrun, and I don't want that asshole to get away with anything. I could maybe find a case of negligent homicide somewhere in that railing."

"Sounds to me, my friend, as if you're looking hard for a reason to charge him. Just keep in mind that if you do, Gudrun, LuAnn, and everyone involved will be scrutinized and vilified by the lawyers and in the court of public opinion. Making an accusation always comes with repercussions."

"So, you think I should just close it out as an accident, and let the whole thing die a natural death?"

"Up to you. Maybe everyone's been hurt enough, though." Arvid and Doc rose and shook hands, clasping each other's shoulders. Arvid stood looking out at the lake after Doc had walked off toward the ferry.

When he got back to the room that served as his headquarters, Mrs. Gendron was sitting in her car outside waiting for him. She rolled down her window and asked if she could come in. Her eyes were red and swollen. *Like everyone else involved in this case.* Arvid thought to himself.

"I've just finished talking to your husband, and I've about decided to write LuAnn's death off as an accident." He thought to forestall any excuses she might be prepared to make for her husband or son, but she spoke before he could continue.

"I was the one who loosened the railing on the widow's walk." She paused while he stared at her, not even trying to conceal his amazement. She had done her crying while making the decision to confess, as she now spoke loudly and clearly. "I was aware of my husband's plan to help LuAnn either trap Jimmy into a love affair or force him to admit his sexual preference. We fought bitterly over the matter, but I'm a very weak woman, Arvid, and am not used to opposing my husband." She paused to drink from the glass of water he'd provided.

"I was also conflicted over involving LuAnn in this kind of business. She was my dear little girl, and even though she had changed into a teenager I barely knew, I hoped she would pass through this wild phase. All my friends on the Island brought me tales of her excessiveness. She paused and took several deep breaths. Arvid thought she might not continue, but she regained control. "But I couldn't tell Gudrun. She wouldn't have believed me, and I could hardly admit that it was true myself. I argued with Jim that he was hurting and manipulating both the young people to no good end, but he was adamant."

"But what was the point in loosening the railing? Who did you want to fall?"

"I didn't want anyone to fall. Oh, believe me, I was just desperate to find any way I could to keep them away from each other. I knew Jim wanted them to use the walk as a meeting place, and I thought if I made it too dangerous, he'd give up the idea. I knew he was going to check the place out, and thought he'd discover how loose the railing was and lock the walk off."

"But he didn't go up to check the place out?"

"No, and when I told him what I'd done, he was furious and grabbed the screwdriver and went up to fix it, but he wasn't up there long before he came down. When I asked him if he'd tightened it, he said he'd done the best he could and if anyone got hurt up there it was on my head. That will stay with me for the rest of my life."

"Why didn't you tell Jimmy what was going on"

"This will sound stupid to you, Arvid, but I didn't want him to think badly of his father. His father was strict and hard on him, but I didn't want him to know that he would scheme and plot against him. Now he knows, and I don't think they'll ever be father and son. I don't think we'll be husband and wife either. Families have been torn apart."

"You do know that your husband didn't tell me you had loosened the railing. He said he found it wobbly and tried to fix it."

"I know, but it doesn't matter now. Will you be charging me with negligent homicide?" He was surprised at her use of the term, then thought that her husband had probably threatened her with the possibility.

"I can't really see that this new information changes anything. The whole case would hinge on the intent of the negligent person, and I don't believe your intent was to harm anyone, let alone a girl you loved or your own son."

After she'd left, Arvid opened his desk drawer and gathered the storyboard, ripping it to pieces before depositing it in the wastebasket. He sat for awhile in thought. He remembered the old saying: "It is said, Lake Superior never gives up its dead."

"Nor its secrets," he said aloud to himself.

Epilogue

"Who cannot be crushed with a plot?"
(ALL'S WELL THAT ENDS WELL) WILLIAM SHAKESPEARE

he Gendrons left early that summer, not waiting for their usual departure on Labor Day weekend. They didn't say goodbye nor did they reveal their future plans to anyone on the Island or in Bayfield. Several weeks after their disappearance, a Minneapolis realtor's sign announced that the beautiful home on the lake with the enchanting widow's walk on the roof was for sale.

Gudrun tried to remain with her friends in Bayfield and on the Island, making her living with her handiwork and baking; but there were too many memories to haunt her dreams and too many vicious tongues that wouldn't let the tragic story die. She eventually drifted back to St. Paul, finding a small apartment close to where she and her mother had lived, supporting herself by cleaning offices in downtown buildings.

She liked to work at night. It was quiet, and she didn't have to talk to anyone. She didn't sleep much anyway, and it gave her plenty of time to think about the path her life had taken.

She did make a friend of another cleaning lady who worked in one of the larger buildings with her and sometimes met her at break time for coffee. It was pleasant to have adult conversation with someone who didn't know her past. She was kind and didn't pry.

The woman lived with her aging mother near Gudrun's apartment, and one day she invited her over for supper on an evening they both had off from work. "We don't have any other family and never have company. I think mother would enjoy having someone come over."

So Gudrun spent the day making her crown of rolls to take for supper, remembering all the times she had made it for complimentary crowds of diners at the Gendrons, and presented herself at the appointed hour. The mother was very old, in her nineties, and didn't seem to take much notice of anything until her daughter brought the crown to the table. Then she sat up straight, looking at the rolls and shaking her head.

"I've only ever seen that once before when my friend, Anna Carlson, used to make it for church suppers. Anna was such a good baker, none better." Gudrun was so surprised and opened her mouth to say Anna was her mother, but the old woman droned on as if in her own world. "Such a shame, what happened to Anna. She fell for this man who was no good, and he got her pregnant and left her in the lurch. She never did get married. Died young, I think. I don't know what happened to the child. Such a shame!" She relaxed back into her other world, shaking her head and repeating, "Such a shame."

Gudrun forced herself to eat and visit but finally feigned a headache and excused herself early to hurry home. Her mother had always said that her father died in World War II. Strange that there were no pictures, and Mother refused to answer questions about him or even want him mentioned. Gudrun just thought her sad because he had been killed.

So mother had never had the much-touted Christian husband, and had sinned and lied about it just as Gudrun had. At last she understood her mother and cried for the pain of the rejection and humiliation she must have endured. *On top of it all, I was a thankless child,* she thought as she lay in bed that night, *and she didn't even have what I had: a born again life on the Island.*

Gudrun was easier in her own mind after that, and gradually softened and forgave herself for a multitude of sins she had been harboring in her soul. "Beating yourself up about the past don't do anybody any good," Willow had tried to tell her. Sometimes she heard her mother say, "Remember, girlie, what goes around comes around."

Eventually the *tants* and Einer were gone, followed in time by Willow and Arne, so Gudrun had no reason to make the long journey back to the Big Lake. She never lost her ability to slip into her fantasy world, however, so every

June she "saw" lupine blooming in the fields and on rocky cliffs. She saw that great expanse of water freeze and thaw with the seasons and then she happily experienced that born again life.

Bayfield forgot the tragedy of the handsome fisherman and the little Swedish cook. The coffee drinkers at The Pier and the beer drinkers at Junior's Bar found more timely subjects to discuss but occasionally one old timer would suddenly remember the ice harvesting days and relate the sad details of a true-to-life Bayfield tragedy. But then, no one put much stock in anything old Danny Miller said.

About the Author

Laurie Otis raised four daughters while following her husband's teaching career through several moves throughout Minnesota, Wisconsin, and Canada. She earned a B.A. with an English major from Northland College in 1973 and did advanced work in Library Science at the Universities of Wisconsin and Minnesota.

Laurie worked for over 30 years as a librarian for Wisconsin Indianhead Technical College, Ashland campus, and later as a communications instructor and public relations representative. Retiring to her country home in Wisconsin, she enjoys writing, gardening, reading, pastel painting and yoga.

A major influence in recent years has been an affiliation with Washburn, Wisconsin's StageNorth Theater. In addition to working as a stage manager and also with lighting and sound, she has had major roles in several plays: *Last Lists of My Mad Mother; Old Ladies Guide to Survival; Song of Survival; A Christmas Memory*, and *Moon Over Buffalo*.

CPSIA information can be obtained
at www.ICGtesting.com
Printed in the USA
FFOW01n1953100717
37547FF